BUILDING NUMBER FOUR

an Amira Margaret Alexander Thriller

Susan Anita Jones

BOOKS BY SUSAN ANITA JONES

Beauty and Ashes
SEA CHILD series
Creating Emotional Ambience Within
Anxiety An Inclusive Approach
The Backward Mirror
Go Schralp It!

Personality, Politics, and the Prince
A Biography of Lady Winifred Maxwell
Countess of Nithsdale

Not For Everyone The Uncrowned Stuart Queen
Louise de Stolberg Comtesse d'Albany
and Conte Vittorio Alfieri
Volumes One & Two

Building Number Four An AMA Thriller
The Number is Thirteen An AMA Thriller
A Number in the Heart An AMA Thriller

Reformatted February 2026
Text copyright © 2019 by Susan Anita Jones. All rights reserved.
Published by Susan Anita Jones
Title: Building Number Four. An Amira Margaret Alexander Thriller.
Government of Canada Copyright.
Courage Endures Love Is Never Abandoned   susananitajones@gmail.com
ISBN Canada 978-0-9959996-7-1
VISIT website: https://www.susananitajones.com

All characters are fictious, except for factual and historical figures. Any connections and storylines connected to these individuals are likewise fictious. No references are made to any real persons or circumstances in the story line with one exception: all events relating to the treatment of individual Palestinians are true and based on the author's personal and first-hand experiences. Place names, individual names, and locations have been changed to protect the innocent and their families. Other place names and locations in this work of fiction are based on accepted factual information and only confirm their existence.

Dedicated to my many friends,
Here and abroad.

If I have met you,
You are a friend.

Peace be upon you.

Egyptian Inscription

CHAPTER ONE
1988

I love to watch people. I try to imagine what they are like, what their lives might be. Some people you can pigeonhole right away. Others are a bit more curious.

She arrived in Tel Aviv from Frankfurt.

I thought to myself, "What do you know, there she is. I've seen that lady before."

Everyone goes through Frankfurt it seems. So, I had no way of knowing where she had been. She was carrying a green plastic bag with gold print. Harrods Department Store. London was a solid bet.

It was a miscalculation anyone would have made.

I am not making excuses, just stating the facts. She looked rich. So obviously in need of care. How could she possibly exist in the Middle East without servants to torment?

It was so evident she couldn't that I thought she was a sure thing. She was neat, trim, and slim, with perfectly coiffed light brown shoulder length hair. The logical thing would be to catch her at the airport before she had time to settle in.

Like I mentioned, she was familiar to me. I equated familiarity with safety.

It was a mistake.

Besides, she really did look like she had cash. I am a very practical person.

My name is Amira Margaret Alexander.

I am good with faces. When I bump into someone again, I can actually know quite a lot about them.

It always astounds them when I say things like, "I saw you at such and such a place" or "You were with so and so."

The majority of people don't like it. They think I am some kind of sneak, a stalker.

I am not. I am just observant.

I believed she was British. She seemed British through and through, tight, precise, tea-on-time type of presentation. She definitely thought she was well above the rabble. Her accent was British or at least like someone who has lived in England for a good chunk of their life.

I remembered her.

The open market in Jerusalem is where I had first seen her. She was pretty and had that air of class distinction like she had stepped out of a Dickens novel.

Honestly, you would have assumed she was British. Her clothes, her shoes, her handbag, her tweed. I know English tweed when I see it.

She was just shopping and then she disappeared into the crowd.

After my excellent memory, my other true skill is that I am an artist, a real artist, and hence economically poor.

But I will try my hand at anything because I have to.

I live in a small flat in Jerusalem with Hazeer. It's stressful. He's been getting hysterical about the price of everything lately. Granted, it was expensive to live in Jerusalem, but honestly, shut up already. The plants needed watering and the rent was due. He complained about everything.

Like I said, we needed cash.

Hazeer took the transit hubs in Jerusalem. I branched out and hit the airport in Tel Aviv. We could do any kind of work, chauffeur, tourist guide, house cleaning, and so on.

She sailed through customs with only a handbag. She didn't even have any carry-on luggage. She waved her declaration card, but I already knew her name. I had heard it when she had been in the Jerusalem market speaking with the vendors.

One of the counter girls made an announcement over the system that there was a taxi waiting for Miss Balgrave right outside Exit Door D. I have never had any problems with arranging rides. Travelers are tired, and in the Tel Aviv heat, they are just grateful to get out of the airport. This day was especially chaotic.

As she approached the taxi, I motioned to her, "This way, Miss Balgrave."

She didn't even break stride as she looked me up and down and got into the back seat of the taxi. I sat in the front beside the driver. It wouldn't do to cuddle up with her in the back.

"I didn't arrange for a taxi," she said with surprise.

We had scooped her off the curb before she could call another taxi from the long queue.

Putting an equally surprised look on my face, I said, "It is a service we provide, ma'am."

This was not the time for downcast eyes, so I smiled instead, but not too much.

I made my offer.

"I can help you with anything you need."

Now was the time to drop my eyes, but just a little.

She stared at me again, shrugged, and said, "Fine. Let's go to the hotel."

My scam was working like a charm.

My manners were impeccable thanks to my British private school education. My former school was in Egypt, on the east side of Alexandria, the favourite city of philosophers. At the entrance, the copper letters announced *The British School of Alexandria founded 1859.*

The school was very complete in the sense that it had an entire staff for every need you could imagine. It was very good employment to be attached to a private school. The local workers made the most of it. Cleaners were willing to run extra errands. Teachers were willing to give extra tutorials. All for a fee of course, but not much.

We even had our own troupe of health care professionals. Some doctors were extra attentive. I recall a particularly unfortunate incident. One of the doctors took it upon himself to make a late-night patient visit. Instead of waiting for the morning hours, he showed up and began tapping on the French door window of the dormitory. The doors were open to the terrace because of the heat, but the mosquito screen was shut. All the students had private rooms. My room was right by the door.

"Amira, Amira."

I wasn't in my room but in the washroom directly across the hall. I was just going to cross in front of the door when I froze upon hearing his urgent whisper. I knew it wasn't good, but honestly, I stopped thinking. I sat on the edge of the bathtub and held my breath.

He pulled at the latch of the screen door. The doors had been secured on the inside, but only with a flimsy wire.

What had I done to deserve this?

The doctor had flirted with me. I guess I had smiled and laughed at what I now knew had been, on his part, foreplay. He was a regular visitor to the school. The *Boabs* must have just winked and let him through the front gate to the terrace.

I was petrified.

Just when I thought I was going to pass out from holding my breath, the visiting doctor gave up pulling on the screen door and went away.

The next day his wife showed up at the school. I was called down to Miss Beatrissa's office to have tea. The headmistress wasn't there, just us two. The doctor's wife wore pearls. A sure sign. She had on a yellow loose knit sweater with a round neck, dark pencil skirt, and white shoes. She crossed her feet and chatted about this and that. All the time, she was sizing me up.

Of course, I didn't mention her husband's creepy behaviour, but she must have known, somehow. My best manners showed up to play the game. After a suitable time spent evaluating me as a potential threat, she left, but her message was clear. I never went close to or chatted with him again.

After all, it's best to stay far away from a doctor who laughs about how his clients pay him in hashish.

The whole affair had taught me how to pick them better. She was a good pick.

Miss Balgrave hadn't told me which hotel. I gave the driver directions to the Plaza Tel Aviv, the most expensive hotel. Once we had pulled out into traffic and were waiting for a traffic light she said to the driver, "Take the road to Ashkelon, the Migdal hotel."

A few hours later I was sitting in a hotel on cheap street in Ashkelon, not the Migdal Villa Hotel where Miss Balgrave was staying.

She had dismissed me once the taxi dropped her off at the Villa and told me to call back later that night. It was early afternoon; I had plenty of time. I always carry an overnight bag in the taxi, part of my arrangement with the driver, Ahmed.

While waiting, I had arranged some evening entertainment plans for Miss Balgrave. Ahmed had dropped me off at my superior hotel of the shoddy type and had gone looking for an even shoddier bar, by my recommendation of course. I always consider it best to be at the top of whatever low class you are in.

I telephoned Hazeer and told him of my luck. I didn't have time to explain the entire situation because he had to go out with his friends. I don't know who his friends are. I never ask. I don't like lies, so I don't ask questions. Soon he would find someone else, someone younger; it was only a matter of time.

I sat down on the lumpy mattress and went through my bag. I had shoved all my personal mail from the Jerusalem flat in my bag thinking I would open it later when I had the time. There was a request from a French Art magazine to send in some of my sketches. It was an insult. I am an artist and a good one. All they would do was take my work, keep it for a year, and tell me no. I am not an idiot. I know a scam as soon as I see one. Money first, art delivered second, otherwise no deal.

I made a few more phone calls to the clubs I had decided on, just to make sure. Then I went to grab a bite to eat. The prices were expensive, but with the quote I had given Miss Balgrave for my services and the taxi, it would be clear sailing.

When I got back to my room, the phone rang. It was Hazeer. His friend had stood him up. More likely she had found another man, someone with money. I told him more about Miss

Balgrave and laughed at all the stupid questions she had asked me on the drive down to Ashkelon from Tel Aviv.

Hazeer didn't laugh with me.

I didn't let on that she had actually annoyed me quite a lot. It had started with her first question about my personal life.

"Is there a husband, Amira?" Miss Balgrave probed in a sweet sappy sort of way.

The question was unexpected. They don't usually get so personal. I told her about my first husband and how he had been shot in a freak incident in an Israeli settlement in the West Bank.

The taxi driver had slid me a glance. The first time Ahmed had heard the story, my husband had been killed by a grenade. I didn't mention Hazeer. I just wanted to keep men out of the conversation at the moment.

"You did say you were French, didn't you?" she inquired.

"My father was Canadian ma'am. I was educated in Canada and Alexandria." I told her the story as if I were talking about someone else.

I disliked the conversation. It made me feel like I was back in Miss Beatrissa's office discussing my many misdemeanors.

Undeterred, Miss Balgrave went on.

"Well, what nationality are you?"

"I have a Canadian passport."

That part was perfectly true, but not the whole truth. I also have an Egyptian passport thanks to my mother and grandparents. It was none of Miss Balgrave's business.

"Was your husband Canadian?"

"No, German."

I should have picked a different nationality. Ahmed's hands tightened on the steering wheel. He doesn't like Germans. Ahmed is Egyptian.

During World War II, the German ideological fervour came to his village and consumed his family. The rest of the villagers were immune to the dogma. They lived in mud huts with straw roofs. There was no running water, not even a well. The water had to be carried up from the river. Basically, the village was run on a feudal system. The family owned the farming estate. The villagers worked for them.

Ahmed's father was thrilled with the right-wing Nazi propaganda, but Ahmed didn't see it that way. He saw the German worldview as upsetting their way of life, full of false promises. The Germans were a nation of soldiers who stomped around, and gave orders.

Ahmed imagined the Germans as the type of guest who would eat every single pigeon from the pigeon coop.

Those coops are dome-shaped clay structures storeys high. The pigeons fly in the round openings and perch on the wooden sticks fastened on the inside of the coop. Want a pigeon? Walk through a wooden door, climb the inside pegs spiraling up the inside walls.

I always find the whole production fascinating. The pigeons just sit there. Pluck them off. Take them away without a fuss. One pigeon will give you about one teaspoon of meat.

So to eat them all, that's quite a feat.

"Oh, German," insinuated Miss Balgrave. "Where is he from in Germany?"

"I don't know exactly, we met here."

"Do you carry a photograph of him?"

Ahmed cleared his throat. Of course there was no photograph. It was an unfortunate question. Ahmed's grandfather had loved the Nazis even more than Ahmed's father. There is even a photograph of Adolf Hitler on the wall in the family home. Still.

Ahmed hates photographs.

He hates them for another reason as well. Even if the people are smiling and hugging in the photograph, he knows after the picture is taken, they will immediately be at each other's throats.

"They're false representations," he always says. "Not the way things actually are."

My argument is that life is made of moments, special moments. Ahmed thinks that's nonsense; life isn't stop and go, but one big swoosh to the cesspool.

"Do you have any children?" asked Miss Balgrave.

Now this was getting to be a bit much.

I had stared out the front window and shook my head.

Naturally, I didn't repeat every single word of the conversation with Miss Balgrave to Hazeer during our telephone conversation.

"This doesn't sound right," Hazeer concluded.

"She has money."

"How do you know?"

"I checked which villa she is in. It is the most expensive one in the complex."

"Sounds like you are having fun," he mocked me.

"Why do you say that?"

"You like to find out about people. Are you going to sketch her face?"

"Perhaps. That is what an artist is attracted to, the unusual."

Hazeer didn't sound convinced. I didn't like having to explain myself. It only triggered senseless recollections and arguments leading to nowhere.

I could hear Hazeer sigh on the other end of the line. "Are you taking her clubbing?"

"That's what she wants."

Hazeer made an attempt to give me good advice and said he would see me after I got back. I wondered if he would be there when I returned to Jerusalem.

But I am not one to ponder misfortune or even good fortune when it happens. If it happened, it happened. If not, it didn't.

I poured myself another glass of wine and tried to figure out what Miss Balgrave was up to.

She seemed much like any other traveler. In the taxi, she had listened absently, nodding now and then while I spoke. As soon as she looked like she wasn't listening anymore I had stopped talking and relaxed. Everything was going to be all right, I figured.

She hadn't inquired about how I came to be in Tel Aviv or what it was I actually did, as they usually do. I figured those questions would come later. Instead, I had tried to find out more about her.

"Are you visiting family ma'am?" I had asked politely.

She had stared at me.

"Business?" I pressed on.

"Maybe."

Her stare told me to mind my own business.

"I am not prying of course, but if you wish anything, like a car for instance, I can make sure one is available. I can also do whatever you wish. I am an excellent tour guide."

"Really."

It wasn't a yes. It wasn't a no. I quoted some quick prices off the top of my head. I told her all about Tel Aviv.

"The city of Tel Aviv was founded in 1909 by the Ishuv on the edge of the ancient port city of Jaffa. It was first called Ahuzat Bayit but the name changed to Tel Aviv in 1910. The name means ancient hill of spring. The population was mostly Jewish, whereas Jaffa was mostly Arab."

I didn't know her political bent so after I finished my pamphlet recitation, I steered clear of Palestinian and Jewish issues. She didn't look Middle Eastern, but you never know. Ahmed knew better than to interrupt me. He would get his cut at the end of the job as usual.

There were red flags waving in the back of my head about Miss Balgrave which I had ignored all day, big warning signs. I pushed them aside.

Although tourism hadn't come to a standstill, tension was high. The *Intifadeh* had begun just the year before. Demonstrations against the Israeli occupation had erupted in Gaza which was only a stone's throw from Ashkelon. I didn't expect the Palestinians to keep it up but considered it the usual riots since Israel had been created and had occupied the West Bank.

It became clear to me, however, that the disturbances were different from those of the previous twenty years. The rioting continued. Defense Minister Yitzhak Rabin identified the problem as a political one, not a military one. The whole situation makes me extremely sad. That's when they began to call it the *Intifadeh,* the uprising.

Some argue Palestinians don't exist, that they are not a people, just the same as other Arabs in the area. I have to laugh at that.

What makes people think they can tell other people how to identify themselves?

Whatever.

I'd like to ask them, "How do you explain the existence of a Palestinian passport and a Palestinian Citizenship Order?"

The Certificate of Nationality was provided to those born in Palestine and to those whose fathers were also born in Palestine. Those documents existed until the state of Israel and the United Nations abolished all paper identities — together.

Being a minister in the Egyptian government, my grandfather made sure I was well versed in the crisis.

Having dual citizenship myself, I wonder what it would be like to be stateless. After the creation of the state of Israel in the late 1940s, a significant number of Palestinians found themselves exactly that, stateless. Israel and the UN called the documents *treasured mementos of identity.*

But that day in Tel Aviv, the day I picked Miss Balgrave out of the crowd at the Ben Gurion airport, I wasn't looking for trouble. I didn't need to belong or have any particular type of identity. I was merely checking out the newly arrived people holding passports. I didn't care what kind of passport they had.

In fact, I never did get a look at any of her papers or legal documentation.

I was merely searching for gainful employment while Hazeer scoped out the prospects in Jerusalem. You can't hold a grudge against someone on a quest for an honest day's work no matter what the political situation, now can you?

When I look back, I can see I didn't have a choice.

Even at the beginning, I had to do what that wretched woman wanted. Later her requests became the kind of suggestions which mean if you don't do exactly what I want, well then life was going to get pretty miserable.

My situation was totally her fault.

The drive from the airport to her hotel had taken about one hour. The Migdal Hotel is a type of villa arrangement near the seashore. Each suite is self-contained with a private pool and garden. A short distance from the hotel was the centre of Ashkelon. The marina was close by too. Miss Balgrave didn't have any luggage so she waved the porters away while paying the taxi fare.

"All right Amira, here's my offer. I'll be here for a few days and could use someone."

I had been pleased and blurted, "We can visit the Tomb of Sheikh Awad which dates back to the 13th century. It's high on a hilltop and is one of several sites built by the Mamelukes along this coast. You'd enjoy this ancient domed crypt. There are sweeping views over the northern beaches."

I had no idea what she would enjoy. I just wanted to make it last as long as possible to earn a higher fee.

"Maybe. Right now, I'd like to visit the town. Know any good spots?"

She said it with more emphasis than was really necessary, so I gathered she wasn't looking for a convenience store. I assured her I did. While she was checking into the hotel, I quickly conferred with a local about the entertainment hotspots in Ashkelon.

"Amira, pick me up at ten o'clock this evening."

"Yes, ma'am."

That's how it happened.

I looked at the clock. I had two hours to kill.

I'm not ungrateful. My education was designed to give me a solid upbringing, a place in society. I found that all right. My place was right at the bottom of the social ladder where I was taking any kind of employment I could get.

My schooling had taught me impeccable manners, a sense of justice, and I could present myself like a lady. Unfortunately, my years at the school were rather painful in a way only youth can feel.

You see my mother was Egyptian and my father was Canadian. Since Amira is Arabic for princess, my father always

11

thought it was funny to call me Princess Margaret. He was a monarchist. I'm not.

My father had met my mother during the war. He had been stationed in Italy originally. How they ever met is beyond me. He had driven a tank and called himself one of the Crunchies.

I always believed it was like Captain Crunch, the yellow crispy cereal so full of sugar it stuck to your teeth for days. It was not like that though. He was a Crunchie because the tanks could roll over the soldiers and crunch them to their death. Nice. His work was a revelation to me, one of many.

My mother could have gone back to Egypt of course. She had a ton of relatives there, but she would rather eat donkey meat than make that trip. She married my dad and worked in Canada. After he died, she collected my dad's pension, cleaned houses and whatever else needed to be done, and she could cook. Yes, indeed. She could cook a splendid dinner, baked tarts, pies and chocolate Yule logs for Christmas.

Rather than fostering a relationship with me, my mother put education first. Hence, she thought my education would be enhanced by spending some time with my relatives in Egypt.

Sure thing, Mom.

My grandmother, who lived in Cairo, was so thrilled to have me that she promptly sent me to the British boarding school in Alexandria. I think it was punishment for my mother having married my Canadian father, Jason Alexander. Yup, my grandmother thought it fitting.

I never did see my mother again. She was a free spirit. Apparently so was I. Happiness is not being where you are not wanted. In Alexandria, I was away from the constraints of family, but not the constraints of boarding school rules.

The British School of Alexandria wasn't posh but it did its best to turn out real ladies, women of society. There were a handful of girls who had managed scholarships and a few who attended the school on a daily basis only.

The headmistress of the school was Miss Beatrissa. She was tiny, not even five feet tall. Formidable. Students collapsed at the idea of being called into her office. She had a toothy grin made more ridiculous by all the missing teeth, but she knew how to run a school. Donations went straight into a new carpet for her office. Behind her desk hung a massive portrait of Hosni Mubarak, the president of Egypt. Of the two dictators, Miss Beatrissa's frown was the winner.

The school was where I learned when to smile and when to drop my eyes. I learned which girls to ask for extra pocket money and who to avoid. I got along fairly well with everyone, and then there were the boys.

There weren't any boys at school of course, but there was a whole slew of them outside. On the weekends we would wander down to the local clay tennis courts. We soon found out what the boys wanted, a little feel, a little kiss, sometimes more. My friend and I hung around, but not too much. We would disguise our outing by stopping at the local kiosk across from the courts where we could observe and be observed.

We couldn't just stand there. We had to buy something. One time, my friend drank fourteen Cokes in a row to prolong our stay. Needless to say, she was pretty ill afterwards.

In the final year at school as a young woman, I was hampered in many ways. My prospects were supposedly linked to finding the right man, the right husband.

This was a no go.

It was a dangerous situation to be in.

What if my grandmother decided to marry me off to an old fat friend?

What if I got saddled with an abusive heavy hander?

The only thing to do was to convince my grandmother that I was far more useful to her single than married. I did this by writing anonymous letters to her.

By the time I was finished with my scheme, she was so afraid to keep me around lest something dreadful happen to me and to her. She put an allowance in the bank for me to draw upon and granted me permission to leave Egypt.

I had a Canadian passport and could travel freely. But she could have made it difficult for me to go, but hadn't.

Bless her heart.

I had a lot more freedom living here in the West Bank than I would have had in Egypt, even today. Some of my Egyptian friends had not been so fortunate. One ended up married to a fifty-year-old miser. The other retired to her parents' apartment never to be seen again.

At ten o'clock the taxi was waiting for Miss Balgrave outside the hotel. She was late by thirty minutes.

I got out of the taxi and went to the front desk.

"Taxi for Miss Balgrave," I announced.

"Oh yes, she left a message for you."

She was a no show.

Tomorrow night, same time, ten o'clock.

I cursed under my breath.

Ahmed and I went for a drink. Then he escorted me to my hotel room. After we had finished, he went to sleep in the taxi.

I'm a married man. I have morals he always says.

Whatever.

I took a shower and went to bed.

CHAPTER TWO

The next day was bright and sunny; the way it always is here. I had a headache and was hungry. Not a good combination. I didn't have any cash and I don't have a credit card. Those companies can be so picky about credit risks.

Again, not my fault.

I have been to Ashkelon before. I adore the sea. The harbor is a pretty place. I love watching the boats coming in. The marina entrance is tricky in strong winds, taking skillful navigation.

Ashkelon is an entry port. It is a preferred harbor for boats coming from the South, the Red Sea and the Suez Canal. Once the boats enter the marina and are through the breakwater, there is a gated dock immediately to port.

That's where Customs and Immigration are waiting. They are very thorough, only the way Israeli security can be. The mooring lines are secured by them. Everyone leaves the vessel without taking anything until they finish their checks.

The Ashkelon marina has full services. Plenty of boats in the marina with people of all nationalities. I figured the marina was a good bet. Once the security checks are done, people carelessly leave stuff lying around all the time on the wharf. Security is more interested in the boats themselves rather than what's out in the open.

Getting on the wharf is easy if you know how to get in, which I do. It's even easier to pick up something useful with a good resale value. It's what I would call sharing the wealth.

I passed by some American travelers and then some British travelers. Have you ever noticed how British humour is not the same as American humour?

At the British school in Alexandria, we would sneak out of the building to the local café and watch Monty Python on the television. We absolutely killed ourselves laughing. Americans in the café ogled us. The only expression on their faces was absolute disbelief. No sense of humour. They were puzzled.

That's how Miss Balgrave had looked at me in the Tel Aviv airport when I offered my numerous services.

Curiosity and disbelief.

At least that's what I supposed she thought at the time.

Sneaking out of the British School in Alexandria to get a peek at the Telly wasn't the only naughty thing we did. You have to appreciate how tricky it was to get away with anything when everyone in a town of two million people knew who went to the British boarding school.

We did manage to get our hands on a video of soft porn. It was all the rage back then. The camera would zoom up and down the bare legs of sweaty young women, arms were flailing, torsos gyrating to the beat. It was exhilarating. It was an American exercise tape. Tight spandex bodies, long muscular legs, heaving breasts. I can still see it in my head.

My friend told me her aunt showed the tape as a special treat at her wedding in Qatar. Viewing the tape in a large gathering, even a private event, would never have happened in Egypt. The secret police would have descended upon the festivities or something, but we schoolgirls had managed to secure a copy. From then on, we called it Gamalia's wedding tape. It made the rounds. We charged five pounds per viewing.

My grandmother had agreed to make a sizeable monetary donation to the school when my scheme came to light. She even paid them extra to solve my manner problems, as she called my many awkward dilemmas. She had a saying, *to heck with them*, when she was displeased with someone.

I applied that philosophy to the world.

I was educated far beyond the regular curriculum.

I knew all about the Boabs at the gate and their families. I knew which teachers lied about their relationships. I knew how desperately Mister Assad, one of the new teachers, wanted a wife from America and what he would do to get one.

I watched Mister Assad move around each day in abject misery. No wife forthcoming.

It was hardly a recipe for a truly successful education but I did have my moments. I discovered the teachers loved chanting and singing which I would engage in regularly, especially when I didn't like the lessons being taught. The teachers also appreciated precise handwriting and absolutely perfect notebooks. I became a great scribe. I also had my hand up all the time to answer any question, but I rarely was called upon, probably from the fear that I would start a chant or break into song.

It is true that I did not devote myself to my studies. With all my active socializing, I would, at times, fall behind in my homework. But I could always copy from Safa who had no friends at all and was just plain grateful for my attention.

Top grades were elusive, but I was smart enough to not copy Safa's work exactly. My homework was filled with numerous mistakes. I had been suspected once of cheating and received a sharp bamboo caning on the back of my calves as a warning. It was a valuable lesson.

Never make them suspicious. Never try to pretend to be someone you are not.

I look out for number one, me. Everyone does, don't kid yourself.

I'd love to say the years flew by, but they didn't. They dragged on and on. The moment I was finally free, I went back to see Miss Beatrissa, to let her know I was leaving Egypt.

This time my fate had been decided by me.

I remember the day clearly. I walked into the office to find Miss Simopee, the headmistress's sidekick with her skirt up and her underpants down. Not a pretty sight I assure you.

She was receiving her monthly antibiotic injection in the rear end. It was being administered by a colleague but I don't think Miss Simopee liked me even before I caught them in the act. She had always made a point of being as unhelpful as she could when it came to me. After Miss Simopee had pulled up her underwear, I was ushered into Miss Beatrissa's office for a lunch of pickled eggs and sweet tea.

After I left Alexandria but not before, I sent Miss Beatrissa an anonymous letter concerning Miss Simopee.

I travelled to Kenya and worked for a tour company booking safaris. Then I travelled to Greece where the nude beaches opened my eyes and my legs. After losing my bloom in Greece, I travelled to Cyprus where I met Cypriots and Turks, and flew around on the back of plenty of motorcycles.

I did learn to cook and I met Hazeer.

What did I learn from my boarding school education and my various travels?

I learned people with power, secretaries, headmistresses, grandmothers, and the police can affect my life in unimaginable ways. What's a girl to do?

You just learn some things from experience but not everything.

How could I possibly have known what type of woman this Miss Balgrave really was?

As I stepped on the wharf, I thought I had the day to myself. I had no idea where Ahmed had gone but I wasn't worried. He'd show up for ten o'clock tonight.

Although I didn't see Ahmed, I did see Miss Balgrave.

She was looking very jaunty. She was wearing white slacks, a blue and white striped shirt, complete with canvas loafers on her feet. Seriously?

Do people actually dress like that because they are near water? Her luggage must have arrived or she already had the clothes at the villa. She was moving her hands, gesturing toward the Mediterranean Sea. The man she was speaking with was listening closely. At last, there was an exchange of farewells.

Miss Balgrave noticed me before I could move away.

She acted as if it was the most natural thing in the world to come across me at the marina. She spoke about this and that, and pointed out the different boats in the marina while asking me various questions about them.

I had been a cook once aboard a yacht, so I actually knew what the charter rates were like. It had been an initially exciting and demanding job; one I grew to hate. The pay had been exorbitant. They think they own you. I was required to cook anytime day or night; I was solicited for many things and never allowed to be unavailable.

I quoted her a high price for chartering a boat, figuring I might get a commission out of that too. I wanted to see how much money was too much.

She didn't even blink at the price I quoted for a boat with a full crew. She nodded and inquired about sailboats and motorboats without a crew

I got a strange feeling her conversation on the pier with the mystery man hadn't totally been about boat rental.

Considering how this entire thing turned out, I think her fascination with boats was certainly noteworthy and would have pointed me in a certain direction. Again, a red flag I paid no attention to, but I was only thinking about the money, not the consequences.

When I casually asked if we were supposed to pick her up at ten or at half past tonight, she stared at me. I considered perhaps she had had more wine than I had the night before, but she didn't seem to have a hangover like me. Not her. She became very precise and started questioning me.

Was I French? British?

I reminded her I was Canadian.

How much had I travelled?

I sidestepped that one as usual. My personal history is none of her business.

Did I own a car?

That one I could answer. I lied and declared, "Of course I did."

It was just that my car was in the garage at the moment, hence the taxi. I described my car in detail, right down to the blue and white BMW decal.

I know what you are thinking.

Never pretend to be someone you are not.

I wasn't. I was talking about the car not myself. Besides, why shouldn't people be told what they want to hear?

She didn't even look at me. I didn't dare look at her for fear she would cancel our whole arrangement. She didn't. Luck was on my side.

At least that was what I thought at the time.

She asked more questions about my husband. Where had he been killed?

Did he support the *Intifadeh*?

What was his name?

I gave vague answers and feigned grief. She stopped talking. I guess she was thinking about more interesting things than my life.

In truth, I couldn't even remember what my husband, Yanni, looked like anymore. I had become so used to his death that I didn't even think about how he had cheated on me with my best friend and was now living in some obscure Greek village with a brood of children.

It was no big deal. I had just wished them both a great deal of misfortune and moved on.

Miss Balgrave was obviously done with me. She waved me away with her hand. It was a gesture I didn't like.

I don't like being dismissed.

"Ten o'clock tonight," she directed.

"Do you have plans for today?" I innocently asked.

"Friends. Lunch," she answered as she absently waved her hand in the other direction.

"Very well ma'am. See you at ten."

I was annoyed. She had thwarted my plans of wealth accumulation from the marina wharf. I was still very hungry with no cash. But I had an idea.

The Migdal Hotel Villa was just around the corner. I made my way to Miss Balgrave's room as fast as I could. It was easy to slip by the concierge and make my way to her private garden. The blazing sun beat down on my back. Although I wasn't nervous, sweat was already running down my body.

There was no one around. I went straight to the French doors. I took my time. There was no rush. She wouldn't be back for hours. It was quick work; French doors are my specialty.

Like I said, I'm an artist.

The cool interior was welcome after the outside heat. It took my eyes time to adjust. There they were. Two beautiful suitcases. Louis Vuitton no less. I didn't have to worry about moving things around because the maids had already been in and she would assume they had done it.

I did have to be careful about what she was going to share with me though. It would have to be something not readily missed or at least not missed until she and I had parted ways.

The suitcase locks were even easier than the door. Sure enough, there was a nice little cache of bills tucked in along the side of the suitcase. She hadn't looked like a traveller's cheque kind of gal. She wasn't. The hundreds were too obvious, and the fifties too. I took two Jacksons. Forty dollars would be enough.

I heard the click of the gun as I was putting the cash in my pocket.

I hadn't heard her come in, but in my defense, I wasn't expecting her either. She had a small pistol in her hand.

"It's amazing what you can get into a handbag these days," I scoffed.

"You are so predictable, Amira."

She seemed rather pleased with herself.

"Sit."

She motioned toward the bed while she sat in a chair. It was an arrangement I didn't like because I had to look at her sideways. She was keeping a good distance between us, just in case I might do something stupid. On the other hand, if I had known at the time that she had paid Ahmed to tell her all about me, I might have done something stupid. The F-in sod, he hadn't even given me a cut of the cash.

"It was a short lunch," I said.

She ignored the remark and started to ask me questions about the marina. She was surprisingly nonchalant. She wanted to know how difficult it was to sail away and return. It was a strange thing to be talking about given the circumstances, but I was staring at her pistol so it didn't register. I said I didn't know. It was the truth. I had only ever sailed in the Greek islands.

"How much?" Miss Balgrave asked.

The question confused me, so I didn't answer.

She grew impatient. "How much money is in your pocket?"

There didn't seem to be any point in lying about it, so I told her forty dollars. She was pleased about that and nodded her head slightly as she decided something…

"Just the right amount," she concluded. "Not too much, not too little. I had you pegged the first time I saw you at the market in Jerusalem."

My astonishment sent a jolt through me, but Miss Balgrave hadn't noticed. She stood up and motioned me to move to the end of the bed. She retrieved a microcassette from the suitcase and tossed it to me.

"Dictation?" I was rattled and tried to cover up by being flippant. It was ridiculous on my part.

"Don't be stupid, Amira," she snapped.

She looked at me the way Miss Beatrissa always did before she gave me a good caning across the calves. I should have taken note of Miss Balgrave but didn't.

"Make your confession good," she sneered. "Details. Right from when you broke in."

I knew what she wanted. After I had finished my confession, she motioned to me to stop the recording and toss it back on the bed near her.

After she had listened to it, she smiled. "That will do."

It was obvious she wanted it as leverage. I waited for the next event. It took about fifteen seconds for her to speak.

"Where have you been in trouble?"

The question caught me by surprise. I couldn't figure out what she was up to. She was an attractive woman, even though she was about twenty years older than I was. She hadn't made a move on me, so sex wasn't it.

She mistook my hesitation and jeered, "Your type is always in trouble with the police."

What an insult. I'm a lady with impeccable manners.

She had no call questioning my integrity. I took extreme offense at the remark. None of it had ever been my fault.

"Out with it Amira. Where?"

Again, there wasn't any point in lying so I told her. When I was done, she seemed strangely satisfied.

"Never in Egypt?"

I feigned being shocked. "Never! It is the land of my forefathers."

She didn't need to know everything. It was none of her business. Besides, white lies don't count.

"Get the suitcase," she commanded and pointed to a regular looking suitcase in the corner.

I hadn't even noticed it up until now.

"Put it on the bed Amira. Open it."

I did as I was told. The dark green suitcase contained an assortment of clothing and two rectangular boxes of chocolates, the type you can buy at any local store. Nothing special. She laughed at the expression on my face.

"What were you expecting Amira? Drugs?"

I felt foolish and angry. What was she playing at?

"My friend needs her suitcase. You are going to take it to her. She lives in Cairo."

The clothes were soft, nothing special there. I picked up the boxes of chocolate. They were individually wrapped in cellophane. There was another box just like it on top of the dresser.

She motioned to the third chocolate box on the dresser, and told me to open it.

"You can have as many as you like Amira."

I shook my head.

"They won't bite, take some."

"I can't eat chocolate. I'm allergic to caffeine," I said sullenly.

She seemed to think that was very funny for she sat down again in her chair and laughed, "It's my friend's birthday. She loves chocolate. You will take the suitcase with her gift."

"How am I supposed to get it there?"

"Bus."

I nodded. I told Miss Balgrave I had made the trip from Jerusalem for my grandmother's funeral in Cairo not that long ago. I thought that was a nice touch. It might garner me some sympathy from her. The bus makes a stop in Ashkelon, but Miss Balgrave knew that. It then goes to the Rafah border crossing, the only crossing between Gaza and Egypt. Even the military personnel use the bus. You can literally have a weapon in your face as you're sitting on the bus. It is always packed, standing room only.

She knew I didn't believe anything she had said about the suitcase. It didn't matter. She was still holding the pistol.

"There's two thousand dollars in it for you," she announced.

My eyebrows shot up. Seriously?

At what time was I going to get that money?

I wasn't expecting anything good to come out of this.

"Sure," I said. "I would have done it for free. Why not? I haven't been to Egypt for years. It will be a nice trip."

She didn't believe me either.

"I'll do it for two grand, and you can give me the recording back." It was worth a try, but she wasn't interested.

"Let's call it incentive," Miss Balgrave mocked. "The police here would find your confession very... compelling, shall we say? I'll keep it. You had better get going though. Ahmed can take you back to Jerusalem to get your passport. Be here tomorrow evening. Six o'clock sharp."

I was already out the door when I heard her say, "Oh Amira, keep the forty bucks."

There certainly wasn't anything left for me to say. Her sarcasm grated on me. She knew enough about me to have the authorities pick me up. I was so deep in thought walking back to my hotel trying to figure out how to get out of this mess, that I didn't even see him coming.

He grabbed me quick and dragged me behind a building. The first punch was to my stomach. I crumbled like bad cake. He kicked me viciously. I wrapped my hands and arms around my face and head.

"Don't worry," he hissed in my ear. "She said not the face."

He sat me up and then pulled me to my feet. I was in so much pain that I couldn't even focus on his face. He was a massive square blurry shape. I heard his voice though. The last thing he said before he was gone was the word incentive.

The funny thing about beatings is how they start to become the same. I hadn't been close to my father, probably because he beat me quite regularly. He died of a heart attack while playing volleyball at the local Legion. Physical activity was part of his rehab as an alcoholic. I guess the exercise wasn't a good idea.

Being Egyptian, my mother never told me my father had died. She hated misfortune and preferred to pretend it hadn't happened. When I asked where he was, she replied he was on a business trip and would be home soon. Then he was on another trip and another. Pretty soon, he had been gone for a while.

I didn't think much of it when I found out he was dead.

The only thing I could think of immediately after this beating was finding my shoe which had come off. At least my attacker had been considerate; he had attacked me only a block from my hotel, so I didn't have far to walk.

I now knew that Miss Balgrave was definitely not a lady. She obviously lacked any kind of manners.

My British private school upbringing kicked in; I would get even. She wasn't a lady, despite her looks. I hated her with a passion. It was an unusually intense feeling for me. Typically, I just move on.

Ahmed was sitting in the taxi outside the hotel. I told him the job was done, we were going back to Jerusalem, and I just had to grab my things from the hotel room. He asked me why I was holding my stomach. I replied I had indigestion.

I still hadn't had a bite to eat, but I wasn't hungry anymore.

CHAPTER THREE

Ahmed complained about driving me all the way to the door of my house, despite the fact that I said my indigestion was so bad and I wouldn't make it otherwise. His village is twenty minutes from me as the crow flies but an hour as the roads go.

The Israeli government made sure all the roads to Arab villages are like a maze. The main arteries bypass the villages.

It's difficult to be an Arab in Israel. I remember one bus trip when I was working as an assistant to an Israeli tour guide. He was a vibrant guy. Really captivating. The tourists loved him, the tips were good. The sex with him was even better. He would explain the history of the Holy Land to the tourists on the bus. His baritone boomed throughout the tour bus; he didn't need a microphone. When he came to the part about Arabs and Jews, the young couple sitting in front of me couldn't quite grasp it.

There are Arabs here? How is it possible to be an Arab in Israel? We were in the West Bank actually. They couldn't comprehend the word *occupation*.

The couple was Jewish and from South America. I don't know what was up with their education though. The tour guide, who was also Jewish, tried to explain to them that Arabs had citizenship in the state of Israel. Well, I thought they were going to jump out of the window of the moving bus. It was an atrocity they said. The guide was pretty exasperated with them.

I have Jewish and Arab friends. They get along. The bigger picture is not quite so rosy. I spied the newspaper on my doorstep had another horrible headline. I didn't want to pick it up. I didn't think I would be able to in my condition.

I stepped over it. Hazeer wasn't home. Good. It would take a lot of explaining and he would try to talk me out of going to Egypt.

Besides, I didn't have a choice.

I could hear Miss Balgrave's voice. "You could be quite attractive, Amira," she criticized me before I left the Villa. "If you did something with your hair and a touch of make-up. You could be a proper maid."

I hadn't known how to take it, so I didn't say anything. From her expression I couldn't tell if there was a double meaning in the comment or not. My silence had made her snicker.

I eased myself into the bathtub. The steam came up around my eyes and ears. It would have been glorious if not for the pain. The bruises were a vibrant colour. Moving without wincing was impossible. As I lay soaking in the tub, I started thinking about ways to get back at Miss Balgrave.

I had hoped there would be something in the refrigerator. There was, milk that had gone sour. I crawled into bed, hoping tomorrow wouldn't come, but it did. I anticipated feeling better the next day, but when morning came, I didn't. It was the same horrible feeling as the day before. I packed plenty of painkillers, and my passport.

Actually, I should say my two passports, Canadian and Egyptian. The Arab countries surrounding Israel always raise an eyebrow if they see an Israeli stamp in a passport.

I use my Canadian passport, smile and say I'm a tourist. All my misdemeanors are linked to my Egyptian passport, nothing important, just a parking ticket here and there.

I scribbled Hazeer a note telling him I had landed a big fish and would be gone four or five days. I can look after myself. I watered the dead plants just to show him how much I cared and left.

My neighbourhood is a mix of architecture. The bottom floors of most residences have lovely arches, reflecting the gentle influence of Arab culture. After the state of Israel was established, huge numbers of Palestinians fled. They left their charming homes thinking they would be returning shortly; they didn't — actually the Palestinians couldn't.

New Jewish occupants moved in, and renovations ensued. I gazed at the top two floors of the residences which now had square stern windows. Functional. Efficient. It's like the buildings are in conflict with their emotions or with their past.

Strange.

Acquiring land under questionable circumstances isn't unique to the Middle East either. There are many ways to grab someone else's real estate. I dated a real estate scoundrel in Canada, who had an eager eye for land. He would grab a parcel of land from a distraught widow, convincing her the price was a fantastic deal. Then he would flip it for twice the price the seller had been paid. The widow was left with a paltry sum.

Land sale theft, and it is theft, doesn't just happen to widows desperate for money but others as well. There are many ways to get people to sell or leave their home. The claim is it was all done legally. It's robbery.

Just because it's legal doesn't mean it isn't a crime.

To get to the main Jerusalem bus terminal, I have to walk past the Palestinian's hut. It makes me angry every time I see his squalor between the two modern mega high rises. They took his land and built on it. There is a little piece of land left over between the two buildings. That is where he lives with his family. He's fighting it in court of course. Good luck with that. He's Palestinian so he has to apply to the Palestinian court even though he's a citizen of Israel, which he did, but this is a housing matter so it has to be heard in the Israeli state court. See where this is going?

Nowhere.

Further down the street is another Palestinian farmer. They took his land and have built on it as well. They have left him his home, but his house is in total disrepair. He doesn't have the money to fix it because they took his land with the olive trees and destroyed his income. The Israeli state says his house is a health hazard. So, he has to fix it, but he cannot fix it without a permit from the state. There is a huge backlog for permits. He will, maybe, get permission in a year.

I tried to help him but found out that once the state has issued a health hazard warning, you only have six months to rectify the problem. After that they can legally condemn the place. According to the state law, you can't live in a condemned place. So in six months, while he is waiting for his permit to fix his house, the state will claim the house and land in the name of health and safety.

I suggested he could appeal it, but he would have to go to the Palestinian court because he's a Palestinian. His case will overlap with the state court, of course, and everyone will say they are confused.

It's a no win for me and for him, well, if he gets a little agitated about the situation, the state feels he is a threat. I knew the military court and law would then step in.

I understand this guy. His uncle is in sort of the same situation. However, the uncle's olive grove is still intact. He lives in a tent on the land, but his conflict is with the new owner of his property. There's only a small catch here – he never sold it, but apparently some Jewish fellow in California bought it and says he's the owner. Hence, the uncle went to court too, all three courts, Israeli, Palestinian, and military.

Like I said, it makes me angry, and I am usually quite calm.

It's all about the land, owning the land or taking the land. Don't even get me started on Canadian Aboriginal issues.

I don't own land. I don't even own a car.

I got on the bus. My feelings for Miss Balgrave hadn't changed. I felt like I was going back to the headmistress's office for a reckoning. Miss Beatrissa never used the cane. Oh no, she had someone else do that. She would threaten you with humiliation. If she pronounced you a rotten egg then everyone knew. All two million residents in Alexandria would know. Your reputation would be ruined. You wouldn't even be able to buy a train ticket.

I always had to think quick and figure out what improvement Miss Beatrissa's office might need so I could siphon the money off my grandmother. Miss Beatrissa had a beautiful office thanks to me, consequently I kept my reputation.

However, my current problem was that Miss Balgrave didn't need a refurbished office. I still couldn't figure out how to make her pay, but it would come to me. I'm very creative.

I couldn't get an express ticket to Ashkelon. Hence I had to travel south via Bayt Lahm or as most of the world knows it,

Bethlehem, and then travel west to my destination. It was now a trip that would take me three times as long.

The woman I sat beside looked pleasant enough. Older. Scarf on her head. Big carpet bag on her lap.

"Beautiful country," she chatted.

I smiled and nodded.

It's true. It's gorgeous. It always reminds me of the Okanagan Valley in British Columbia. That's Canada by the way. I went there once with my father on a quick trip. It was hot. The lake was fun.

"There are Arab villages near Bethlehem," the woman leaned closer like it was a state secret.

I gave a little laugh at her clandestine manner but said with the utmost seriousness, "Yes. My friend is a teacher in one of them. She lives in terror for her Palestinian students."

"Ahh," the woman gave a knowing nod. "Pity that."

"Four months ago, I visited her. She was shaking from head to toe. The Israelis had come to the elementary school to harass the children, again."

"It's not right," responded the woman.

"This time they had taken four Palestinian boys away with them."

A look of pain crossed her face. "How old were the students?"

"The students were eleven years old. I stayed with my friend all day. The school didn't send the rest of the students home."

"Education is very dear to them. It should be. They were not going to be deprived of their right to learn."

"Yes. You seem to understand."

"It's amazing that normal life continues under the umbrella of oppression."

"Yes," I responded. "People still eat, cook, shop, and go to school. At least, until they can't."

"You waited all day?"

"While I was there, the teacher showed me the school projects. The students raised chickens and had a thriving little industry going. The eggs are marketed in the local area."

"No doubt the students were very proud."

"It was a long, painful day waiting for word about the four boys. At the end of the school day, my friend finally received the news. All four boys were still alive."

"Small mercies."

"The Israeli soldiers had taken them into the countryside, roughed them up by beating them with sticks. They made them lie down in front of the Israeli soldiers so that they could urinate all over the young boys."

"Disgusting."

"No solace could comfort her. I had nothing to offer her but the pledge that I would retell her story."

The woman patted my hand, nodding.

Memories.

They are sometimes painful, hard to bear.

My bus trip to Ashkelon went along the main roads, but in the distance, the villages nestled into the countryside. I had taken many walks up there. It greeted me with a silence on the wind only interrupted by a tinkling bell on a wandering goat or the wavering flute song of a still present shepherd.

It's a beautiful riveting land full of deadly conflict.

I arrived at the Migdal Villa Hotel at six o'clock sharp. Miss Balgrave kept me waiting. Wouldn't you know it. Her stooge, the one with the big fists, walked into the lobby of the hotel. He came right up to where I was sitting in one of those cushy chairs.

"Come back tomorrow morning. Seven o'clock sharp. Don't be late."

It was on the tip of my tongue to quip that being sharp was irrelevant since she was always late, but my body still ached, so I shut my mouth and nodded.

He handed me an envelope which I automatically took. The two thousand dollars it wasn't. Inside the envelope was just enough cash for the night. So, the bargain hotel it was. At least I wouldn't get beaten up on my way there since the Pitbull was staying at the Villa with his master.

I was in a foul mood by the time I got to my hotel. No pain, no gain. That saying is a lie. I live to run away, so I can run away tomorrow. Unfortunately, I had been rather blindsided the night before and was in significant pain. I considered phoning Hazeer but it would cost me money I didn't have. I knew he wouldn't take a collect call. Cheap bastard.

The only thing left to do was take a hot shower and wait for the morning to come.

Why is nothing simple in my life?

After all my years of living on this earth, I still haven't got used to insects.

I took a deep breath before opening the door to the bathroom. After a quick peek around, I decided the coast was clear and stepped in. The brilliant turquoise tile and bright red trim grated on me. Why, why, why was all I could think. I'm a pastel person myself, subtle.

At least the shower was hot. Just when I was starting to relax was when they started to appear. Maybe they liked the heat too and that's what encouraged them to come out of the open drain in the corner.

So, picture this, I'm standing in a hot shower, big sigh, eyes closed, turning around, getting the water cascade on all sides. Then I open my eyes and right there, right at eye level, is the cockroach on the tile in the shower with me. It's a big one, two inches at least.

I nearly broke a leg getting out of the bathtub. I had to step high over the edge. Wouldn't you know it, there were two cockroaches on the floor.

I was dancing and screaming.

My feet slipped on the tiles. I crashed into the bedroom slamming the bathroom door behind me.

I'll never get used to those things.

Imagining those creatures making it out of the bathroom into the bedroom was worse than the thought of an ultimate confrontation.

I had to go back in.

I picked up one of my high-heeled shoes and pushed open the door.

The big one was still in the shower on the wall. I couldn't see the other two smaller ones. I took a deep breath and smacked it.

I hit it right on.

Tough bugger. The impact only cracked his back.

Now he was doing contortions all over the wall with a trail of slime coming out. The excrement left a weaving death trail on the tiles.

I turned around and screamed. The other two on the wall. They'd been flanking me.

Crafty buggers.

Whack. Whack.

I dropped the shoe and stumbled into the bedroom.

I'd have to go barefoot tomorrow.

Sometimes life is just too hard.

There was a cigarette pack and matches left by a previous guest on the bed stand. I fumbled with the pack. It seemed to take forever to open it. My hands were shaking as I grabbed a cigarette and lit one.

I sucked in hard and fast to calm myself. The smoke went straight into my lungs and circulated through my body in seconds.

I nearly passed out.

I don't smoke.

I had to lie down on the bed or else I would have cracked my head open on the wall as I most certainly would have tumbled over. I was so exhausted that I simply collapsed.

When I woke up at four o'clock, it was pitch black. The automatic light in the bathroom had shut itself off. Hell hole.

I was buck-naked and the hair soap I hadn't had a chance to wash out stuck to the bed linen.

What now?

I didn't have an alarm. If I missed being sharp and on time, Miss Balgrave would certainly send Mister Fix-it.

I'd have to stay awake.

Needless to say, when I finally got to Miss Balgrave's room in the Migdal Hotel, I was moving stiffly and looked a mess.

There were some extra people in her suite for this bon voyage party. Two were exiting the room on the far side as I was coming in from the patio via the French doors. I didn't get a good look at them. They had been speaking German, that much I knew.

I know the words *Dummheit* and *Arschloch* when I hear them. English isn't the only language I can swear in.

Miss Balgrave made some comments about me looking the part. She told me her friend would meet me at the bus station in Cairo. Her friend would identify the suitcase and had been given my description.

I only had my own small suitcase to carry and could manage. Whatever was in the lining of Miss Balgrave's suitcase must be pretty valuable.

Drugs, but maybe it was diamonds?

Name of the friend? Nope. She looks like? Nope.

Nothing doing. There was no extra information for me.

The stooge handed me the bus ticket and stated he'd drop me off at the bus stop. On our way there, we passed a post office.

Why didn't they just use the postal service?

I mean, not only mail the contents but the whole suitcase. It certainly wouldn't be any more expensive than sending me with it.

If Miss Balgrave really supposed I had bought the story about her friend and the gift of chocolates, so be it.

I can look after myself, or so I thought.

There wasn't a chance to get a good look at the suitcase before I hit the border. I never touched it. Strong man had put it in the hold of the bus and made sure I had a window seat.

Once I stepped off the bus at the Rafah crossing, I'd be under surveillance by the Israeli border guards with no chance to inspect the bag. I figured the stuff must be in the lining or in the piping trim around the edge, maybe even in the handle or under the locks.

The Israeli border crossing at Rafah is pristine, state of the art. There are lovely palm trees swaying in the breeze, welcoming flowers and immaculate landscaping.

I nearly fell down the stairs of the bus on my way out. No one paid any attention to me. The usual tourists were yakking about the border and where to go.

It's pretty obvious where to go. It's not like the Israelis just let you wander across. Tourists are so stupid.

No one spoke or came close to me. I smelled or at least I'm pretty sure I did. The shampoo had caked my hair together. Well, I hadn't had a shower, had I?

I trundled into the building. The checkpoint officer was a young woman who does the initial questioning. At the border they watch you like a hawk.

Are you carrying anything for anybody?

I'm not an idiot, so of course I said no.

Letters? Nope. Gifts? Nope.

Suitcase is yours? Every inch of it I declared. I was on the verge of getting flippant, couldn't she hurry this up? But she took her time.

"You say you are a tourist, yet there is no recent entry stamp in your Canadian passport."

I indicated an obscure smudge on one of the pages, and smiled. "Just staying with friends."

"What friends?"

I gave a Jewish name and an address. Asher Levin. West Jerusalem. I live in East Jerusalem. It wouldn't do to give that address. Asher is never home. It was a safe bet. They'd have a heck of a time checking it. I dropped my eyes and revealed we were going to be married. I was going to tell my Egyptian family the great news.

She looked at my hair with skepticism.

"So, you're not a tourist?"

"Well, I have never been in love before, so it's all new. I am a tourist of the heart." I smiled.

I'm not a teenager and have been around the block a few times, so her incredulity was increasing. Maybe I was overdoing it, but my usually calm nerves were not co-operating. My torso ached from standing so long.

She stamped my Canadian passport. I put my passport in the outside pocket of my luggage bag.

Going from Israel to Egypt is like being on the back of a snake. The single file line weaves out of the passport office. It's serious business, don't wave at the arm guards. The exit line slithers its way alongside a chain link fence to a gate. It's pretty dramatic.

They have done everything to make you feel like you are leaving the garden of paradise and entering a desert. The gate slams shut behind you. I walked that little stretch before reaching the Egyptian gate with a profound and growing sense of relief.

It was misplaced.

On the Egyptian side of the border, there's not a patch of green anywhere.

Behind me, on the Israeli side of the border, was the chosen land. I was surrounded by giddy American tourists thrilled with having visited God's blessed land, a land belonging to the Jewish people as proven in the Bible. I was astounded at their viewpoint. Modern Israel unabashedly calls itself a secular state. How is Israel's *biblical right* a valid claim then for so many of its supporters who reside outside the Middle East?

A perspiring nationalist of some western country huffed beside me and spoke to me as if I was actually interested in what he had to say.

"The state of Israel claims God gave them the land."

I gave the origin of the voice a glance and retorted, "Sure, if you go for that kind of stuff."

"Stuff! It's not just stuff!"

Heaving a weary sigh, I countered, "For argument's sake, let's say God made a covenant with Abram. That was only one side of the bargain; the other required the Jews to bless the nations of the world."

"I am relieved to hear you know the Bible," he replied.

I guess he had been skeptical since he had profiled me. You know, skin colour, hair colour, eye colour. All dark. He was so pleased to hear the light.

"Well, that hasn't happened," I replied shooting down his balloon. "The religious doctrine also states if the Jews didn't hold up their end of the bargain, then the covenant was null and void."

"Well…"

I held up my hand and continued, "Expulsion is the word used. Expulsion. The Jewish people scattered to the winds."

I waved my hand across the desert.

I never did understand this biblical claim stuff. I've heard it a million times.

I was speaking loudly and hadn't even turned my head towards the man.

He was astonished.

I was on a roll so I said, "Even the New Testament addresses this issue of ownership but moves the claim into a new realm, not the kingdom of land, but the kingdom of God."

"I suppose."

"*La-ah.* No," I waggled my finger. "I quote *all nations and people* being welcome there."

"The Jewish people have a right," he argued.

"That's another thing," I responded. "Judaism also holds this tenet. It's not a nationalistic focus, but a focus on a love for God."

We had reached the door of the Egyptian authorities. I pulled it open and said, "Have a nice day."

The man's stunned silence reminded me of a similar conversation my grandmother had once held with an older couple who lived just outside Tel Aviv.

We were in Cyprus on vacation and were sitting on reclining white lawn chairs by a lovely blue pool. Very idyllic.

The man explained they were Jewish. He told my grandmother how they were living good lives and their children also. He shared all about the nice house they now had, good jobs, just good people all around. He even gave my grandmother his address. Told her to come visit.

It was all very well until my grandmother said, "But what about the Palestinians that used to live in your house?"

That was when the wife left us. The woman was dreadfully upset. It made me feel awful that my grandmother had ruined her vacation time.

I dislike feeling awful. As I was crossing over into the Egyptian sector, I was glad I was leaving all of that conflict behind or so I thought.

As soon as I got into the Egyptian zone, I went straight to the loo to check the suitcase. I started with what I could see and went through all the clothing, the side pockets and palpated the lining like I was looking for a cancerous tumour. I used my metal nail file and slid it behind any section I could.

Nothing. The only thing left was the piping and the hardware but I couldn't inspect that without damaging the suitcase. It was going on close to an hour when I heard the announcement calling Amira Alexander to the passport desk.

What?

I hadn't presented myself to the control officers. How did they know I was in the building?

Then it occurred to me that the Israelis must have let them know. It shocked me actually. I didn't think the two sides even spoke to each other.

It was a miscalculation, that's for sure.

I should have paid attention to the red flag waving in the back of my head. Then I had a flash of inspiration. Miss Balgrave must have realized I would be returning. Perhaps the friend was going to give me something for the return trip? There wasn't anything in this luggage.

I carried my two bags to the line for the Egyptian customs official who was sitting behind a worn counter. I rubbed my stomach and made grimaces at anyone who would look at me indicating I had gastrointestinal issues requiring me to be in the washroom for long periods of time. It wasn't too far off the truth, my stomach still hurt thanks to Mister Muscle. I don't think the officer was particularly interested. He looked extremely bored.

"Yes," he said.

I smiled.

"Your passport?"

"Oh, of course. My name was called. I was just in the loo."

I don't know what I had been thinking, maybe a little flustered by my name being announced, maybe trying too hard to tuck the suitcase behind me. I don't know. Silly me. I gave him my passport.

Your name? Your birthday? Where were you born? Where do you live?

"I'm from Canada. Visiting friends in Jerusalem."

Better to stick with the same story

The officer already had the passport stamp in his hand ready to give me the A-okay. He kept looking at my passport like it was the Koran.

"It says here that you live in Alexandria."

The hand with the stamp slowly came down.

"Just right there, stamp on that page is fine," I pointed.

He looked over my shoulder, back at me and said, "Come with me."

I looked at my passport in front of him on his desk. I glanced down at the outside pocket of my luggage bag on the floor beside me, and could see my other passport looking back at me with exasperation.

My Egyptian passport was in front of him on his desk, not the Canadian passport I had presented to the Israelis.

Oh. Not a good situation. Not on the Egyptian side.

I had no choice but to follow him. There was nothing pristine about this building. It was dusty, dirty, a maze of hallways.

He led me into a room with one chair and a small table.

"Wait here."

I waited a long time.

Another guard came in carrying the two boxes of chocolates.

"Have a chocolate," he offered.

He had already removed the cellophane. He lifted the lid. The rows of chocolate pieces sat in their little individual compartments.

"No, thank you."

"Amira is it?"

I nodded.

"You don't like chocolate?"

"I'm allergic to chocolate," I refused. "Sir."

I was back in school again. Idiot. I cursed quietly for mistakenly giving them my Egyptian passport.

They had taken my luggage. By now they would have discovered the Canadian passport as well. I figured I could explain it away. Egyptians love a good story. They are very curious about what is in your luggage, what is happening in your life, and what is in your personal mail.

I used to get mail packets sent from my father's Canadian sister to where I lived in Alexandria. She would regularly mail three or four packets of Kool Aid. I'm not sure what the post office thought about the powdered drink, but the packets regularly arrived with the corners torn off like someone had stuck a wet finger in there to have a taste. My friends at the British school in Alexandria wouldn't drink the stuff after I had mixed it with water. I guess brilliant lime green liquid with a dubious life span was not an adventure they wished to partake in, but I always tried to share.

"Please. Sir. Have some chocolate yourself."

He looked at me curiously.

I tried all my old tricks. I smiled. I lowered my eyes. I talked about my ailing grandmother. The officer refused to even consider giving me back my passports.

"Wait here."

Not again.

This time, I didn't have long to wait. Two female security officers stepped into the room. My good luck totally disintegrated. My bad luck kicked in.

"Clothes off."

"Now just a minute."

One of them stepped forward.

"All right. All right."

I gestured for her to keep away. *Mahlish.* I wanted to let her know it was fine and not to get excited. You know how people in power get when they think you are not co-operating.

One officer walked around me slowly, peering at my bruises. The work the stooge had done on me was now a pretty shade of purple, blue, green and yellow. I looked like an abstract painting. The other officer checked every inch of my clothing.

"You're getting married?" she inquired.

Jeesh. The Israelis had passed on every bit of information.

I nodded. Might as well stick to the story.

"You shouldn't marry this man. He's a bad man. Put your clothes on."

Egyptians are very sympathetic people.

"You should stay in Egypt. It is better for you."

Well, I'm not sure about that, but I nodded anyway. I deemed we were finished but nothing doing. I waited for another ten minutes when a different guard came and told me to follow him.

The maze of corridors continued. We went out of the passport building, across a cement courtyard to what looked like a warehouse. Lo and behold, it was a warehouse! Tucked deep into its recesses was an office. The room was sparse except for a picture of Hosni Mubarak hanging on the wall behind the desk. Obviously, the office didn't belong to Miss Beatrissa; it wasn't opulent at all. Seated behind the desk was a man in Western dress. He didn't look like a police officer. I think he belonged to the secret police, but you know, I never did find out exactly his position.

"Your name is Amira Margaret Alexander," he said.

"Yes, sir."

He nodded to the guard beside me who pushed me down in the chair and then went and stood by the door.

My two passports were on the officer's desk, along with the two boxes of chocolates. He brushed the Canadian one aside and picked up my Egyptian passport. He waggled it in my direction.

"You have dishonoured the Egyptian government and the right to hold an Egyptian passport."

"I had no intention of dishonouring anybody. I just got them mixed up."

Hey, it happens. What was he so hot under the collar for?

I hadn't been back to Egypt for five years, but now I know why I left. What did it matter that I had presented the wrong passport?

I could just give them the Canadian one with the Israeli stamp in it. I said as much.

I have never been able to keep my mouth shut.

He glared at me. In a land of bribers, he didn't look like the type you could, not with sex, not with money. I admit I was starting to feel like there were monkeys on my back.

Deference Amira. Remember you are just a woman.

I lowered my eyes.

"You are causing a lot of trouble, Amira."

Story of my life.

"Yes sir," I appealed to his softer side. "I am so sorry."

"Amira, it says in your passport, in your passports," he corrected himself, "you are a student, an artist?"

His tone had changed.

"Yes sir. I am an artist."

I felt encouraged. Misperception on my part.

His tone had changed for the worse. "What do you do?"

Hold on here, no need to get sarcastic. I am an artist and a damned good one.

I didn't need to justify myself to someone who couldn't appreciate it.

"I paint."

"You told the officer you were getting married. You are not getting married are you, Amira?"

My heart sank. I pleaded, "I am travelling for inspiration. Back to my home. I must work and create."

"You lied, Amira. You are not getting married."

He frowned at me.

I felt like frowning back and mocking him, but I reined myself in. "Not really. Sir."

"You're not going to meet your family to tell them about your engagement, Amira. Who are you meeting?"

I couldn't think of a name they couldn't check. Like I said I haven't been back to Egypt for a long time. I replied I was meeting a friend.

"Like the friend you met at night, on…" he stopped to peer at a paper on his desk, "…on May 7, 1980? Is that right, Amira?"

It was a date in infamy.

It was the date I'd been arrested and plunked into an Egyptian jail.

It wasn't my fault.

How was I to know the car had parked on restricted access territory? Okay, okay, it wasn't a parking ticket. My friend and I had been there, in the car, for hours but whatever.

"It was a misunderstanding," I asserted. "Sir."

He tilted his head sideways.

I didn't try to explain it to him, but I will explain it to you.

The seventh of May was a day just like any other. This lovely guy invited me to go with him for a drive. I said sure. He had seemed attractive enough. I don't even remember his name.

I was lonely. It was a little late for an outing, but you know, he was cute. It was tennis court stuff, nothing heavy. The problem was he had parked his car in a military zone.

A restricted military zone.

If I had known what an imbecile he was, I never would have gone necking with him in the first place. The Egyptian military was not impressed. While they were checking us out, well, yeah, they put us in prison. I was only in there a few days, but it is an experience I would rather not discuss. Thank you.

"I can only say I am terribly sorry about the whole thing," I implored. "Sir."

"Amira, now you are going to meet another friend?"

Why does he keep saying my name? It was giving me the creeps.

"Amira, are the boxes of chocolate for your friend?"

Sure, why not? I said it was for the friend I was meeting.

"Yes, because you don't eat chocolate, Amira."

There was that strange smile again, followed by a truly unpleasant pause.

"Where did you get the boxes of chocolate, Amira?"

Ahh. A store. Where else do you get chocolate from? Maybe he wasn't as smart as I initially supposed he was. I was wrong there too. He saw my hesitation.

"Did you enjoy your time in prison?"

I gulped.

"A friend got it for me to give to my friend," I explained.

"We're all friends. Friendly, you know. Sir."

"Where is this friend?"

"Ashkelon."

"What nationality is this friend?"

The question caught me by surprise. Of course, I had been thinking about Miss Balgrave, but I didn't know what nationality she was. I didn't know much about her at all. I shrugged. When he probed about my friend in Egypt that I was supposedly meeting I started to get tongue tied.

He didn't get upset though and he had stopped saying my name. He switched to asking me where I had lived in Egypt, about my life, and about my painting.

He had an easy manner about him. We were getting chummier by the minute. He started to remind me of the vendor in Alexandria where I always went to buy a Coke.

He looked over my shoulder and nodded.

Suddenly the guard grabbed both my arms, pulled them behind my back, and slapped handcuffs onto my wrists.

The officer picked up one of the two boxes of chocolate.

"These aren't chocolates, Amira. These are plastic explosives."

I gaped at him.

"No wonder you don't want to eat them, Amira."

He nodded to the guard who yanked me out of the chair.

He was using my name again.

"Amira Margaret Alexander, you are under arrest."

CHAPTER FOUR

Naturally the whole story came out. I'm not a martyr.

I didn't get to tell him right away because of the call to prayer, the *Adhan*. Muslims are called to pray five times a day. The *Adhan*, which means to listen, is called out from the mosque by the Muezzin who stands either in the mosque's minaret tower or turns the loudspeakers on for the recording.

Allah Akbar! Allah Akbar! Faithful followers begin the ritual of prayer on the prayer rugs by touching their foreheads to the ground repeatedly.

My grandmother had been a bit lax when it came to religion. Some of the loudspeakers are located right next to apartment windows. They are booming loud, but it's amazing what you can sleep through once you get used to it. When I had questioned my grandmother about my grandfather, who had been Muslim, she scoffed.

Personally, I had always considered the prayer ritual of touching your forehead to the ground a good exercise regime, at the very least.

I asked my grandmother why my grandfather rubbed sandpaper on his forehead. She didn't know what I was referring to, but it became clear after I pointed to the round spot in the middle of his forehead. She had given me a slap across the head and told me not to be so insolent.

I'm not insolent, just curious. I got the same slap across the head when I told my father that I wasn't going to church anymore.

I don't have much use for religion.

I can look after myself, which is what I was doing in the interrogation room. After I had finished confessing, my interrogator left the room to give me some more time to ponder life. While I was waiting, I thought about all of the things I would like to do to Miss Balgrave for getting me into this mess.

I wasn't sure what was going to happen next, but my grandmother's advice jumped into my head.

You should go through life expecting nothing from anyone That way you will never be disappointed.

I concentrated on not being disappointed in the hope that I would get nothing from anyone, especially the authorities, and that nothing would equal no charges pressed.

I was transferred to Building Number Four. I have only a vague idea of where that particular compound is located. I was transported in an army truck. I estimate it must have been a two-hour drive, but who knows. They could have been driving in circles for all I know. I was actually trying really hard not to think about anything at that time. Number Four was located among a collection of buildings, all of which were surrounded by a high stone wall.

It certainly looked like a jail. My knees crumbled. My new escorts dragged me inside. I was taken to a stone-cold room with no windows and a bucket in the corner. My case was being processed. What I mean by that is I was examined, poked, prodded, fingered, photographed, and fingerprinted.

After everyone had left the room, I sat in the corner and cried. I sounded like the starving cat I had heard outside my grandmother's balcony in Cairo. The teeny kitten had been wailing from starvation and could barely walk. I remember looking over the balcony to see it wobbling through the garbage in the alley four storeys below.

It had upset me so much that I ran to get an egg from the refrigerator. I figured my aim would be pretty good. I'd save the cat and thereby make the world a better place. My aim from four storeys up was perfect. Well, almost. The egg didn't land beside the kitten but right on top of it with significant force. There wasn't a sound or any movement after that.

So much for good intentions.

I was totally disoriented in my cell. There were no windows or anything to indicate the time of day. I collapsed in the corner.

A rough hand shook me awake. I followed the hand of the shape it was attached to along endless corridors. This office was different. There were embroidered chairs and proper lighting. The entire décor was of good taste and affluence. The Canadian Embassy must have come through. I praised the Israelis for being so efficient and relaying the information to the proper authorities.

Like I said, I was disoriented.

The man who entered was a match for the office. This official was trim, elegant, and well dressed. He was in no hurry and moved with a natural ease. He sat behind his desk with the confidence that only power and influence can give.

The door opened. A tray of hot tea and bowl of Ful was brought in. The official made a flick of his finger. I was poured a glass of steaming hot tea by the guard. Did I want sugar?

I looked at the guard who lifted a teaspoonful of sugar. I nodded eagerly and put up my hand. Five. He smiled and put in five heaping teaspoons of sugar into my glass. I judged it would be my last cup of tea and wanted it to be good.

Another one finger flick. The guard moved away.

"Amira."

Oh no, another name caller.

"Would you like some Ful?" the official asked.

I shook my head. The beans looked like they had attitude. For sure it would make me vomit. I didn't want to disgrace myself. I have some dignity you know.

He flicked his finger again. The guard took the Ful away.

"I will be handling your case."

I could see his name on the brass desk Toblerone. It was Omar Mohammed.

"That's good. The Canadian government will be eager to speak with you," I said.

"Oh? Why is that?"

"Well, now that they know I have been wrongfully arrested, they will want an explanation."

It must have been all that sugar that made me into a motor mouth. He leaned back into his swivel chair and moved side to side.

"The Canadian government does not know you are here," he murmured. "You tried to enter the country on an Egyptian passport with explosives. This is a domestic matter under my jurisdiction, my control."

My bravado cracked.

"When was the last time you were in Egypt, Amira?"

"Five years ago."

"Now then, let's not waste any more time. You are being charged. Held as a terrorist. That carries a life sentence, in some cases, even a death penalty."

"I'm innocent."

"So you say, but your story is nonsense. A friend of a friend of a friend. It means nothing," dismissed Omar Mohammed.

"I tell you I don't know anything about Miss Balgrave." I tried not to sniffle.

"Tell me what you do know. What does she look like for instance?"

I described her pretty well, I think. I'm an artist and observant. I didn't volunteer to do a sketch for him though. *That* would have been a bit too much co-operation.

Always hold something back. I'd make him work for the information. If I gave every detail up right away, he'd think I was lying.

He wasn't interested in how I got my bruising though. Compassionate sort of guy he wasn't. That hurt my feelings a bit and I got a little peevish about it.

He considered the information I had given him and I suddenly thought maybe I had overdone it or in this case underdone it. I couldn't tell.

"There is something else. I just remembered."

I wanted to make sure he believed I was fully cooperating. I told him about the other people who were in the room at the Migdal hotel the morning I had left Ashkelon.

"I didn't get a good look at them but they were speaking German."

"Male or female? What did they say?"

"I couldn't tell. I didn't hear what they were talking about."

"Then how do you know it was German?"

He was getting annoyed I could tell.

My face grew red. "They said I was stupid. They called me an asshole."

Omar seemed to relax. "You don't know anything else?"

I shook my head.

"Tell me again what her instructions were to you."

He questioned me this way and that way, but I didn't have anything else to share. Eager to show I was on his side, I ventured my original theory about diamonds and drugs. He waved it away with a flip of his hand and called for the guard to take me back to my stone cell.

This time we went through the outside courtyard. There was a flickering yard light on. The white bulk of Building Number Four loomed to the right of me. A work detail was crossing the compound. It was a chain gang of ten prisoners heading to the railway station.

They were linked together like animals going to market. The clank of the chains made a scraping sound. The guards hit the prisoners to keep them in line. The prisoners swayed unsteadily and leered at me. Their gait became irregular as they grabbed their dirty cotton clothing and groped their genitals. Seeing a woman probably gave them all instant hard-ons. They made lewd gestures and licked their lips as they lurched by me.

My guard pushed me on by. I had to come to terms with the fact that I was in dire straits. The charge against me was serious. I only had my wits to get me out of the situation. I would have to do better the next time I spoke with Omar Mohammed. If there was a next time. I'd have to convince him that I was innocent.

"Let me give you a piece of advice," my guard said to me before locking me in. "You should smile more, co-operate more. Don't be so sullen and angry. It will get you nowhere. You should be nicer."

Nice? Nice! This wasn't an F-in tea party.

"If you know something you should tell them. Especially since these are crimes against the state. President Mubarak doesn't take kindly to that."

It was true. My travelling from Jerusalem certainly fell into that category and didn't help my defense. President Hosni Mubarak of the Arab Republic of Egypt, was notoriously anti-Semitic. He had come to power after the assassination of President Anwar Sadat in 1981 at the parade of the October 6th celebration.

"He is our president," the guard announced proudly as if I wasn't aware of that fact. "The October 6th festivities were about Egyptian empowerment."

"Well, Mubarak certainly rewrote the history of the 6 October 1973 events or at least his role in those historic events."

"What do you mean rewrote?"

Ohh, but I was on shaky ground with that comment.

I quickly responded, "If you mention the date in Israel, they say that was the day they saw the outskirts of Cairo, decided no way, and withdrew. In the Mubarak version of history, it was the day the Egyptians decisively drove the Israeli's out and reclaimed the Sinai."

"Bah, they are losers," scoffed the guard. "Mubarak was a national hero because of October 6th."

Personally, I always laughed at that when I was home in Jerusalem on that date.

I didn't share that information with the guard. But he looked like he expected me to say something patriotic.

"I was in my final year at school in Alexandria when the attack occurred. I wasn't at the Cairo victory parade, of course, I was enjoying festivities in Alexandria, but my grandmother had gone. It was the most horrific thing she had ever witnessed. The Fundamentalist militants had used automatic rifles to gun Sadat down."

The guard nodded with satisfaction at my nationalist sentiment.

Again, I didn't share that I thought Mubarak's heavy hand was also behind the State Security Investigations Service which is where I currently found myself. The SSIS's job was to keep an eye on, well that would be inaccurate, let's say crush underground deviant networks and opposition groups.

The network of the fundamentalist Muslim Brotherhood did grass roots development, health clinics, social supports in destitute villages, and banks. Clever I thought. They had millions of followers.

"Egypt's poor are in dire straits," I mumbled a bit of social commentary.

The guard shrugged with indifference.

He didn't seem to care that the country used to export food but now the population relied on half of its food from imports.

It made me feel guilty that the farmers had to work harder too. There used to be marked growing seasons and times when they could recuperate from the exhausting work. But since the annual flooding of the Nile River didn't occur anymore, thanks to the Aswan Dam, the *Fellaheen* worked all year under harsh conditions.

One time, I was in Aswan lounging around a pool. The sun beat down upon me with a staggering forty plus Celsius weather. Like I said, I felt real guilty.

Even though the Muslim Brotherhood tried to help the poor, Mubarak had a professed hatred toward them. It was a political gambit.

"Mubarak is a great leader," said the guard.

Mubarak had to tread with care.

My grandmother didn't think the SSIS should only be concerned with national urgencies. She telephoned them when she suspected one of her servants of theft. It was a little bit of overkill, but hey, my grandmother could be very persuasive.

The SSIS hired the man instead of arresting him. The entire time he was being interrogated about theft in my grandmother's house, he smoked. His cigarette was dead still in his hand, the smoke travelling straight up. He was the coolest cucumber you ever saw.

You don't mess with the Egyptian police.

It was a lesson I understood. I gave my guard a look.

"This situation," I said as I waved my hand around my stone cell. "None of my unlucky interactions have ever been my fault. Not really."

I am just surrounded by idiots.

"We only have so much patience," articulated the guard as he slammed the prison door shut.

It is always the same when there is trouble. Everyone wants you to feel guilty. They will blame you for things that aren't your fault. I had had that all my life.

The problem with being in jail though was that I was trapped in a corner like a rat.

After a few hours, I heard my door screech open on its hinges. The head honcho wanted to see me again.

I was ushered back across the courtyard filled with loose flagstones and concrete rubble everywhere. Back into Building Number Four. Back to the office.

Omar Mohammed was at the desk. He motioned with one finger. I was pushed into the chair.

For a moment nothing else happened. I was smacking my lips together because the guard gave me a bottle of water which I downed in two seconds flat. When I was done, Omar was staring at me.

"Good evening," I greeted him. "Or is it, good morning? Sir."

I was on dangerous ground here. I should have waited until he spoke first, but he seemed to have other things on his mind. Lucky for me, I guess. As I look back, I realize if I had not been arrested by Omar Mohammed, if they had refused me entry and sent me back across the border, I would have been arrested by the Israelis.

Now which would have been worse?

He took a cigarette out of the packet and lit it. He smoked for a bit, all the while looking at me silently. He had all the time in the world apparently. I wasn't going anywhere. There was a knock on the door. A guard came in with a tray of falafel and some hot tea. I was starving.

Omar bent one finger in my direction. The guard gave me a plate. I tried not to disgrace myself, I truly did, but to no avail. I nearly choked on the food because I was eating so fast.

"Do you want to stay here, Amira?" Omar Mohammed spoke quietly.

I stopped eating mid-gulp. I put down my plate.

"No. Do I have a choice?"

"I would like you to do something for me."

It wasn't quite what Miss Balgrave had said when she had caught me with her cash in my pocket but the sentiment was the same.

What was I going to do, refuse?

"Of course, anything."

Omar, my best bud, my favourite authoritarian secret police guy out here in the middle of nowhere.

Omar Mohammed did everything deliberately. He poured himself a glass of water and drank it slowly.

He made me wait. I squirmed in my chair.

"Your type can be very useful."

Now wait a minute. It was Miss Balgrave again. What's with this your type stuff?

It was extremely unfair. It even occurred to me in a lightning flash that he might be working with Miss Balgrave, but why would he have stopped me at the border then?

Perhaps that had been a mistake and he would let me go?

If I got released, I would go straight to the Canadian Embassy. That's what I would do.

"The Canadians agree," Omar divulged.

"What!"

"They will not interfere in this case, not while you are co-operating that is."

Nice to know. Those sons of bitches. You can't trust anyone.

"My grandmother is no longer around. I don't have any family here. I don't have anything, no money, nothing."

"Amira," he spoke just the way Miss Beatrissa always did, right before she pronounced sentence. "Don't think you can fool us, Amira. That is a dangerous game."

I was on the verge of saying danger was my other middle name when I was saved from being buried alive by my own folly by the sound of his telephone ringing.

"We will go over your story one more time."

I told him everything that had happened. Well almost. I sensed he wasn't particularly interested in my personal life. Besides, it's none of his business. I spoke with feeling, just to keep him focusing on the other stuff.

"You searched the bag?"

Again, I went over how I had been in the loo for an hour trying to find the drugs.

"Are you stupid, Amira?"

"No. I'm not!"

How was I to know that the chocolates were explosives?

I don't do explosives. If I had known would I have gone to the loo for an hour? Obviously, he had come to that conclusion as well.

"You think she is European?" He was referring to Miss Balgrave.

"Well, she must be. She knows a couple of languages."

It was a lame deduction. Plenty of people speak more than one language in the Middle East. The official language of Egypt is Arabic, but French and English are so widely used they might as well be considered official. I speak all three languages, but I didn't let Omar know that.

We had only been conversing in English. I always find it comes in handy if people think you are monolingual. You can glean a lot of information that way.

"This Miss Balgrave has made a huge effort to recruit you and try to get the explosives into Egypt. We watch the border very closely."

Obviously.

"You are no help to us here. You're going to work with us."

I knew it.

Miss Beatrissa had done the same thing to me in school. If I told her which teachers were slacking off or if I heard them complain, she wanted a report. I had the lowdown on everyone, even the cleaning ladies. They never knew how Miss Beatrissa knew everything. They thought she was a Goddess with mighty powers.

It's not like I was betraying close friends or disclosing secrets, well, not usually. I didn't even like these people. I was simply sharing conversations.

I was surviving; it's not the same thing.

I smiled at Omar.

What else could I do?

The politics in the Middle East were simmering. Many were against peace negotiations with Jews. That wasn't the only thing. It's hate, pure hate. Fundamentalists and extremists hate anybody that is not them.

There's a joke about Fundamentalists concerning holy days. They say Friday is for Muslims, especially Palestinians. Saturday is for Jews. After that it's Sunday when we do the Christians.

Looking for the weekend massacre? Just follow the joke.

I find the real tragedy is when these extremist groups gain political power. That fervour destroys lives. Huge populations, such as the Palestinians, are manipulated by their leaders. Even Hitler was initially elected in Germany.

Omar shifted in his chair.

Was I supposed to say something?

Like the last words of the condemned or the spouting sounds of a grateful servant?

All I could think about was that history repeats itself.

I'm puzzled by that yet it is so difficult to identify evil. I picture it as dressed up in clothes of freedom. Sort of flowing all around and accessorized with culture. Maybe chuck in some ethnicity and the search for a national identity. That sounds about right. It's a real jumble.

I'm just waiting for some democratic country, like the United States for example, to elect a real right-wing idiot. Many leaders have gained power through supposed fair democratic elections.

I tried to clear my throat. I'd die for a glass of water.

It's amazing what you think about when you are in circumstances with only one way out.

I stared at Omar Mohammed and thought about European history, indeed world history, no less.

Omar poured himself another glass of water.

None for me.

I pictured the world full of malevolent rulers and suffering populations.

It is almost impossible for a population to rescue itself without outside support once this occurs. Like me. Insignificant. Caught. Trapped.

It was certainly happening in Palestine, and Israel. The Israeli state, not even a decade after the end of the Holocaust, was well on its way to becoming an apartheid country I thought. It would be committing human rights violations against the Palestinians as an official state policy.

All in the name of what?

"We need to know more about these people," Omar finally spoke.

"These guys are extremists, you think?" I asked while hopefully motioning to the jug of water.

Actually, I wasn't sure which people he was referring to — the Israelis or the Palestinians?

Nevertheless, it certainly looked like I was in with a group of people whose activities were equally hostile. Not the voice of the Palestinian people. Many were intent on destruction.

That type of thing leads nowhere good.

"These groups take it into their head to commit violence. You will find out for us."

Yup, I was spying again. Miss Beatrissa all over again.

"Yes Sir."

I had a huge knot in my stomach. It didn't quite feel like grade school. I knew better than to ask what was in it for me. That might sound ungrateful.

So, I smiled.

"I will need to continue on my journey to Cairo."

"Indeed, Amira. Now for your passports. They will be returned to you. The Canadian passport will be stamped arriving on Egyptian soil at the appropriate time."

"Yes Sir."

He handed me back my two passports and a glass of water.

"You will continue on your journey to the bus depot. Make contact as directed. Figure out an excuse for coming late on your own. I'm sure lying will not be a difficulty for you."

Omar Mohammed turned his back to me and walked away.

He knew about the bruises on my body. He also knew I wouldn't warn Miss Balgrave about my deal with him and the SSIS.

There was nothing in it for me in that direction.

I figured I would be murdered between Saturday and Sunday, probably at the stroke of midnight.

CHAPTER FIVE

They plopped me onto the bus to Cairo, only it was twenty-four hours later. I had plenty of time to think, even with my undercover SSIS tail sitting beside me. It felt strangely reassuring to know I wasn't going it totally alone.

"You haven't asked why the Canadians are so willing to let us deal with you?" Omar had said slyly as he tapped his pen on his desk just before I got up to catch my bus.

I had only replied, "I don't know."

To which he had chided me. "Oh come, come, Amira. Surely you haven't forgotten."

It's genuinely annoying when people keep bringing up the mistakes of the past. I wish they would move on, like I do. I actually thought I had been quite clever considering I hadn't ever been caught or even charged with a crime. It must have been a note on my file from that Canadian MP who was out to get me.

See, I can't live anywhere in peace.

I had gone back to Canada after my schooling had ended in Alexandria. I couldn't find my mother. To be truthful, I hadn't really looked. Besides, I hadn't communicated with her in years, so I stayed with friends of my father.

Winterpeg, in the province of Manitoba, is a brutal place from the standpoint of the weather. In the winter it's minus forty. In the summer it's a vicious moist heat and mosquitoes. There's no spring or autumn to speak of. You can have a blizzard in September and in June. It's actually not called Winterpeg. It's Winnipeg. I just call it that. Get the picture?

My father's friends lived on a farm. I had to commute by bus into university. I actually wasn't attending university but I needed to make them think I was. I had come up with a great scheme. North Americans are so gullible. All my Egyptian friends thought so. They would laugh and laugh as they told me stories of their travels to Canada or the United States.

Right on cue, my SSIS buddy Haris said to me, "I have travelled to North America."

Of course you have. And no I don't know Maria in Montreal.

"Those foreigners," he laughed.

My Egyptian friends would always mimic the foreigners in their storytelling. Really? Wow! No way!

Haris continued, "Those North Americans believe anything they are told about how poorly we live in the Middle East. It's all made up. Do Canadians feel sorry for us?"

I feigned ignorance but I know that when my Egyptian friends travelled they gave them money. Not that they needed any money, the Egyptians were all travelling in style, funded by their family's business or university grants. My Egyptian friends would give a hearty laugh and look at me. I always felt they were laughing at me as well, some private joke between them.

"Canada is a wealthy and healthy country," I responded with a shrug.

My get-rich scheme in Canada was quite simple. Based upon my wealth of worldly knowledge, I applied for Unemployment Insurance, student grants, loans, and student assistance. I had some friends help me with the interviews. I couldn't keep showing up under different names, but most of the applications were completed online or through letters. Of course, you can't be a student and apply for unemployment, but there was so much money to be had that I did it anyway.

I believed the wealth should be shared, so I was on firm moral ground there.

I think I messed up when I became quite vocal about the farmer down the road. He was an old chap, a dreadful abuser of animals. I couldn't stand it. The horses were skeletons. They stood in the unkempt fields amid the abandoned farm machinery and old trucks. I started a campaign against the miser which did result in action.

Unfortunately, one of the consequences was action towards me. You see, the old codger was the father of a notable Federal Member of Parliament. When the story broke, it was all over the news.

At the time, it didn't help this guy's political career. He turned his eyes on me. The Member of Parliament didn't like it that I had called the whistle on what I saw as an injustice. He was telling me to mind my own business.

I had quite a few identities for the Unemployment scam going when it all fell through. I managed to quietly make my way across the Canadian border. I couldn't access the thousands of dollars I had accumulated under various accounts in the banks, but I had enough to make it to Europe.

It was all very unkind of Omar to bring it up again.

Sadly for me, the MP was now linked to the Minister of Foreign Affairs. In Canada, we have a saying. *It's duck hunting season.* I guess the MP figured this was a good shot at me. I learned to tread more carefully after that, especially since I live in Jerusalem where minding your own business is a national pastime.

Haris looked at me with interest. "So you were travelling from the West Bank. Hmmm. Never been there. We are not encouraged to visit that area."

"I totally understand," I replied.

"So many protests," Haris noted.

"I make my protests on a more personal level and tell my stories about the treatment of the Palestinian people in the state of Israel one-to-one," I explained. "You know like this."

I indicated to him by waving my hands back and forth between us.

"Do you have many stories?" Haris asked.

I hesitated and then jumped right in. "Yup. Mostly met with incredulous stares and awkward comments about Jewish destiny. The comeback is Palestinians are terrorists."

"Ah yes," Haris rubbed his forehead and said, "It all gets to be ... I don't know."

"... rather heated," I said. "Like the 1972 massacre of Jews, Munich Olympics. The hijacking of the TWA jetliner ... "

"The Italian cruise ship the *Achille Lauro* in 1985. I condemn those acts," said Haris.

"Absolutely," I agreed with him. "Horrible acts but they're not the voice of the Palestinian people who are clamouring for justice."

Haris nodded his head thoughtfully. "No one seems to listen to that voice. Every society has its extremists, a truly regrettable fact, and never excusable."

I was jolted out of my political musings by the bus bumping off the highway and pulling into the El-Arish bus terminal. I had been on the bus just over an hour and got out to stretch my legs.

I had to smile to myself. There were memories in El-Arish. Some of them were actually good memories.

There was a family I had gotten to know whilst in Alexandria. They had a beach home in El-Arish. I had been invited for a visit once when I was a teenager. We had made the trip in what was basically a four-seater Fiat. The little orange car had taken the eight of us with all our bags strapped to the car roof to El-Arish's glorious, long white sandy beaches. Lazy days. Swimming.

We frolicked on the sand, swam in the Mediterranean Sea. The water was warm but deceptive. There is an incredibly strong undercurrent quite close to the shoreline. You can be swept into the sea very quickly, before you know it.

Tarek, my friend's father, knew this. When he saw me casually drifting further and further away, he swam to me and hauled me back. He's a very strong swimmer, which was a good thing because I am not. I hadn't even realized I was in danger, so the incident hadn't even alarmed me.

I spent the rest of the holiday being watched over.

Soft evenings. Quiet nights.

It is the only time someone in my life has saved me.

"All that matters is life as it is lived," my friend's father shared with me. He was a wonderful man.

After my overnight sessions with Omar, I felt absolutely miserable on the bus. My headache was pounding but at least they had let me have a shower in the prison and had washed my clothes for me. A surprising courtesy given the circumstances. I slunk down in my seat and tried to get some shut eye.

My own suitcase was in the inside overhead bin. Miss Balgrave's suitcase was down in the outside hold beside a huge pot of already-made soup.

Honestly, what do some people think or don't they? Why would you travel with a pot of soup?

Whatever the contents of that cauldron were, they would be ruined by the time that pot got to wherever it was going. The bus engine was right next to the baggage hold. Along with the Egyptian heat, that soup concoction was probably already foul.

It wasn't my problem though.

I closed my eyes, tried to stop my memories and think of nothing as the bus sped down the two-lane highway. Suddenly, the brakes of the bus squealed. I was forcefully thrown against the back of the seat in front of me, all the passengers were. There was a void in time.

There was no terrible crunching noise, no impact rippling its effects down the bus. The bus was dead silent. Everyone held their breath.

"Alhamdulillah."

Nervous laughter and clapping erupted. A goat trotted off the highway. A life had been spared.

In addition to my pounding headache and aching body, I now had whiplash. I was getting grumpier by the minute. On top of that I had to come up with a story to cover my delay in getting to Cairo. The bus pulled into its next stop, near the Ahmed Hamdi Tunnel.

I turned to Haris in an attempt to relieve my anxiety and said, "When I was a kid, my father and I always played a game going through the tunnels in Canada. You had to hold your breath all the way through the tunnel until you emerged from it on the other side."

"That's crazy," said Haris. "This is one long tunnel."

"Whoever accomplished the feat was the winner. Usually, we burst out laughing before the end of the tunnel at the sight of our faces going red and our eyes starting to bulge."

"That's a gimmick to keep you from being scared about possibly being buried alive down there," observed Haris.

Great observation. Thanks.

There was no way I could hold my breath that long through the Ahmed Hamdi Tunnel. The tunnel is 1640 metres long. It was named after an engineer killed in the Yom Kippur War. The two lanes of traffic zip by each other, down there, in an already dug grave.

I shut my eyes, concentrated on slow breathing and retrieving happy memories of the October 6th victory celebrations.

I figured the success of my new mission, now that I was an unregistered operative, with the SSIS was practically zero. Omar had made me memorize a phone number so I could *call to report* as he said. It was totally unrealistic to set a time for contacting him. It wasn't the movies where I could have a ten o'clock rendezvous each night or failing that, the next morning. I was to call when I had something of note, preferably not longer than 24 hours between contacts.

Omar had no idea where the chocolate explosives had been made. It was possible Miss Balgrave had smuggled them into Israel.

That didn't make sense to me. I had told him so. Then I remembered she hadn't had any luggage with her at the Tel Aviv airport but that it had come later. He had looked at me with exasperation but I could tell the information was important. One point for me in my corner.

Omar Mohammed hadn't wished me luck or patted me on the back. He had said, and I quote, "Don't fail. Staying out of prison is your incentive."

Seriously, I am not making that up. That is actually what he said. Had he conferred with Miss Balgrave and her stooge about common language used to bully the unfortunates, me, of the world?

At El-Arish, my shadow Haris changed to a stern-looking young man. It was good they were swapping surveillance duty, but I hoped it wasn't obvious to anyone else.

The bus coughed me out at the bus stop beside the colossus of Ramses the Great.

"Madame! Welcome to Cairo!" A man materialized at my elbow. "Official guide. Very official. You need history?"

I know a scam when I see one.

"I've got plenty of history," I said, shifting my suitcase. "Isn't the main bus station in Tahrir Square?"

"Yes, yes, of course. But Ramses Square is the heart," he flung an arm dramatically.

A peanut vendor leaned in. "Best view of the statue from here. Five pounds."

"I can see it already," I said. "Nice try."

"But you cannot *understand* it," the guide insisted. "Behold! Ramses the Second. Most powerful pharaoh of ancient Egypt. Builder. Warrior. Legend."

The statue towered above us, a mega stone planted in the middle of taxis, buses, and human folly.

"They dragged the colossus from the ruins of ancient Memphis," the guide went on, undeterred. "Twenty-five miles. Imagine! In 1954, President Nasser himself brought it here. Second anniversary of the Revolution. A symbol of strength."

"Ah, huh," I muttered.

"Strength," the guide repeated. "He watches over the station."

"I know," I said. "He always has."

The peanut vendor squinted at me. "You're not a tourist?"

"I'm not."

The guide tried another angle. "Cairo! Very mysterious. Yes?"

Behind him, Ramses Square was a blaring apocalypse of traffic noise.

"You see? So alive." He smiled nervously and followed my gaze back up to the statue.

"You like him?" the vendor asked.

"I do," I laughed. "He stares into eternity, unimpressed. At least he makes me feel like someone is in charge."

The guide laughed. "In Cairo? No one is in charge."

I adjusted my suitcases.

Whatever. I wasn't going to argue with the man. I found the statue pleasing. When I was younger, I believed he was watching over me. I suppose part of me still does.

Beautiful.

Cairo, the name of the city sounds exotic. To me, it was simply home.

Dusty, donkey-driven, luxury car lined streets. Noise. Exhaust. Smells. Wailing cats.

Real life. Raw life.

Miss Balgrave hadn't given me a lot of instructions. Just get to Cairo, check into a hotel and go to *Le Chantilly* on Baghdad Street in Heliopolis, the city of the sun.

I knew the street well. My grandmother had had a flat and a house in Heliopolis, a suburb of Cairo. She often went to *Le Chantilly*. It was her favourite restaurant, mine too.

Baghdad Street is a lovely wide street with columns and covered walkways. I especially remember the Lego store across the street from the restaurant. As a child, I thought Baghdad Street was the best place in the world.

I was starving and got a bite from the *Shawarma* stand on the corner before hopping on the tram to Heliopolis. I could have taken a taxi but I'd make Omar's man work for his money.

On the tram I stood by the door with my back to the wall. If you sit down, you get all the creeps beside you trying to feel you up. I put the suitcase in front of me, my smaller one on top. That way no one could press their hard-on up against me when we were standing.

The tram is actually quite efficient and cheap. If you can bear to put up with the crap.

I made my way to the Sphinx Moon Hotel on Nazih Khalifa Street.

The first thing I had to do was secure the contents of the suitcase. I took a piece of clothing from the suitcase, wrapped it around the two boxes of chocolates, put the whole thing in a plastic bag and went down to the concierge.

"I need to place something in your safe."

"Of course, madame."

Easy. Peasy. I didn't need explosives in my room even if there was no detonator. Next, I took a shower and sifted through the clean clothes from Miss Balgrave's collection.

What of it? I had carried that suitcase all the way from Ashkelon. Besides, I couldn't go to *Le Chantilly* in my own clothes. They would have kicked me out. I selected a skirt and a blouse. They fit okay, not perfect, but it was better than my travel outfit.

The restaurant on Baghdad Street hadn't changed much since I had last been there. Oh, that must have been about seven or eight years ago on a very brief visit to see my grandmother. I sat at the same table, the one in the middle. It's a small restaurant, quite intimate. The menu hadn't changed much either.

I didn't know what else to do except sit, wait, and eat.

So, I did.

I was hoping my contact might be in the restaurant waiting since I hadn't arrived yesterday when I was expected. There wasn't anyone there that fit the profile. But I figured, at the very least, the contact would have to keep coming back. She did. She sat down at my table at about ten o'clock. I was just starting my third dessert.

"Hello Amira."

"Hello."

I wasn't certain if this was Miss Balgrave's friend or a member of the Heliopolis welcoming committee.

"You were supposed to be here yesterday."

Ah, so I was. I had a mouthful of Crème Brûlée, so my snappy comeback got lost in translation. Miss Balgrave had indicated my job was to bring the suitcase to Cairo and hand it over. I would get my recording back and the two thousand dollars. I hadn't trusted her in Ashkelon.

I sure as heck didn't trust the woman sitting across from me.

"We stopped at the Suez Canal."

She waited for me to continue. "Shaluffa?"

"I think I heard that was the name of the place. That's not conclusive."

Conclusive? Really? What was I trying to do, impress her with my vocabulary?

She tapped her fingers on the table with impatience.

"What of it?"

"Would you like some coffee?" I asked her.

I needed time to get my story straight. I certainly wasn't going to just hand over the suitcase. I had to get in contact with who she was working with and I wanted my two thousand dollars. Money for the meal I was eating I didn't have. She'd have to take care of that. The hotel was on a tab. Still, unpaid bills irritate people.

I didn't want to have anyone calling the police, now did I?

She signaled to the waiter to bring her coffee.

"It's quite silly really," I began while I mustered my most embarrassed look and dropped my eyes.

"The loo," I whispered.

She shook her head and widened her eyes. I could tell the suspense was killing her.

"I went to use the facilities. You know, it was a hole in the ground behind the single building at this stop. Really gross. This place was out in the middle of nowhere. There was just dust and desert for miles and miles."

I paused for effect.

"Not a loo at all. I took the suitcase with me of course because you can't be too careful. Would you believe it!"

I slammed my hand on the table so that the cutlery jumped.

"Sorry," I said in true Canadian fashion, "but I am still upset about it. That damn bus driver left without me. I guess he assumed since I had pulled my suitcase off the bus that I had completed my trip."

I was nodding energetically.

She looked at me like I was the dumbest person on earth and muttered something about useful idiots.

"I guess it was a mistake anyone could have made," I said.

"Which mistake? Yours or the bus driver's?"

"Both I guess, but here I am."

She was slim with dark long straight hair and brown eyes. She was well dressed, and spoke English with only a slight accent. She wasn't local I'd say.

I was writing dictation in my head for Omar Mohammed.

"Where did you spend the night?"

"On the ground! There was no place else. It's only a canteen stop with a hole in the ground around the back. The shopkeeper let me stay on his floor. There wasn't even anyone there to serve tea. I had to wait until the next day for the next bus."

"Hence your sorry state," she enunciated.

Hey, I thought I looked quite good since I had had a shower and was wearing new clothes. I adjusted my too large blouse and stared her in the eye. Her clothes were tailor-made; that much was obvious. Even her shoes were perfect with slim soles and black patent leather. I pulled my clompers under my chair.

"Where's the suitcase?"

"Oh yes, your gift! It's your birthday isn't it?" I clapped my hands together. "Happy Birthday," I said loudly.

The waiter whipped his head around and hurried over to the table like a butterfly.

"Birthday? Do we have a birthday girl here?"

"No. We don't," she spoke evenly as she glared at me.

"She doesn't like getting older," I said apologetically to him.

The waiter backed down. I smiled my best birthday smile.

"What's your name?" I inquired in my friendship voice.

"Nancy."

I have always hated that name ever since a girl named Nancy whacked me across the head in elementary school. It's amazing how some things stick with you.

"What a lovely name," I said.

"Where's the suitcase?" she said through her teeth.

"Where's my money?" I said through mine.

"You were to hand over the suitcase when you arrived in Cairo. You're here. Hand it over. The money arrangement is between you and Miss Balgrave."

"Well I don't see Miss Balgrave, do I?"

"You can talk to her tomorrow for all I care," Nancy snapped.

"She's here, in Cairo?"

Nancy paused and shrugged.

"How do I know you are the right person?" I feigned suspicion. "I was supposed to be here yesterday, but there was a glitch, though no fault of my own."

Never admit you made a mistake.

I continued, "I'd have to get confirmation from Miss Balgrave before I hand over the suitcase."

We both knew she wasn't dying for a taste of chocolate. The restaurant was full of delectable treats far better than any box of chocolates purchased in Ashkelon.

"She's not going to be pleased to have to spend more time dealing with you," she sneered at me as she leaned over the table.

"So, she is here. She is in Cairo."

"You don't know?" she expressed surprise.

Was I supposed to know? I could tell she sensed she had made a mistake.

She abruptly declared, "Get the suitcase. Bring it here. I'll meet you in the street."

She stood up to go.

"Nope," I said.

What else could I do? I had to stall. I had to get more information out of her.

Desperation makes you take ridiculous risks.

A gentleman came into the restaurant and made his way toward us. I say gentleman because I didn't identify him at first. Mister Incentive from the Ashkelon beating alley had arrived.

"Either you give me the chocolates now or you can continue the conversation with my friend," she threatened.

"I don't like the conversations I have had with him. The chocolates?" I repeated innocently. "What's so special about the chocolates? Don't you want the whole suitcase?"

It happened so fast that the pain didn't come right away. She slapped me hard across the face. I don't know how I maintained my composure when the waiter hurried over to whisper perhaps it was time to go now.

I stood up, announced, "My friends will take care of the cheque," and walked out the door.

Mister Muscle followed me out.

"Tell Miss Balgrave, please, I would like my money. I am just being careful with her items. I'll be here again tomorrow night. Tell her."

I turned, walked away, and spoke over my shoulder, "Don't follow me either."

That was for Mister Heavy Hand, not my SSIS shadow who had been waiting hours for me to come out of the restaurant.

Regardless, I don't know how I found the nerve to behave that way. After I got back to my hotel, I threw up everything, the hors d'oeuvre, dinner, and the three desserts.

CHAPTER SIX

Early the next morning, I phoned the number Omar had made me memorize. I had gone down the street to a shop. After indicating to the owner that I would buy a whole bunch of stuff, I casually requested to use his phone. Afraid I might change my mind about the purchase, he grudgingly consented. It wasn't particularly private but it would do.

I couldn't use the phone at the hotel for fear that Miss Balgrave was keeping tabs on me.

The phone number was a direct line to Omar. I told him I had made contact but he probably already knew that since he had me under constant surveillance.

"What has happened?"

I gave my description of Nancy and the conversation. There was another point for my corner when I told him Miss Balgrave was most certainly in Cairo.

"Find out where."

No kidding. Good plan. I hadn't expected a great big thank you, but I wished he would appreciate my tricky situation. He didn't have any information for me. The SSIS were still trying to figure out who exactly Miss Balgrave was, and my new information would help, but the investigative wheels were sluggish. She must have come in through the airport. I suggested they could check the manifest.

Omar ignored my constant advice and instructed me instead.

"Whatever you do, don't hand over the suitcase until you actually know something valid."

That was a bit harsh. Everything I had said was important. I was doing the best I could. I told him my plan for tonight which was to refuse to hand anything over until I was taken to Miss Balgrave and saw her face to face. He seemed to like that idea by giving me a backhanded compliment.

"See, you are not so stupid after all."

Then he hung up.

I left the shop without buying anything. I'd have to find another telephone location for my next call.

A touch of nostalgia hit me as I wandered down the streets of Heliopolis. Cairo is a tangle of noises, of human cries and laughter. It is also a jungle full of sights. Its inhabitants move in an ageless manner in bright colours among the warm mist. Everything mingles. The sights of people, donkey carts, live sheep in the markets. The scent of fruit and vegetables, the teas, the whiffs of cooking. The smell of dung.

It is a lazy eternal experience.

I decided to have a morning tea in Merryland, the park on the other side of El Hegaz Street.

I used to go there and visit the lion in the zoo. It was a pathetic setup actually. The lion keeper sat in a wooden chair outside the small iron cage all day. The lion lay inside, depressed I'm sure.

The park was huge with a type of grandstand cement area with round tables and chairs. I used to sit there with a summer treat in my hand, probably ice cream or something, and watch the big wild street cats play with the little cats or so I thought.

They were actually tomcats screwing the females. The little kittens didn't have a chance against those brutes.

Harsh world.

At the opposite end of the scale, you could always find someone in the park who wanted to share their hot Chai and picnic food with you and create a fond memory.

After I had finished with those recollections, I walked the kilometre to the Heliopolis sporting club. It felt good to stretch my legs and just wander.

Inside the grounds, the club is an oasis of fun and relaxation. Swimming pools, tennis courts, my kind of place.

Outside of the grounds is the maze of the city. Wild dogs sleeping on top of the hoods and roofs of the warm cars. The dog packs would roam the streets at night. When you heard them coming you made sure the gate to your home was shut.

I carefully navigated my way through the dogs but they were zonked out from their habitual midnight revelry.

Omar's new man stayed well clear. I didn't go into the club; my grandmother wasn't a member anymore and the cost of a day ticket was stiff. I hadn't brought my bikini with me anyway, so I gave it a pass.

I headed over to the French Cultural Centre to see what was playing in the cinema. I had seen the most memorable movie of my childhood there, Tintin. It had shocked my pants off to hear the captain yelling, *Merde, merde!* As you can tell, I had been a very impressionable youth.

From there it was only a half hour walk to the Cathedral Basilica. I was wearing a white cotton shirt and as I looked down at it, I noticed it had strange short dashes of black on it. A rare misty rain had started to fall. The soot in the air was making marks on my white shirt. A consequence of the modern world.

I knew *la Basilique* would be cool inside. The hot weather was already making me work too hard. The cathedral had always been a wonderful place for me, not for the religion, but because of the building. Even though my grandmother wasn't much of a follower of anything consistently, she would occasionally visit a mosque and she did visit this majestic cathedral.

I always light a candle for someone when I visit any holy place. I'm a bit superstitious that way.

Today, I lit one for myself, and tried not to think of Omar Mohammed. I would need all the luck I could get.

I spent the rest of the afternoon in bed. Just before five o'clock I got up and got dressed. I wasn't quite as pleased with my outfit as I had been the day before after seeing neat Nancy, but I didn't have a choice. Short of theft, I would never steal clothes, I was stuck with my attire.

There was a large plastic bag at the base of a tree right as I came out of the hotel. At first, I didn't know what it was. When I peered closer, it was a suffocated and very dead cat. The knot on the bag was tight. There was condensation forming on the inside. Someone must have choked the thing in a fit of anger. I hoped it wasn't a bad sign.

I walked down to *Le Chantilly* and took a table in the corner. It was half past five. A bit early maybe, but I was willing to bet Nancy would show up before too long. The food was superb, as always. It was going on seven o'clock when I noticed Mister Bulldog walk into the restaurant.

Wouldn't you know it, behind him was his master, Miss Balgrave. They sat down opposite me and ordered two coffees.

"Where's the suitcase?" she queried.

"Safe."

She looked at me just the way Nancy had looked at me the night before, like I was an idiot.

Omar Mohammed was expecting results, something vital was the way he had put it. I could feel the pressure.

"Where's Nancy?" I quipped.

"Recovering."

"From what, excessive ego and stupidity?"

Wouldn't you know it. Nancy was more careless than I imagined. After leaving me, she'd been hit by a car. The driver had lost control. The car had driven up onto the sidewalk and taken a good swipe at her.

I know you hear stuff like that all the time, but not about people you have just met. I was suitably impressed.

"You have caused us a fair amount of trouble, Amira."

I could tell Miss Balgrave and Nancy were close by the amount of sympathy she was showing for Nancy's accident.

"It's not my fault, besides, she hurt my feelings."

"You're not a child, Amira."

"No, but I want my things back."

Miss Balgrave looked at me with amusement. "Oh, you mean your tape recording."

"That's right, and the two thousand dollars. I don't think that's too much to ask for a couple of boxes of chocolates."

Slip up number one.

Miss Balgrave's eyes narrowed.

"Two thousand dollars is a lot of money, Amira. How would you like another job?"

I couldn't seem too eager to stick around because she certainly would have wondered about my change of heart.

"I'm not interested in being a mule again."

"No, nothing like that. I need a cook. In a few days I will be taking possession of a flat in Heliopolis and could use someone like you."

"I don't know. I just want to pack my bag and say goodbye to the Sphinx Moon Hotel."

Slip up number two.

I caught the quick glance between Mister Fix-it and Miss Balgrave. He immediately got up and left, no doubt to search my hotel room now that he knew exactly where I was staying.

She stood up to leave.

"Where are we going?" I asked. "Have you had dinner?" I wanted to make our time together to be as long as possible. "We can eat here."

"No. Let's go somewhere else, shall we?"

Indeed, we shall I thought to myself. She could send her goon to retrieve the suitcase but the contents were in the safe. She'd find that out when Mister Heavy Hand returned empty handed.

I was confused by her insistence to join her. We walked along the street a short distance to a Korean restaurant. There was one gleaming Mercedes Benz after another parked along the curb. The entrance to the restaurant was down a dirty flight of stairs. You wouldn't have seen the place from the street level if you hadn't known it was there.

The restaurant was busy. While we waited near the front desk, I watched the inhabitants of a huge fish tank by the restaurant entrance. There were all sorts of fish in there, a different world. There was a Wanda, a huge angelfish. I laughed when I saw it. It was a private joke between Hazeer and me.

We had taken his niece to the cinema in Jerusalem to a showing of the film *Wanda.* I know, I know, not particularly a kid's show, but we were babysitting and hadn't wanted to stay at home. Besides, his niece was only five years old at the time. Any of the gritty stuff she wouldn't understand anyway.

Spoiler alert. The thieves in the show hide the key in the fish tank where the Angelfish lives. For various reasons we thought the film was pretty amusing.

My SSIS shadow had stayed up on the curb. I had an irresistible urge to leave the restaurant and check he was still hanging around.

No chance.

Miss Balgrave took a private table in the corner and had me wedged in pretty good. I suggested maybe a less nefarious location another block over, some place with visible exits.

"No. You'll eat with me here."

"Really, I'm not sure about Korean food."

Miss Balgrave was quick with the retort, "I said, you will eat here with me."

I stayed.

When the cheque arrived, she paid with a hundred-dollar pound note. Maybe she was into forgery?

I tried to hide the curious expression on my face from her. I was sure I would give myself away.

The clock was ticking towards midnight. We didn't have to take a walk anywhere. This place had everything. The entrance to the disco nightlife was down another long dark flight of stairs at the back of the building. The space was packed with people. Everyone looked blue in the lights. The music was pounding. You couldn't talk but I signaled to Miss Balgrave that I needed to go to the loo and would be back shortly.

She wouldn't have any of it. She insisted I stay with her. She ordered drinks but I am sure I drank far more than she did. We joked about some of the guys behind the bar. Too fat, too thin, too short. When I pointed out a tall athletic dude and nudged her to make a move on him, she turned and stared at me.

"Is that the one you like?"

"Me?" I was confused.

I had a significant feeling of loathing for her at the moment.

She swore at me like a trucker and ordered another drink. She was really pissed off and had been watching me all evening. Obviously, things weren't going the way she liked, but I had no idea what she was doing. I considered rectifying the situation by making chit chat but decided against it. You couldn't have a conversation in the disco anyway.

Abruptly she stood up to leave.

"There's nothing more to do here, Amira. What's with the look on your face? Are they going to start slapping naked behinds and start yanking on each other?"

She was in a foul mood. I decided not to argue, but suggested we go to a discreet massage parlour around the corner from my hotel. Perhaps she fancied a quieter and more private outing. She sneered at my suggestion and reconsidered.

"Fine. Fine Amira. Let's go see what you suggest."

Wow, she could switch gears faster than I could blink, but we never got there. Once we were back on the street, the bulldog was waiting for us.

"Nothing," he muttered.

Miss Balgrave turned to me. "Where's the stuff from the suitcase?"

Her voice was dry like the desert wind before a sandstorm.

"In the safe, of course!" I feigned being insulted.

I know how the game is played. There is no other country in the world where an insult is considered the height of brutality.

Egyptians know this.

Words are all powerful.

Greetings are effervescent. A word of love is tender. A curse is final. I pretended to be super shocked.

She motioned to my favourite guy and ordered him to go back to the Sphinx Moon Hotel with me to retrieve the contents.

I shook my head.

"That's not possible; it's in the safe. The guy in charge of the safe isn't there in the evening. He comes in the morning."

Miss Balgrave let out a long sigh.

"Come to the Marriott tomorrow. Nine o'clock sharp. Don't be late, Amira. Make sure you bring everything."

She sashayed away.

Once I was sure they had gone, I went to the nearest open café in search of a telephone. There are always people around in

Cairo, so I wasn't worried about my safety. Besides, I had my faithful SSIS watchdog nearby.

I'd been successful at prolonging my usefulness to Miss Balgrave or perhaps she just wanted to keep an eye on me because I already had too much knowledge. It was a stressful situation. My stomach hurt as much from the two dinners as the anxiety I was experiencing.

There was no way to know what would happen in the flat once Miss Balgrave moved in there. I told Omar as much. After I finished enlightening him about the Marriott and Nancy, he was silent for so long that I thought the connection had been broken.

"We have traced Miss Balgrave's movements from Europe. We must meet tonight to prepare you for your meeting at the Marriott."

I was dead tired and wanted to wait until the morning, but he wouldn't have it.

"Go up to my man and say my name. He will take care of the arrangements."

I didn't like it but did as I was told. In five minutes, I was speeding through the streets of Heliopolis in a black sedan. We slowed down by a tall orange-coloured cement wall surrounding a compound. The armed sentries at the gate admitted us quickly. I'd seen the area many times, but of course had never been inside.

The closest I had ever come to the enclosure was my grandmother's friend's flat just down the street. The flat had been on the third floor of the apartment building. The place was above a grocer. They used to drop a wicker basket down on a string and have him fill it up with the items they shouted down to him. I was always amused by their shopping.

But this experience in the old neighbourhood wasn't quite as quaint as my memory of housekeeping techniques. The familiar streets surrounding the enclosure disappeared behind me as I entered the complex.

The walls of the compound reminded me of the walls around the British School of Alexandria. One time, a dog had made its way into the school grounds and was running around in a crazed manner. The Boab had been called to get rid of the poor creature which he did by cornering it and promptly shooting it underneath the window of the classroom I was in.

The shotgun blast had made my heart stop with terror. More so than any other student because my desk had been right by the window. When I had looked out, I saw the Boab slinging the black dog over his shoulder and carrying it away. Its tongue was hanging out of its mouth. Its head was lolling back and forth.

That wasn't the end of it though. For lack of a better disposal site, the Boab had the bright idea of stashing the carcass in the abandoned bunker at the far end of the playground. The bunker had been a leftover from the war.

It was definitely out of bounds for us. However, the stench got so bad that someone reported it to Miss Beatrissa. For once, I wasn't the one being called down to the headmistress's office for something foul.

My midnight excursion with Omar Mohammed definitely had the same kind of unpleasant odour to it, so to speak. I don't like the feeling that I am aimlessly wandering down long corridors flanked by closed doors in the dead of night. The tall walls were hung with large haunting portraits of Mubarak.

I was short-tempered by the time we reached our destination. It was clear my escort was a staunch supporter of the current regime. He snapped to attention the second Omar walked into the room.

"Did you know that this used to be a palace?" asked Omar.

Every grand building in Cairo used to be something. The room I was in was opulent with red drapery over every window and gold leaf as a trim along the ceilings.

"I hadn't ever really thought about it."

"Well Amira, that is what I do. I think. That is lucky for you."

I didn't feel very lucky at the moment and grumbled I would rather be in bed, asleep.

Omar placed a row of photographs on the desk and had me look at them. A few of the people were familiar to me. Miss

Balgrave, her stooge, and Nancy. The others I had never seen before.

"Look closely. You may meet them tomorrow. It is of vital importance that you let us know immediately if you do."

"Who are they?"

"They work with the Muslim Brotherhood."

He tapped one of the photos. "We suspect this one has been in contact with the Palestine Liberation Organization and Yasser Arafat."

"Arafat leads Fatah, one of the largest PLO groups. The recent rumblings of the *Intifadeh* are signs he is gaining momentum," I threw my arms in the air. "Honestly Omar, that's all I know. Let me go home."

"Correct," responded Omar. "The *Intifadeh* is hitting every front. Some call Yasser Arafat the ultimate freedom fighter; others see him as a thug."

"It's complicated. Two peoples. One land."

Omar snorted, "It's not that complicated. The area was under the Ottoman Empire for centuries. Muslims, Christians, Jews — living there in peace long before Europeans started drawing lines on maps."

"Yeah, but the British, ya know, after World War II," I said with annoyance.

"The British," Omar bristled, "The Mandate for Palestine. Jews arrive. Violent conflicts between immigrants and locals."

"After the Holocaust, someone thought the solution was to take someone else's land," I said, my voice flat. "Do we really need to have this conversation now? I mean okay, Arafat doesn't like what happened in 1947 when the United Nations divided the area."

"Not many do," said Omar. "The Golan Heights, West Bank, and Gaza were to remain Palestinian. The state of Israel would take the other half. It is no surprise that the Jews said yes, and the Arabs said no."

I rubbed my face and propped my eyes open with my fingers.

"Are you even listening to me?"

"Barely," I muttered.

80

His jaw tightened.

"Why don't other countries just butt out?"

Omar gave a small indulgent smile at my childish comment.

"The Arabs saw it as colonial interference aimed at stealing land," he said.

"Why do you care about what happens in the West Bank?" I uttered the question.

My fatigue made my voice barely audible.

Omar glared at me. "Sadat is the first Muslim to be a Nobel laureate for his negotiations with Israel."

This was true. Mohamed Anwar al-Sadat shared the Nobel Peace Prize in 1978 with Israel's Prime Minister Menachem Begin for the Egypt-Israel Peace Treaty.

I nearly fell off my chair. To steady myself I laid my head on my arms over his desk.

I mumbled, "Yeah, yeah. It's been a long road since the establishment of the Jewish state in 1947. You do realize this is a really long night for me too."

"The point is Amira," Omar shoved my head up. His fingers dug into my shoulders. "You need to know what is at stake!"

"Yeah," I said grudgingly. "And the next year, 1948, the Arabs declared war. War is a terrible thing."

Omar's response was sharp. Personal.

"Israel won. By 1967, Israel had claimed all the Palestinian lands and the Sinai. The West Bank and Gaza Strip are called occupied land by the international community. Yet Israel continues to build and install settlers."

"Not exactly a success for some," I quipped.

Omar continued, "Sadat was a great man."

"All hail Sadat," I chanted and clapped my hands. "Egypt is becoming whole again."

"I will excuse your disrespect, Amira. You are tired. But understand that the Egyptian forces had victory. The Sinai has been returned to us. The Muslim Brotherhood rejects Sadat's peace. They accuse him of abandoning the Palestinians. If Arafat works with the Brotherhood, it threatens the Egyptian state. Mubarak carries on the great work of his predecessor. That is why I care."

I shrugged.

I look out for myself.

The Egyptian government would do the same no doubt.

One time they say this, the next time they say that. Egyptian-Palestinian relations would be no different.

"I'm sure the Secret Police are working diligently to counter the growing influence of the Muslim Brotherhood and its allies," I said sarcastically.

Some Egyptians regarded Palestinians as the root of all Egypt's problems. Travel to Gaza is discouraged. The fact I had departed from Ashkelon and travelled across from Israel to Egypt was starting to look like it really would not end well.

Little did I know how bad it could get.

I settled back in my chair to listen, or not listen as it were, to Omar's continuing rant about Imperialism, Americans, the 1978 Camp David Accord, and the supreme leader Hosni Mubarak.

It was all the same to me.

Egypt's ruling class has its own interests.

I have mine.

I really thought everyone should just get along and share the wealth.

"I am here to protect," announced Omar. "Mubarak was wounded during Sadat's assassination. He has made security an absolute priority by arresting or imprisoning Islamists and their supporters. The Muslim Brotherhood must be stopped."

Omar had obviously absorbed the president's passion for order and control.

"Yasser's wife lives in Paris. Miss Balgrave," Omar tapped her photo, "is a close friend."

"You don't say," I came out of my foggy state.

I attempted to whistle, but I don't whistle.

I don't know why I even tried.

"Until we know what exact move they are planning and what the explosives will be used for, I want you to stay as close to Miss Balgrave as possible."

"She wants me as her cook, not her confidante."

"Food is the gateway to the soul."

Oh no, now he was getting really philosophical.

"Whatever," I retorted. "I'm not getting myself killed."

"Information, Amira. You are no good to me dead. You have a job to do."

I was so glad to be useful.

A lieutenant walked into the room with a manila folder and gave it to Omar Mohammed.

"The bulldog, as you call him, is Josef Hakim Steinman. He is of Palestinian and German descent, aged thirty-three. Lists his occupation as a construction manager."

After the creation of the state of Israel, Steinman's family had been displaced in the great expulsion of Palestinians. *Al Nakba* or the catastrophe the Arabs called it. The Zionist campaign used torture, kidnappings, deportations, collective punishment, and confiscation of Palestinian property.

Omar continued reading from the dossier.

"Miss Balgrave, her real name interestingly enough, is of British and French descent. No obvious occupation."

Omar stared at the photo of Miss Balgrave.

"Divorced. Wealthy. Her age is forty-seven."

He murmured, "Really? She doesn't look like forty-seven. She looks your age,"

Omar shook his head but didn't look at me.

I'm in my twenties.

She's ancient.

I wasn't going to forget that insult.

"We are working on the information about Nancy," Omar said. "There is one final detail to go over."

He handed me a small radio.

"Seriously?"

I was flabbergasted.

"Omar. You're giving me a radio? What am I supposed to do with it?"

"It's a transmitter, you idiot."

He showed me how to switch it from being a radio to a transmitter.

"You will only use this in emergencies. It is imperative we know what is happening."

"You mean it's a walkie-talkie."

It was the dumbest idea I had ever heard of. Just use it in an emergency?

An emergency is chaotic, unpredictable, a catastrophe. He wanted me to be prepared for it with a walkie-talkie?

It was ridiculous.

"What if they find it? You don't think they will suspect I'm transmitting to someone?"

"Make sure they don't find it, Amira."

Oh, that was a great plan.

Mister Muscle aka Steinman had already searched my room at the hotel.

"Why don't we just use pigeons?" I wisecracked.

Omar Mohammed didn't think that was funny and issued my final order.

"Continue to phone in."

Obviously, I was dismissed.

The driver dropped me off near my hotel with a disdain that made me wonder if he thought I was one of Omar's favourite prostitutes. However, my SSIS shadow who was still following orders and waiting in the street outside the Sphinx Moon Hotel, made sure I got inside safely.

It was the last time I would have supervision.

Omar had pulled the SSIS watch off me since I now had my trusty transmitter.

CHAPTER SEVEN

I was bagged by the time I got back to the hotel. Needless to say the next morning, I was still sound asleep at nine o'clock sharp. By the time I got hold of the concierge to get my items from the safe, it was pushing ten o'clock in the morning.

From the Roxy circle, I took a minibus. Three stops later, two disciples of the Muslim Brotherhood got on. There was palpable fear. All of the passengers averted their eyes. The men were dressed in perfect white from head to toe. They had long dark brushed beards and piercing eyes. Everyone dug into their pockets. Not a word was spoken.

The people on the minibus collectively reacted like a dog who closes its eyes, rushes through the electric fence to escape, sustaining immense pain but only for a moment.

They just had to place their piastres in the cloth donations bag and escape the scrutiny. At the next stop, there was an immense and audible sigh of relief after the Brotherhood stepped off with the collection bag full of coins.

I had to make one transfer on Lotfi El-Said to get the bus across to Gezira Island. Zamalek, along with the suburb of Heliopolis, is one of the more affluent residential districts in Cairo. It's gorgeous, like so many things are in Egypt. The island is an oasis of quiet wide streets, tall leafy trees with spots of sunshine and shadows. It's a hub of culture, art, and galleries. My bus made a right turn onto Gezira Street once it was over the October 6th Bridge. The street runs alongside the club of the same name.

My grandmother was a member of the Gezira Club. The club was founded in 1882 by the British. In the 1950s, Nasser nationalized the club and my grandfather joined. My grandparents had a passion for horse racing. I used to come down from Alexandria for the prestigious Nasser Cup. The horse races ran in Cairo in the winter and in Alexandria in the summer, although the number of races was steadily declining by the time I started attending.

For some reason, I only ever went to the Gezira Club races with my grandparents. My grandfather used to say the difference between a horse and a donkey was that the horse raced and the donkey bet on it.

I descended from the bus in a hurry and walked the last few remaining blocks to the Marriott.

I passed the silver shop, my silver shop. I still have my silver bracelets from that shop, that is if Hazeer hasn't sold them by now. I love jewellery. I bought all my silver jewellery there.

My silver shop is the tiniest shop in the world. You opened the door. That was it. There was no more space for anyone else. The owner had been an old craftsman from a bygone era.

He sold me four Bedouin dowry bracelets when I was sixteen. A Bedouin bride's wealth is her jewellery. It was not uncommon for her to have several of these bracelets. One bracelet I kept for myself, the other three I gave away as gifts. They were two-inch wide bands of crafted silver cuff bracelets with a braided row of silver in the middle.

You can make all the jokes you want about me getting ready to be married because Yanni no longer counts.

At least I am worth my weight in silver when I meet Mister Right; Hazeer doesn't count either. Much of the silver I have is from that shop.

It was gratifying to see the shop was still there, but sadly, the owner had long since passed away.

Historically, Gezira Island was called *Jardin des Plantes* for its vast collection of exotic plants. In 1869 the Gezirah Palace, designed by J. F. Pasha, was constructed. The palace was used for guests attending that year's opening of the Suez Canal. Emperor Franz Josef was one of the aristocrats who graced the Neo-classical building.

The U-shaped mansion is now the central part of the Cairo Marriott. This Marriott hotel was one of my favourite places as a child, not because it was a grand palace which I love, but for the Roy Rogers restaurant.

I was big into the wild west back then. The Roy Rogers served hamburgers and fries in red plastic baskets, accompanied by endless milkshakes! The waiters and waitresses wore jeans, red and white checkered shirts, and bandanas around their necks. They even wore cowboy hats and cowboy boots.

The Roy Rogers was still there, but my return visit would have to wait.

I hurried into the lobby and there was the scowling Steinman. I'd have to be careful not to call him rock man or something and give away that I now knew who he was. Ironically, his face did match his name. He didn't say a word, but I knew to follow him into the elevator. The clock indicated it was high noon.

Miss Balgrave was on the balcony being served lunch. Lo and behold Nancy was with her and another man I didn't recognize. The stranger was sitting, but I judged him to be of medium height, quite fit, with an expansive forehead, dreamy eyes and full lips. He was a looker, but not one of the men in the row of photographs Omar had me study the night before. Omar would be disappointed and frustrated about this new accomplice.

Miss Balgrave didn't introduce me, so I had to introduce myself to the newcomer.

"Amira." I beamed my best tell-me-your-name smile.

"Enchantée."

That was it. Anyone could have said that. It wasn't even a clue if he was truly French or not. Before I could ask him for his name, Miss Balgrave jumped in.

"Where is the suitcase?"

I indicated the green bag by the couch in the living room. Miss Balgrave walked over to it and told me to open it. The two boxes of chocolate were inside.

"They were wrapped in cellophane. Why is it off?"

I explained the customs on the Israeli side had inspected the boxes.

"No doubt they were looking for drugs but when they saw they were chocolates, they just laughed and through I went."

"And the Egyptian control?"

"Didn't even look."

I gave my best carefree laugh and made sure I had eye contact with her as I spoke. Nothing generates suspicion more than lack of eye contact, a lesson I had learned with Headmistress Miss Beatrissa. Bless her heart.

Miss Balgrave seemed to accept the explanation. It was after all logical that someone would want to check the contents of the boxes. Nancy sat down on the couch opposite me. I could see she was hurt. Her hand was in a sling. It looked like she had a collar bone fracture.

Nancy didn't like me eyeballing her.

"It was pretty stupid to get left behind at Shaluffa," she barked at me.

"I'm not the one that got hit by a car," I shot back. "That's pretty stupid."

She was a quick fuse. Her indignation was evident, but I couldn't leave it alone.

I dug deeper and heckled, "I'm surprised you're insulted that I said you were an idiot. I already thought you knew."

"Enough!" Miss Balgrave snapped. "Amira, go sit on the balcony with Yasser."

Yasser? Really? Well, I had the first name. I moved out of the living room and onto the balcony with a nonchalance I certainly didn't feel.

"It's hot," I babbled to cover the reason for my perspiration.

Yasser merely waved his hand at the weather Gods in the vast blue sky.

"So, Yasser."

He looked at me and smiled.

I tried again. "You look familiar. Do I know you?"

He shook his head. "I doubt it."

His English was perfect. British accent.

"Sure, I do. What's your family name?"

"Arafat."

"Very funny."

"Amira. Come here." Grrr. Miss Balgrave really needed to stop interrupting me while I was playing detective.

"We are moving into the flat tomorrow and need a cook. You will come with us."

The way she said it, I knew it wasn't a request.

"You will need some cash to purchase supplies."

She made a motion to Steinman.

"Give her what she needs."

He gave me a wad of cash and wrote down the address of the flat. Bingo. Omar would be pleased. Yasser had drifted in from the balcony. The other three were speaking quietly among themselves. I couldn't hear what they were saying.

Miss Balgrave looked over her shoulder at me.

"What are you standing there for Amira? Get going! *Imshi ya bint!*"

They all broke out laughing. I laughed along with them like a good servant would. I gestured toward the facilities with my hand and moved in that direction. No one paid any more attention to me.

I flushed the toilet and let the tap run as I slowly pulled open the door. I still couldn't hear what they were saying so I slipped a little bit closer. I heard Miss Balgrave say she would go to the Egyptian Museum for the afternoon while the others, and then I lost my concentration because Steinman stepped in front of me. I never did find out what they were up to.

"Oh," I laughed.

Try explaining why you are creeping toward the living room to this guy.

"Ah, I left the tap running."

Tapping my forehead like I was crazy, I rushed back to turn it off. Quickly I waved goodbye and escaped into the hotel hallway.

There was no time for Roy Rogers or Dizzy Gillespie who was performing at the Omar Khayyam Casino in the hotel that night. I walked out of the hotel via the pool route.

The pool is set down at the bottom of a series of terraces. It must have been an oasis of palace gardens and trees at one time I guessed. Now, it was a bunker of cement levels with no shade.

It was a heat stroke arena. I was sweating by the time I made it back onto the minibus.

The night before, Omar had decided having me shadowed was a waste of time and money. I can't say the pronouncement made me feel valued as an asset, quite the opposite. It had been somewhat reassuring that the SSIS had been close at hand.

Now I was totally on my own.

I had to get to the museum before Miss Balgrave. Otherwise, I would have no chance of knowing when or if she was in the building.

I certainly hoped she was going there, although for the life of me, I couldn't figure out why she would. Maybe she was only sightseeing, after all.

I patted the wad of cash in my pant pocket and made sure it was buttoned shut. The address of the flat in Heliopolis that Steinman had written on the paper I knew. El-Sobki Street. Near the Heliopolis Club, not too far from the Ittihadia Palace.

There were two places that always held my imagination in Heliopolis. The first was the Ittihadia palace and the second was the Baron Empain Palace or as we called it *Le Palais Hindou.*

I was fascinated by the bewildering palace of the Belgian Baron Édouard Empain who had been inspired by the Hindu temple of Angkor Wat in Cambodia.

My friend and I tried to access it one time when a very angry man came screaming out of the empty palace. We were so terrified, thinking it was some Hindu demon protecting a tomb.

It was an absolutely huge brown edifice, apparently abandoned. It sat like a ruined beacon of a bygone era, full of treachery and intrigue. It's on a slightly raised dais and is an unforgettable structure.

The area around *Le Palais Hindou* was totally bare, dusty dry dirt. You wouldn't be able to sneak in unseen.

One could only stare from a distance at the openings of the palace like they were deep caverns into a mountain.

It stretched up to the sky in contorted shapes. Needless to say, the ghosts of the palace had led to incredible tales of mystery including supposed satanic rituals, orgies, sacrifices, and wild parties. The massive palace had been completed in 1911 and was made out of reinforced concrete.

The mansion is covered with spirals and curls which are exquisitely detailed animals and human figures. It is an amalgamation of Arab architecture and Walloon imagination.

In its heyday it had been a sumptuous residence with magnificent gardens and grounds. That was hard to believe as it stood in the wasteland area of El Korba, Heliopolis.

I never made it inside the palace, but if the interior had been as lavish as the exterior, it must have been quite a treasure trove for modern grave robbers. No doubt the gilded doors had long since disappeared.

Rumour has it there are tunnels connecting it to the basilica where the Baron is buried.

Tragedy enshrouds the place.

His wife allegedly fell to her death from the main tower which is only accessible via a spectacular spiraling staircase. The Baron's mentally ill daughter was found at the other end of the palace, dead in a basement chamber. The son kept the house until the July 23rd revolution in 1952. Since then, sightings of the Baron's daughter and late-night parties have been rumoured.

Death and tragedy weren't exactly helpful or happy thoughts as I reached Tahrir Square in a descending mood that meeting Miss Balgrave had brought on.

I'd have to check my vast volumes of Freud. Signals from my unconscious mind indicated that this woman was having an effect on me.

The Museum of Egyptian Antiquities is a hop, skip and a jump over the October 6th Bridge. I had spent hours there by myself nearly every time I had come to Cairo.

The enormous T-shaped building is a labyrinth of galleries and a museum without a rival. Fascinating. It has a comfortable, almost Parisian appearance on the outside. However, step inside and the treasures of lost worlds emerge before you.

I was starving. But I didn't go get any food as I was worried Miss Balgrave, who could arrive at any minute, would slip by unnoticed. I longed to be on the other side of Tahrir Square chomping down on Aish Baladi stuffed with Tahina covered Falafel.

The Nile Ritz Carlton, kitty-corner to the museum, makes the best Falafel in the world. They have a little stand outside the hotel entrance. Delicious.

After walking through the elaborate iron gate, I picked an obscure spot in the front courtyard of the Egyptian Museum, the far corner by the stone mailbox. I wondered if tourists realized a postcard or a letter in that forgotten mailbox would take four months to reach its destination, if ever.

It was hot in that corner, but it's a dry heat and easier to tolerate than the sweltering humid heat of Winterpeg in a Canadian summer. The tourists were streaming into the pink-coloured building.

True to her word, there was Miss Balgrave, all by herself. White pants, a loose flowery shirt, red scarf around her head. She glided into the two-story museum unperturbed by the throng of eager visitors.

The museum entrance is on the ground floor. The interior of the museum is gigantic. Even though there were many people wandering around the exhibits and large spaces, it was easy to follow her undetected. The artifacts are stuffed everywhere, in every single nook and cranny. It's only a fraction of what is actually inside the museum, most of it is in storage in the basement.

Miss Balgrave really took her time looking at the numerous pieces of ancient papyrus. In the coin section, I thought she would never leave.

There are quite a few gold, silver, and bronze coins inscribed with Greek, Latin, Arabic and the ancient Egyptian writing language of hieroglyphs. I have a special affinity for coins. On the beach in Alexandria, it is not unusual to find ancient coins. I never did, but my friend did.

It always pissed me off that she found a beautiful gold Roman coin. She had it made into a gorgeous key chain which she gave her grandfather. He loved it. I loved it too. It was a piece of jewellery if truth be told. I truly regret that I lost it in my travels since I had gotten quite attached to it.

It was my first real jewellery theft.

Easy. Peasy.

Miss Balgrave didn't visit all forty-two rooms on that floor, thank goodness. She barely gave a glance at the New Kingdom artifacts and sculptures.

I gave a conciliatory pat to the colossal statue of Akhenaton, my favourite pharaoh, as I went by. He was an original, along with his wife, Nefertiti, my favourite queen. They reigned over one of the great periods of Art and adventure. They took an entire civilization and reframed it.

Originally called Amenhotep IV, the pharaoh decreed that Egypt would only worship one God, Aten. He installed himself and his queen in Amarna, now named Akhetaten. Akhenaton worshipped his one God for twenty years.

The Egyptian Museum is considered to be the largest museum in the entire world, and it felt like it. My legs were starting to ache by the time Miss Balgrave sauntered up to the second floor.

She hadn't met anyone. She hadn't even talked to a guide.

The upper floor has smaller displays like tools, funerary objects, smaller statues, jewellery, and most importantly, the wealth of Tut Ankh Amun's tomb. It's not to be missed and she went straight for it.

I was glad she did because I'm not partial to the endless rows of mummies on display.

Dead people don't do anything for me.

The sumptuous collection of Tut, on the other hand, is always stunning. Seeing it always overwhelms me.

Miss Balgrave continued her meticulous inspection of the Tut Ankh Amun exhibit with what I deemed was her typical British thoroughness or French obstinacy, take your pick.

I spent my time staring at the golden diadem of the boy pharaoh. It has a vulture and cobra on the front and apart from the eyes, the vulture's head is solid gold. The cobra's head and hood are inlaid with gemstones. The vulture and the cobra were political symbols of ancient Egypt's unification. Their heads were often placed side by side on the front of the headdresses worn by kings on state occasions, and on the headdresses of their statues.

Seems like you can't get away from politics anywhere.

"It's beautiful, isn't it?" Miss Balgrave whispered into my right ear.

I shut my eyes and turned to face her as if it was the most natural thing in the world to be in the museum together.

"Yes, it is. I always love coming here. I didn't know you were coming Miss Balgrave. You could have given me a lift."

I beamed my chummy friendship smile.

"It was a last-minute decision," she spoke just like Miss Beatrissa did, right before she announced my punishments.

I quickly confessed. "Actually, I am not being very honest. I did see you come in."

"Yes, you've been following me for hours."

So much for being a detective. Okay, a detective I'm not but I am a good liar.

"Yeah. I wanted to get up the nerve to ask about clothing."

She gave me a blank stare and looked me up and down.

"Clothing?"

"Hmm. You see I haven't any clothes. New job and everything, maybe I could do some shopping? You did say to get anything I needed. I hoped maybe we could extend that to attire."

She tilted her head the way a hawk looks at its prey before it is going to dive and kill it.

"Sure," she said. "How far is the airport?"

"The airport?" The question caught me by surprise.

"Yes Amira. You know planes, travel, airport?"

"To here?"

"To Heliopolis."

"Oh, twenty minutes I guess."

"The plane gets in at four and then customs." She was ruminating out loud. "There will be six persons for dinner tomorrow. Seven o'clock sharp."

"Guests are coming from the airport?"

"Is that too much for you to handle?" she mocked.

"I only meant I could check the flight to see if the plane was arriving on time and plan dinner accordingly."

She was still checking me out, the prey. I imagined she might take flight and descend upon my head.

"British Airways from Frankfurt," she snapped like a turtle and walked away.

She does like an exit I thought to myself.

There was absolutely no point sticking around. I beat a hasty exit carrying that treasure trove of information.

Back to the Sphinx Moon Hotel on Nazih Khalifa Street in Heliopolis.

CHAPTER EIGHT

Mister Muscle Steinman was waiting outside the Heliopolis telephone exchange for me.

"Have a nice chat?"

I don't think he had ever questioned me before, at least, oh wait, he had strung some words together after beating me up in Ashkelon. How quickly one buries trauma.

"Who were you talking to?"

"None of your business," I responded.

It's amazing how often courage and stupidity look the same.

He stepped in front of me.

"Miss Balgrave will think it is her business or do you need some incentive to talk?"

"My boyfriend, okay?" I gushed.

"Because?"

"I had to let him know I was staying on a bit longer so he wouldn't worry and contact the police. He's kind of an anxious type of guy."

The mention of the police seemed to do the trick. He backed down but just a bit.

"Well, say hello to Hazeer next time you speak with him."

Steinman made my skin crawl. I didn't love Hazeer, but I was fond of him. How did he know my boyfriend's name anyway?

I brushed by him, but I was shaking from head to toe. Of course, I hadn't been talking to Hazeer, but Omar.

The telephone exchange is open to the public. You can pay your money, place a phone call with the operator at the front desk, wait for the connection to be made and go to the private telephone booth for your telephone conversation.

The only drawback to this system is that you have to give your number to the attendant at the counter and wait your turn for the call to go through. That part is all very public.

While I waited, sometimes it takes a long time, the woman next to me leaned over and confided, "You know what I dream of?"

I had no idea. I didn't care, but I have manners so I encouraged her to tell me.

"I dream of being able to pick up a telephone in my own home and dial anywhere in the world."

Wow. The simple things that make people happy. It was a reminder to me of how most of the population in Egypt really had no idea what the rest of the world was doing.

That was definitely confirmed many times during my life.

One time my grandmother and I met her hairdresser at Merryland for an evening tea; the hairdresser had brought her son along with her. He was a skinny, unhealthy-looking man in his late twenties. Very quickly the conversation had come around to his request for an exit visa. A goal he was convinced my family could make happen.

He had pointed at me like I was an undeserving child.

His argument was that if I had a Canadian passport why couldn't he?

He was so desperate. He worked at a menial job in the back of some shop day in and day out. I guess he figured my grandmother could snap her fingers and produce the visa. It didn't work that way. My grandmother told him so. He wailed that he was going to die after having endured a miserable life in Cairo.

I could see his point though.

He lived in a two-bedroom ground floor flat behind a shoe shop in the middle of Heliopolis. The area is considered quite upper class; their place certainly was not.

It stank from all the water dripping down from the flats above. He and his aging father slept in one room, his sister and mother in another.

The kitchen was a cavity with a window opening onto a totally enclosed area. The upper apartments threw their garbage into that four-foot square space and it ended up stinking right outside their kitchen window. It was the only window in the entire flat. The bathroom was worse. Except for another small space that seated four people on wooden chairs, that was the entire flat.

The rent of the seeping infested flat was a whopping five pounds a month. The flat had belonged to the grandfather. Since the law stated you couldn't raise the rent if the same family still lived in it, the rent hadn't gone up for decades. The landlord couldn't collect and hence never did any repairs or upgrades. There wasn't any law about maintaining apartments. It was miserable.

I never did find out what happened with the young man desperate to escape to North America. Nothing good, probably.

Before I took my telephone connection in the private booth, I agreed with the unfortunate woman sitting beside me in the telephone office about her dream.

"Telephones are wonderful," I had said.

Now that I had some money, I had figured the exchange was as good a place as any to call Omar. But with Mister Nosey Parker Steinman milling about I'd have to be more careful and find another location.

Omar had taken my telephone call immediately. I told him everything. He repeated the information back to me, especially the description of Yasser. It didn't seem to irritate him as much as I thought it would, maybe he had a lead on who Yasser was that I didn't know about. The location of Miss Balgrave's Heliopolis flat on El-Sobki Street near the Ittihadia palace was of interest to him as well.

The Ittihadia palace is a gigantic creation of luxury. In its first life, it was the Heliopolis Palace Hotel with over three hundred rooms and fifty-five private apartments. It was known as the legendary Arab Palace. I know it sounds like something out of Aladdin, but this place was stunning.

The design is Moorish Revival with some Louis XIV and Louis XV thrown in, along with a central dome and classic symmetry. The vast building moved into its second life as the Egyptian presidential palace and administrative headquarters of President Hosni Mubarak.

I could tell Omar was considering the Ittihadia palace, the heart of the Egyptian government, as a possible target. It would have great symbolic meaning for those opposed to the current direction of Middle Eastern politics.

There it was again, the political angle.

Omar had a lot to do, especially with the new arrivals coming in from Frankfurt on British Airways at four o'clock. I hadn't seen them yet. I didn't know anything more about them, not even their gender.

The next day was spent shopping and preparing for dinner. I know what you are thinking, but I can cook and I had to make sure I didn't get fired.

I decided on a menu of spicy Koftah with Taboulleh and Wara Anib. I like the grape leaves stuffed with spicy meat pencil thin with very little filling, so I spent hours making them and stacking them in a little pyramid pile. The leaves have to be fresh picked, the first growth of the year, otherwise Wara Anib is like eating cow feed no matter how you cook it. There would be plenty of bread, hummus and tahina to fill in the gaps. For dessert, there was Baklava. I wasn't sure about the menu combination, but hey, it was what I knew how to cook.

I figured I couldn't make Miss Balgrave trust me. I could only feed her Baklava soaked in syrup and hope for the best.

The two new arrivals showed up at ten minutes to seven. I was fussing with the table setting and made sure to have a good long look at them. The two men were Middle Easterners. Spoke Arabic to each other. French with Miss Balgrave.

It was difficult pretending not to understand what they were saying. I am fluent in Arabic and French but only speak with Miss Balgrave and the others in English.

The newcomers spoke mostly about the current political situation. It was difficult to hear them because a music recording of Umm Kulthum was blaring in the background. She was a popular Egyptian singer, referred to as the Star of the East.

Umm Kulthum was still considered a national treasure even though she had passed away in 1975. She had sung one song for six hours without repetition.

When my grandfather had said that was where he had been all night and into the wee hours of the morning, my grandmother didn't believe him. It was inconceivable that he had only been listening to one song. They had had a terrible row. I don't think my grandmother ever apologized when she found out my grandfather had actually been at the night club.

It would have been sacrilege to turn the volume down on the voice of Egypt's fourth pyramid. If Miss Balgrave asked me to leave, I'd just say I wanted to hear the end of the song first.

I was serving the dessert as slowly as possible. I went around with the Baklava for a second time, much to Nancy's annoyance. Her antics were really getting under my skin.

"That's it, keep rolling your eyes, maybe you'll find your brain," I directed the barb at her.

Nancy's jaw hit the floor but not before she had sworn angrily in French. The two guests broke out in laughter. I had embarrassed her quite nicely in front of the two men.

"Shut up Amira," spat Miss Balgrave. "It's time to go. Leave the room."

She was certainly wound tight this evening. I judged it unwise to make a musical request, and got my things. Before I walked out the door, I caught a glimpse of a set of blueprints on the coffee table; but I couldn't tarry, I had to leave as I was still spending the nights at the Sphinx Moon Hotel. I took a long route to the Hotel to make sure no one was following me and to find a telephone to make my report to Omar.

"I don't live in the flat, Omar," I had argued with him.

The kitchen is right at the back of the apartment, the way it is in these old-style flats. It's a hole in the wall really. The woman is supposed to be in the kitchen, out of the way and silent. The location of the kitchen made sure that I couldn't hear anything or see anything unless I was right in the living room area. I hadn't told him about my gaff and how it had got me kicked out of the flat.

"Well, you have to get in there," insisted Omar. "Search the place."

"There is always someone there. It's impossible for me to just pull out the blueprint to study it."

I explained it looked like a large, very large building.

He asked if it could be the Ittihadia Palace.

I replied it might have been but I really didn't know.

Omar did have some information for me though about our two new guests. He had narrowed it down to four people.

When I described them, he felt sure who they were.

"Right. We think Eda Pofem has ties to Abu Nidal, the founder of Fatah. He has quite the résumé. Involved in the planning of the Rome and Vienna airport attacks in 1985, twenty persons were killed. One hundred and thirty-eight were wounded. He keeps ruthless company. Specialty is explosives."

"Makes bombs, murders people," I summed up.

They had traced the components of the explosives and boxes, and were confident they had been made and assembled in Israel.

But why come through the Israeli Egypt border?

Why not just smuggle it into Egypt another way, surely an easier way?

Omar's theory was that the group responsible would want to claim ownership of the attack and thereby increase its prestige.

Homegrown and infiltrated was the way he had phrased it.

"The other passenger is Mohatmed Pofem, fraternal twin of Eda. He is a shadow character and has not quite such an impressive résumé, but we believe he is also an expert in explosives," Omar disclosed.

All right then. It looked like things were moving into the big league. I wasn't sure I wanted to stick around for the fireworks. Something would go wrong and I would get blamed, like always. Omar was expecting results. He wouldn't tolerate not getting them.

The next morning after I had finished serving breakfast, Miss Balgrave gave me a lecture about Nancy. She wanted me to cut it out.

It was a warning to behave.

It of course took me right back to my school days. I didn't smile at Miss Balgrave, but I did drop my eyes and swear I would never do it again.

As if.

I was washing up in the kitchen when I heard Miss Balgrave yelling into the telephone. We were alone in the flat so I took the liberty to see what the matter was. It seemed her driver, which had been arranged by Nancy had not shown up.

"Do you have an international driver's licence?" she fired the question at me when she saw I was listening to her telephone conversation.

"Of course," I lied. "Can't you drive yourself?"

"Ya Humar," she swore. "I don't want to drive myself."

"Where to?" I asked.

Her car was a white Peugeot sedan. It wasn't very far to go to the Sheraton Hotel, but I made an incorrect turn onto Al Ahram Street right at the beginning.

A traffic officer flagged me down.

He wanted to see my licence, which of course I didn't have.

The discussion was escalating when Miss Balgrave rolled down the backseat window, slipped the policeman a hundred-pound note and thanked him for his concern.

A donkey cart clattered past, a polished black Mercedes zipped by. Taxi drivers leaned on their horns.

I pulled out into traffic carefully and glanced in the rear-view mirror at Miss Balgrave.

"Just like my grandmother," I said.

Miss Balgrave glared at me.

It was a short twenty-minute drive. She disappeared into the "S" hotel as soon as I pulled up to the entrance. She was going to see her bombers. I knew I couldn't possibly be anywhere near enough to hear the conversation between her, Eda and Mohatmed Pofem.

Instead, I went to the restaurant to get a bite to eat.

There are three restaurants in the lobby of the Sheraton, two were closed, so it was an obvious choice. The restaurant caters to mostly international travelers. The fare was typically continental. Being the only one open, the restaurant was busy. Guests were expected to share tables. No sitting by yourself.

It's the kind of phony friendly thing I hate, like having to shake hands in church after the minister instructs everyone to say hello.

An American woman and her husband sat down across from me. I had a clear view into the lobby from my table. I kept my handbag on the chair beside me to prevent anyone else sitting down. I wasn't going to be totally surrounded.

Hello. I'm so and so. How are you? Are you travelling? Where from?

It's the type of nauseating chit chat that drives me crazy, but I had been to a British boarding school so I did fairly well.

Etiquette. Miss Beatrissa used to spell it to me, very slowly.

The fellow sitting across from me was a scholar. He had come to research Muslim and Christian interfacing amid the Ecumenical Crisis of the 5th century with regards to the Symbolism of the Holy Trinity.

All right then.

I asked him if his name happened to be Nestorius which he thought was a fine joke. He was impressed I could even mention a controversial theologian of the fifth century. It was the first time in his life anyone hadn't been struck mute by the title of his research.

Well, if that's where you get your thrills, who am I to argue?

His wife was also quite impressed with me after she found out I was living in Cairo with my husband and three children. I explained we were doing missionary work and had an office in Coptic Cairo.

I invited her to come and visit the oldest part of Cairo.

"The best time is in the evening," I said, "when the children are playing quietly and the day is settling down."

The houses are small, simple with narrow windows and single shutters. It is like wandering through another age. There are no visible signs of the modern era there. The Coptic Museum is a peaceful maze of inner courtyards and small gardens set among ancient wooden lattices, the *mushrabiyyah.* It is also home to the Jewish community of Old Cairo.

She was thrilled. Wow. You live here. That is so cool, and with your children.

I was laughing at her on the inside.

What can I say? I live to impress.

It never occurred to Miss America to wonder why I was sitting in a restaurant in a plush hotel by myself?

You know the type of traveller she was. Gullible.

Foreigners are so gullible; my Egyptian friends were right.

I saw Miss Balgrave come into the lobby and excused myself by telling the American couple I had just spotted a donor for our volunteer work.

I left them to take care of my cheque for the meal.

Miss Balgrave had a foul look on her face. I sensed if I didn't tread carefully, I might be donating blood.

"The car?" she sneered at me.

"I'll bring it right away."

I brought the car to the hotel entrance. Miss Balgrave stood there like she wanted me to open the door for her, which I was not going to do. I'm not a chauffeur, I'm an artist.

Don't forget who you are Amira, a voice whispered to me.

Miss Balgrave slammed the door shut and said, "Home James."

She didn't actually say that; she didn't say anything. That was the scary part. She usually watches me and sneers, but not this time.

Obviously, we weren't talking because she turned her gaze to the view outside the car window. There are two Sheratons. There is the one by the road to the airport which is where we were, and one located downtown by the Nile.

I didn't want to disturb Miss Balgrave by talking. Perhaps it had something to do with the bombardier twosome she had just visited or perhaps it was just the experience of being at this particular Sheraton. Half of the hotel building had recently been damaged by a fire.

The hotel had set up huge tents in the gardens for a wedding. The streamers, banners and electric lights had been draped from the hotel balconies to the tents. It looked very festive, but it was also a road map for fire to travel up to the hotel when the cooking tents caught fire. The hotel was engulfed in flames as quickly as you can light a match.

A Swiss air crew staying at the hotel managed to escape by jumping off the balconies in their underwear. That was how they flew out of Cairo too. I am not joking, that's how they left. Luckily only a fraction of the hotel was badly damaged and the tennis courts were fine.

"You don't care for Nancy," came her bad-tempered voice from the back seat.

That was an understatement, but why say it at all?

"Tell me why," Miss Balgrave inquired.

I thought for a minute and spoke carefully, "She has no class despite the way she looks. Her manners are lacking. She draws attention to herself."

Miss Balgrave nodded thoughtfully.

"She's careless and stupid."

I added the last part because it was the brutal truth and where Nancy was concerned, I was going to be brutal.

I wasn't needed after playing chauffeur. I headed back to the Sphinx Moon Hotel. When I arrived at the hotel, there was a message at the front desk. Miss Balgrave had called to tell me to hustle back over to the flat on El-Sobki.

Once out on the street, I slowed myself down to remind myself that I wasn't a jump-to-it sort of girl. I deliberately took my time getting back to Miss Balgrave's flat.

It was a good opportunity to dive into a nearby food shop to make a telephone call to Omar.

He wasn't available. I had never spoken to anyone but him, so I didn't leave a message. What a stupid system.

How could he be unavailable?

The next time I spoke with him I was going to tell him how poorly the SSIS was functioning.

Hence, I was out of sorts upon entering Miss Balgrave's flat. There were four of them sitting out on the veranda. Steinman was looking his usual self, Nancy too. She had her typical petulant pout going. Only Yasser acknowledged I was alive. They all gaped at me. It was obvious they had been having a heated discussion.

"Would you like to discuss today's menu ma'am?"

I always found it better to take the initiative when summoned to the headmistress's office. I was carrying a shopping bag full of food items and lifted it to show her what a good girl I'd been.

"No Amira. You won't be cooking for us anymore," said Miss Balgrave.

"Very well then."

The statement caught me by surprise, but I recovered quickly.

"May I have my…" I paused for a second, looking for the right words, "…my salary and my things."

Omar Mohammed was going to be terribly disappointed. I was going to be in big trouble with the Egyptian authorities.

Suddenly, there was hysterical shouting. Three men burst out of one of the buildings in the lane below. The veranda overlooks the back lane and we had a clear view.

A cow which had been brought into the city to be slaughtered had escaped. It was absolute chaos. The whole thing would have been hysterically funny if it wasn't for the fact the animal already had had its flexor tendons slashed on all four legs and was making a panicked attempt to escape its certain death. The still attached hooves flopped about uselessly. It ran on all four of its severed stumps of legs. It was a horrible scene of abuse. I turned my head away and covered my ears.

"It's over." Yasser leaned over and whispered to me. "They've taken it back into the shop. You can look now."

The scene seemed to have pushed Miss Balgrave to a decision.

"You see what happens when things go wrong and there aren't enough bodies. We need to include her for now."

The statement made me feel like I had slurped a Freezie and was getting a sharp searing pain in my nose and forehead from doing it too fast. I didn't like it. What did the words 'for now' mean?

Enough bodies? Were they going to slaughter me later?

No one objected to my inclusion at that point or at least to my face. I guess that meant I was no longer the cook but what I was, I couldn't tell. I kept a straight face. The only place Miss Balgrave and her pals couldn't see was inside my head. I tried to figure out what they were up to.

My first guess had been drugs. Egypt was a good market, but was it that good?

What were the explosives for?

My second guess was maybe they were running some type of fraud but again the explosives didn't fit in that theory.

What was the target?

The third guess was the political angle. I had to admit all the pieces fit with that, but I still wasn't sure.

"You'll be helping Yasser with a few errands, Amira."

"Take her with you," Miss Balgrave instructed Yasser.

He nodded his head slightly and stood up. "Come with me."

CHAPTER NINE

"You weren't available!" I raised my voice.

"Was it an emergency?" Omar inquired.

"It might have been!"

"That's what the transmitter is for," he said it like he was a genius and I was a numbskull.

There was a long pause.

"I will arrange it. Call whenever you can. If the information is highly significant, tell whoever is on the line. If not, call back later when you can."

I didn't like it, not at this point. I told him so.

"I can't be a switchboard operator waiting for your call, Amira. We have Miss Balgrave and her associates all under surveillance. Relax. You are overreacting."

I told him about my change of status and what Yasser and I had been up to that afternoon. Well, almost, I didn't tell him everything.

Yasser and I had headed down to the Nile Ritz Carlton. At least that was what I believed the destination was when he spoke with the taxi driver, but once we were there, Yasser headed down the north side of the hotel to the Nile River. He wouldn't tell me what we were doing.

It seemed like he was attempting to cross the Nile Corniche Road along the stretch that runs parallel to the Egyptian Museum and behind the Ritz Carlton Hotel. Not a good idea. We couldn't manage it. Instead, we walked the one kilometre from that spot down to a crossing which led to a wharf on the Nile River.

The path went past a boat house, a shack in fact. Just before the wharf, Yasser gave me a sly wink and pulled me inside the shack. He slammed me up against the wall, grabbed my thighs and pulled them apart. He was a little rough but I groaned with pleasure.

You can never overdo it in that department I find. Yasser spewed into me, pulled back, and did up his pants.

"Well, at least that was better than your Baklava," he said.

I thought my Baklava was pretty sweet, so I decided to take it as a compliment. Three minutes later I was following Yasser down to the wharf.

His fascination with boats was the same interest Miss Balgrave had had in Ashkelon. Again, it was a big pointer that I didn't pay much attention to.

"What are we doing here?" I asked.

Since we were now on better terms, he replied, "We're going to take a boat ride."

I turned chatty, "I love being on the water. My graduation gift from my grandmother for surviving an education at the British School of Alexandria was a trip down the Nile River to Aswan."

He glanced at me in surprise at my sudden verbal verbosity.

The cities of Egypt exist on the narrow strips of land on either side of the Nile. Fertile. Lush. Then the endless desert. Egypt is like that, a contradiction. The ancient Pharaohs called their country black and red. Red was for the desert sands. Black was for the fertile soil by the Nile River.

"When my grandmother and I arrived in Aswan, we stayed at the Old Cataract Hotel. Yes. Now, that was style."

Yasser raised his eyebrows.

"It was built in the elegant Victorian era in 1899 by Thomas Cook. The legendary hotel is like a palace. It is an enchanted building of lovely Moorish arches and *mushrabiyyah* windows," I said.

"Ah yes, windows for the discrete," Yasser laughed.

I kept on talking.

"The chandeliers are exquisite, plush carpets, soft armchairs, and hand-carved gilt chairs. My grandmother picked a favourite and so did I."

Special memory.

"So it's a treasure," Yasser mocked and chuckled at his own private joke.

"Yes," I said feeling slightly offended. "It stands like a gate to Upper Egypt's treasures of Abu Simbel. The glittering majestic Nile. The warmth of the amber desert reflects onto the Hotel which is built on a ledge of pink granite. It sits grand, comfortable, and opulent,"

Just to spite him, I finished my recital with a flourish.

"Next you're going to tell me you had the best," teased Yasser.

"My room in the old palace wing was one of the best in the original part of the hotel," I shot back. "The doors to the private balcony opened onto a sumptuous view of the Nile where my grandmother and I drank ice cold glasses of *Karkadé* and gazed over the Nile to Elephantine Island."

Historically, Elephantine Island stood at the border between Egypt and Nubia. It was a natural defensive site as well as a trading location.

"My grandmother told me the island was the dwelling place of Khnum, the ram-headed god of the cataracts. He guards and controls the waters of the Nile from the caves beneath the Elephantine Island. The island is also home to a Nilometer."

The ancient device measured the level of the water in the Nile River with remarkable accuracy.

Yasser was disappointingly quiet about the Nile River.

Embarrassed by my defensiveness, I asked, "Did you know that the Old Cataract Hotel has hosted the *haut monde* for nearly a century? I stayed in the same room as Agatha Christie. Don't laugh. Whenever I had had a particular bad day and felt the need to kill someone, I could always count on Agatha to take care of it by diving into one of her novels for a few hours."

Yasser looked at me like he was considering killing me if I didn't shut up. He certainly wasn't considering reading a book.

"Naturally, my grandmother and I took a memorable sail in a sleek Felucca on the dark blue Nile across to Elephantine Island at breakneck speed. The island isn't named after any existing elephants now or ever. It's probably just named that by someone who imagined the large gray granite boulders looked like a herd of elephants standing in the water. Have you ever been on a felucca?"

Yasser finally spoke, "Actually I have."

"The sailor of our felucca in Aswan was an old man and his deckhand was his grandson. They tacked across the Nile with amazing skill and speed. The winds were really blowing. Usually, the felucca moves with gently swollen sails filled by tepid winds. That day, the craft clipped the waves. I could feel the felucca pulling across the river."

"Sounds exhilarating."

"Oh it was! It was two different worlds meeting, theirs and mine, and I was only sailing through. I had just completed my schooling; the grandson didn't even know his age when I asked him how old he was. *Mahlish.* Who needs to keep track of stuff like that?"

Yasser gave a little nod and mumbled, "Who needs to tell everyone about it?"

I bristled. Just to drive my irritation home, I kept talking.

"It is amazing who you bump into though. In the Cataract Hotel lobby, a very enthusiastic young man ran up to me. Ah huh. It was a shop owner's son from Alexandria. I'd only ever spoken to him a few times."

"A long-lost love?"

I gave an expansive smile and leaned into him. "Naturally. He was thrilled to see me. I mean absolutely effervescent. We spoke in French."

"So, he was a tour guide. How original," quipped Yasser.

I blushed slightly. "He *was* a tour guide. He had reached the pinnacle of success and wanted to share."

I stopped there because the guy had then grabbed my hand, and pulled me close. What? Hey buddy we're in the lobby. What room was I in? He would come later, wink, wink. Just to get him away from me, I gave him room number 119 in the New Cataract Hotel wing. Yuck.

I'm sure the old lady in that hotel room would have no trouble getting rid of him or entertaining him when he showed up, whatever she desired.

Despite Yasser's response, I was truly enjoying myself. We walked back along the river, taking the same activity route via the boat shack.

"Do you still think this is better than my Baklava?" I whispered in Yasser's ear at the apex of his crusade to assert his masculinity a second time.

My legs were wrapped around his hips.

"I wasn't thinking about your Baklava," he panted. "I wasn't thinking of anything. I was just glad you finally stopped talking."

It was a comment I had heard before.

Unfortunately. But I was thinking, and not about Yasser's performance.

I was thinking about the chocolate explosives and the beating Steinman had given me.

My personal emotional thermometer went cold.

Later, I told Omar about the boat ride, the one with Yasser, not my graduation gift from my grandmother. We didn't discuss my Baklava either, but Omar did find the turnaround point of the boat excursion interesting.

Yasser and I had only taken the motorboat down the Nile to the Marriott hotel. Yasser hadn't said anything more about it. I hadn't asked.

Omar made a possible connection to the upcoming visit by Israeli Foreign Minister Arens and Soviet Foreign Minister Shevardnadze who were to meet in the Marriott conference centre in the coming days. Various meetings were also being conducted with high-ranking officials in the Egyptian government and affluent Arab businessmen from neighbouring countries.

I could see Omar's point about their objective being a political one. On the other hand, Miss Balgrave seemed to be more consumed with herself than politics.

There wasn't any useful information Omar could give me, which seemed to make it quite a one-sided phone call.

The owner of the flat on El-Sobki had leased it on a yearly basis to a businessman named Miguel Gonzales. His name and address were checked, fictitious of course. There were no other people or servants linked to the lease.

Miss Balgrave was still at the Heliopolis flat when Yasser and I returned. Evidently, I was residing at the flat now. It wasn't going to be a friendly sleepover that much I knew.

My boss supposed that by threatening to release my recorded confession to the Egyptian police she had my compliance.

She wasn't as clever as she thought she was. Now that I was part of the group, she was going to try to keep me in her sights, day and night.

But with Omar telling me to stop overreacting, a comment that always sets me off, and just being physically close to her, I didn't feel very relaxed. Nevertheless, I had to play it right, so I made a pitch for more money.

"This wasn't the original deal," I pouted.

"What of it?" asked Miss Balgrave as she leaned back against the sofa.

"A deal's a deal. I held up my end of the bargain. I even cooked, but this…" I let my voice trail off in abject misery.

She shrugged. I'm not sure how much she assumed I had figured out. It didn't look like she cared, if I had figured anything out or not.

Perhaps she thought I wasn't dead certain that the boxes of chocolate were not candy for example. Maybe I thought I had transported drugs. She must have realized I knew something illegitimate was in the works.

I had to be careful about the information Omar had given me. Any indication I knew about the explosives and the Pofem brothers would send me straight to the executioner.

"How much is your precious time worth to you?"

That was better. Her sneer was back. The look on her face gave me confidence.

"Four thousand pounds," I swanked.

I hoped I wasn't overdoing it. That's a lot of cash for running errands around town.

"Fine."

A good deal? I hadn't even seen any of the original cash yet.

Miss Balgrave instructed Steinman to accompany me to the Sphinx Moon Hotel to get my things.

Steinman didn't say anything to me on the way over. At the hotel entrance, he didn't even open the door for me but followed me into the elevator and down the hall to my hotel room. I took out my key and made a sweeping gesture to let him in first. I was hoping he'd react to my cheeky behaviour, but nothing. He walked into the room without a word.

I pulled the chair to the wall, climbed up, and popped off the wall grill. My two passports were sitting in the vent. It was a big opening, much larger than it needed to be for a vent.

"I had a friend who lived in an apartment with a mammoth opening in her kitchen wall, much bigger than this vent," I made motions with my hands.

He wasn't even looking at me.

"Well Steinman, you'll be interested to know that it was an older building with fourteen-foot ceilings. The opening didn't have a cover over it either. The cave, as she called it, was at a height of about ten feet off the floor. A bear could hibernate in there; it was that large. She had hung a blanket over the opening and told me she didn't even want to know where it went to or what was in there."

Steinman gave no reaction to my tittle-tattle.

I went into the bathroom.

The radio transmitter was gone from under the white towels.

Maybe I had put it somewhere else?

I stepped out of the bathroom. Steinman was waiting impatiently.

I glanced over to the bedside table. The ashtray was on top. I had put my silver bracelet in that ashtray. Gone.

My eyes focused on the little sign on the wall. Please place valuables in the hotel safe.

I swore. The maid, the F-in maid.

Steinman threw me a quizzical look.

"The maid," I griped. "She does a great job cleaning up, don't you think?"

Now that I was really getting information, I had no way to get it to Omar. The transmitter was in the hands of the maid. I could only hope Omar's surveillance would report my activity since I wouldn't have a minute to myself once I was in Miss Balgrave's flat and wouldn't be able to get to the phone.

Once Steinman and I returned to the El-Sobki flat, dinner arrived from the restaurant down the street. I can only assume Miss Balgrave didn't want to tire me out with extra duties such as cooking, so I appreciated the gestures.

"Now this is food," Yasser commented. "Finally."

I let the insinuation slide. I didn't want to cause waves. The explosive twins weren't with us. I was beginning to wonder if the chocolate boxes were a gift for the bomb-bomb brothers and had nothing to do with what Miss Balgrave was planning.

I hadn't considered that before. It opened up a whole new world of possibilities. Too many in fact.

If you took the explosives out of the picture, they could be planning anything. The lease on the El-Sobki flat was for a year.

Could it take that long?

Maybe Miss Balgrave wasn't in charge, but was working for someone else?

The following morning, I headed out to take a stroll to Merryland. In the lobby, I knew the occupants of the apartment on that level were awake too. It was seven o'clock, but not too early for the American Boss. Bruce Springsteen was screaming out, *Hey, little girl, is your daddy home?*

The lobby reverberated with bass. I always cringe at that song. *Did he go and leave you all alone?* I guess it strikes too close to home.

Steinman was right behind me when I hit the street. There was no way to lose him without explaining why I needed to be alone. I gave up trying and had my tea at the park café while watching the feral cats. My telephone call to Omar would have to wait.

I had just gotten back to the flat when Miss Balgrave came breezing out of her room.

"Good morning, Amira," she hailed me.

She was wearing a flowing dress of peach with a matching tailored jacket.

"Good morning, Miss Balgrave."

She flicked her head to Steinman. He disappeared.

"You will accompany me today, Amira. We will take the white Peugeot sedan."

"Am I driving?" I asked.

She gave me a withering look.

I didn't even have time to put a pretty bow in my hair. She had a chauffeur today. She insisted I sit in the back with her. I was beginning to realize she was quite an odd character. Distant and cold one minute. All chummy the next. Weird.

I was perspiring slightly, not because of the heat, although it was already quite warm, but because she had caught me off guard. I didn't know what was coming. I smoothed my wet palms on my skirt, trying to cover my agitation with conversation.

"Are we meeting Yasser and Nancy there?"

Wherever there was.

Miss Balgrave snorted, "Nancy has a complication with her injury and has to see a doctor. Yasser is sleeping."

What a team. No wonder she pulled me into the group. Bombs and amateurs. I started to get a nauseous feeling in my stomach.

"Yes, ma'am," I said for a lack of a better comment.

"Stop calling me ma'am."

Wow. We were certainly getting chummy.

The chauffeur was heading downtown or so I supposed. He stuck to the El-Nasr and took the road past Mansheyat Naser, also known as Garbage City.

It's a Christian slum area, and it is growing. It is like an assault on eternity. The poorest of the poor live there. The *Zabbaleen* collect all of Cairo's garbage in donkey carts. They take it there, live there, sort it, breathe it, recycle it.

Swarms of barefoot children spill into the streets among the donkeys, goats, cats, and yellow dogs. The air stinks of grilled food and dirt, spice, incense, and rotting garbage. Narrow shops are wedged into recesses in the walls.

It's home to over a quarter of a million people. A city within a city. The area even contains the church of Saint Simeon the Tanner built into a vast cave which seats 17,000 worshippers.

The driver connected with the Ring Road and took the bridge across the Nile River. We were headed to Mena House.

"Is this your first time in Egypt, Miss Balgrave?"

Might as well try to find out something about her.

Miss Balgrave didn't answer the question, but I found out she knew something about history, and I thought she was just a pretty face. Surprisingly, she made a fleeting reference to a daughter, and got a real odd look on her face.

I had a real moment of déjà vu. There was a red flag in the back of my head, but I didn't pay attention.

"How long will it take to get to Mena House?" she asked.

"From Heliopolis just under an hour, I guess. It depends on traffic," I replied. "The former royal hunting lodge, the core of the Mena House Hotel, was originally built in 1869 and coincided with the opening of the Suez Canal. Kings, Queens, foreign diplomats and Hollywood stars have stayed there."

Miss Balgrave made some flippant comment about useless information. We finished the drive in silence.

My grandparents had been nuts about Mena House. It was where they had met. In 1943, my grandfather was totally consumed with the events of the War. He had booked himself into Mena House due to a high-level meeting taking place.

How he managed to secure lodging he never divulged but he was there, waiting in the wings so to speak.

It was the get together of Winston Churchill, Franklin D Roosevelt, and General Chiang Kai-Shek of China. The conference discussed *Overlord,* the invasion of Europe even though the war was happening in Asia as well. It was at Mena House that the Big Three announced the independence of the Korean peninsula.

My grandparents had met in 1925 at the festivities hosted at Mena House by King Fouad. Since that time, my grandparents stayed at the Mena House often, even though they had a house in Zamalek and in Heliopolis.

My grandmother considered it the height of fashion to be in the shadows of Khufu, Khafre, and Menkaure, the three great pyramids. They would wander down to the Sphinx to a nearby stable full of spirited Arabian horses for their morning ride out into the desert.

Very cool, I always thought.

In 1954, when Cecil B. DeMille and Charlton Heston showed up to film *The Ten Commandments*, the film company used Mena House as their base for three months. My grandparents were there too.

Miss Balgrave called my name, "Amira."

I didn't hear her.

I was admiring the view, the city of Giza, Cairo in the background, the majestic pyramids, the Sphinx, the endless blue sky. The beauty of Cairo, the land, the generous people, mesmerized me. The hotel stands right in front of the Great Pyramids, the last remaining of the seven wonders of the ancient world.

Miss Balgrave must have uttered my name a few times before I responded.

"Amira. I'm meeting a friend here. Go and sit by the pool."

She disappeared into the hotel before I had a chance to think up a reason to go with her. This failure wasn't going to help my espionage résumé. I headed in the same direction.

I don't know what I was thinking, something tactless no doubt. I headed upstairs to the suites. The door was open to the Churchill room, where the historic meeting had taken place.

Just a maid in there. I lingered in the room. Very classy. The pyramid loomed right outside the window. What a setting, like a movie set, but it had been real.

There was nothing for it. My attempt at stealth was not a success. Down in the garden, I took a white and yellow striped towel, and flopped myself into a lawn chair by the pool.

I had come to Egypt when I was about seven years old. Most of the memories of my father before his death are unpleasant or odd recollections. I have one clear memory that falls into that latter category.

I was travelling with my father in the car. We were on a driving trip to British Columbia. Beautiful hilly land, green and open, land mixed with scrub brush, wildlife, and scraggly trees full of singing birds. All of it was gorgeous. There is only so much agricultural land in British Columbia. There are plenty of mountains, so I thought it was just the type of land you would want to preserve for posterity and manage carefully. There wasn't a person for miles.

I don't think that was a silly deduction of an uneducated child, I think it was rather astute, given my age. However, my father's perception was quite different.

"Look at all that wasted land. You could make a pile of money out of that if you would just build on it."

I vividly recall my shock. He supposed you could simply come, take the land, and make it more useful. It was as if it didn't belong to someone else. Because it wasn't humming with activity, he deemed it a waste. Where would people grow food if not there?

He didn't think about anything except the ownership and the money. It has always puzzled me, even to this day.

I'm not sure why I had that particular recollection at that point of the day but right at that moment, the Mena House waiter came by to take my order.

"You are not from here," I said to him.

"No, from Palestine," he whispered to me.

"Really?" I was surprised. "How did you get into Egypt?"

He shrugged, "Luck."

"How do you find it here?"

He shrugged again. It was okay, but his family was back in the West Bank.

"We had some land, but not now."

My father's words had shaped my perception of what people or a nation will do to acquire land. Living in the Middle East for so many years, I knew it was a huge issue.

"They say we never owned it."

His face was a sky of sadness that went on endlessly, right down to his soul I imagined.

He spoke to me, "The mysterious empty land myth has been perpetuated by the state of Israel. They announce Palestine never truly existed or that the land was basically empty or that the Israelis rescued the land and made it more fertile and useful."

I nodded in agreement and added, "Another myth is there are only super rich Arabs and terrorists there anyway. No matter how you look at it, even if you don't want to take into account land ownership, the fact remains the Palestinians are refugees and live as second-class citizens."

"True," he said in a small voice. "Many argue the Jews were entitled to a homeland especially after the Holocaust. I am not comparing the plight of Jews and the Holocaust with the unwanted Palestinian refugees, for they are different, and both situations are morally reprehensible."

I commiserated, "Being unwanted is something I am keenly familiar with thanks to my mother. The final words my mother spoke to me were that I was the meanest person she knew. That was saying quite a lot because my mother knew plenty of nasty people."

The waiter remained silent.

What my mother said to me has stuck in my head through all the years along with those odd memories of my father.

For a second, I thought the waiter was going to pull up a chair and stay there all day by the Mena House pool with me. Luckily, he snapped out of it and ran off to get my drink.

My grandmother was, I believed, my refuge, but she had a number of houses and moved around regularly, especially after my grandfather passed away. My time with him had been incredibly precious and pivotal. At first, my grandmother had taken me with her, but I suppose she didn't really care to have me around that much or something. She sent me back to the British School in Alexandria.

It makes me sad when I think how much I longed to be close to my family and couldn't. No matter how many times I left the school in Alexandria and showed up on her doorstep, she usually thought it was "a bit much" as she would say. Circumstances would dictate that I couldn't be physically close to her on a daily basis.

I often wondered what it would be like to have your family intact, a mom, dad, brothers and sisters, and cousins too, I suppose. Then there would be grandparents and everyone would be close because they chose to live in the same place, being part of each other's lives.

What a dream.

But my life wasn't that. I was seized by true feelings of regret and sadness. Sorry for myself some would say and call me pathetic.

My drink came. I repositioned myself in the reclining lawn chair. I didn't have to be careful about the bruises Steinman had christened me with anymore. When the waiter dropped by to see how I was doing ten minutes later, I ordered another drink.

I was doing plenty of thinking. My life was what it was, sort of like Mena House. The hotel had no say in its life. It had been remolded and changed; people used it for their own purposes. Guests came and went regardless of how Mena House felt. Sitting in the garden pondering about it,

I felt like an empty house that gets sold because all the memories have already been made and no one wants to go there anymore.

When another waiter came, I was quite melancholy. The towel was folded underneath my head. My eyes staring into the blue sky. He asked if I would like yet another drink.

I thought sure. Why not?

I sipped my refreshed cocktail and reflected more about Mena House and my life.

I suppose my grandparents hadn't given me what I wanted, but what they thought I needed. I didn't hate my grandmother; in fact, it was just the opposite, but I had learned to live without her most of the time. I'm not sure my emotional distance and self-sufficiency was a particularly good thing. Some people will say I was too needy and had to be fixed.

121

Part of my education, my grandfather had believed, was to know the political history of Egypt. By the 1950s Egypt's monarchy had, unfortunately, become equated with scandalous decadence. In revolt against the monarchy and the British, the Free Officers conspired against King Farouk. In 1953, Egypt was declared a Republic.

I took a long slurp of my drink.

Mena House is a fitting location for a political anything.

Is that why Miss Balgrave was here?

Mena House was the venue for the 1979 Egypt-Israel peace talks. President Sadat stayed in the Montgomery suite, Menachem Begin occupied suite 908, and President Jimmy Carter took the Churchill suite.

I had always deemed it rather tactless to stick Begin in suite 908 and not in a suite with a grander title. Tact is an acquired taste, and as Winston Churchill had said *it is also the ability to tell someone to go to hell in such a way that they look forward to the trip.*

Was there a connection between Mena House and the Marriott Hotel?

The hotels did have political links, even if it was only as venues. What could be more of a political statement than blowing up one or two of them?

Politically, Mena House had as much historical political significance as the upcoming meetings at the Marriott.

Were they going to target a series of hotels and co-ordinate the attacks?

What was with the boat ride Yasser and I had taken?

That's what happens when you drink too much, there are more questions than answers.

Right about that time, Miss Balgrave showed up with her friend in the garden. They took two lounge chairs in the far corner of the garden. It must have been some discussion because they were quite agitated and both stood up at the same time. Then they began walking on the gravel path that goes around the garden and the grounds of the hotel. It takes about twenty minutes to complete the route.

They were so deep in conversation that Miss Balgrave had left her bag behind on the chair.

I'm not sure I was seeing straight, but I become possessed with the crazy idea that I had about twenty minutes to find all the answers I would need in Miss Balgrave's bag.

Hairbrush, lipstick, pen, a pamphlet from the Egyptian Museum of Antiquities, and a thick wallet stuffed with plastic cards and hand-written notes was what I found.

I had hit the jackpot with the notes when I happened to glance up and saw Miss Balgrave approaching. She had ditched her companion.

The walk had taken ten minutes not twenty.

She hadn't seen me yet, thanks to the chairs and umbrellas, but she was headed right for me and her handbag.

I had one piece of luck, a waiter, so eager to be of service, stopped her. I flipped her bag back onto the chair and headed towards her like a long-lost friend.

Unfortunately, I hadn't had the time to put everything back into her wallet.

"There you are," I said with my best gosh-I-missed-you smile.

It worked perfectly because she couldn't talk to the waiter and me at the same time and therefore didn't even glance at her bag. The waiter didn't give up on offering his services, but geared it up a notch with suggestions from the food menu.

"Perhaps another time," Miss Balgrave said.

"Will you be here later? Perhaps I could arrange for a table."

The waiter was certainly vying for a big tip, *Baksheesh*.

I'd seen the tipping game many times. Sometimes is was sheer intimidation. On one visit to the ruins of Saqqara, the famous step pyramid of Zoser, I saw a local guide corner an innocent young couple in the ruins.

I wagged my finger at the waiter and came to Miss Balgrave's defense.

"You are asking for *Baksheesh*, and a lot of it. I have seen people fork over at least forty pounds. This young couple I once saw was clearly terrified. Considering that the monthly wage of a teacher was about fifteen pounds a month, I can see why *Baksheesh* can be a problem."

"Madame…" the waiter tried to stop my tirade.

"It is a strange phenomenon," I continued. "Egyptians are a wonderfully generous and gentle people transformed by this compelling obsession with a tip. Not only are foreigners targeted by the tourist industry but some of their own Egyptian taxi drivers as well."

It was Miss Balgrave's turn to step in and stop my flow of words.

But I was having none of it.

I pointed my index finger to the heavens and said, "Those enterprising types who have a monopoly on a certain hotel like Mena House, park their taxis immediately in front of the hotel. These guys charge twenty-five pounds per fare. Across the street you could hail a regular taxi for twenty-five piastres. There would be some pretty fierce retribution for taxi drivers if they picked up a tourist who had figured out the taxi rates and skipped across the street for a ride."

"Alright Amira," said Miss Balgrave sternly. "We didn't come by taxi. So relax."

Some people get more talkative when they are drunk, and I had had a lot to drink.

Miss Balgrave and I left Mena House fairly promptly after that.

Both of us sat in the back seat of the car. Miss Balgrave's bag, containing the messed-up wallet, was beside her. She hadn't looked in her bag. I had my comments ready about skanky staff at the hotel and how you couldn't trust anyone, just in case she discovered someone had been rummaging through her bag.

"Did you have a nice time at the museum the other day, Miss Balgrave?"

The alcohol was kicking in and in my misty mind I deduced I needed to talk to keep her away from her bag.

"It was interesting."

"The Tut Ankh Amun exhibit is the best, and the statues of Ramses II."

"Truly," commented Miss Balgrave.

"All that gold. It is an amazing amount of gold. Don't you think?"

I was sitting fairly close to her. She must have noticed I was tanked but she hadn't said anything about that.

"Well, they are all replicas," she said.

"They are?" I was totally astounded. "Really? How do they carry them around and get them in the building? They are far too heavy. Well, I never!"

I was making a complete ass out of myself, but I couldn't help it. I was really scared she'd find out I had been snooping in her handbag.

"That Mena House is a great place," I prattled.

I made a big deal about our outing and thanked her for taking me along. I supposed that if I kept talking, I might calm down.

We made one stop on the way back to El-Sobki Street at a bookstore.

"I have a book order Amira. Hop out and tell the clerk. It's under my name. The account has already been settled. The parking here is atrocious. We'll make a loop around the block."

Right. I launched myself out of the vehicle.

The shop was like shops are in Cairo. Tiny, but packed with merchandise. The clerk knew exactly what I had come in for and delivered the massive book into my hands.

I was taken aback by the size of the volume and the topic. I hurried out onto the street to look for Miss Balgrave's car.

She put the book beside her on the seat without a word.

"So, Amira, what kind of work do you actually do in Jerusalem? Have you always been a no-brain drifter?"

I guess she wanted to control the topic of conversation.

"I'm an artist," I articulated with dignity.

I didn't condescend to her level by acknowledging her insult.

However, her surprise at my artistic talent declaration was insulting. I was sorry I had told her. She patted my hand and stroked my thigh when she saw the look on my face.

"Are you going to kiss me," I slurred.

She sneered at me. She was back to her old self, watching me keenly, in an amused sort of way. Maybe she had known I'd been through her bag. Maybe she had left it on the chair exactly for that reason. She had called me predictable.

I started to squirm and felt very uncomfortable.

"What do you think of Yasser?" she asked.

I squirmed some more. He hadn't! Had he?

I groaned inside. Of course he had. He had probably described the sex in detail to her. Miss Balgrave was looking at me like I was irrelevant.

All I could do was be pissed off.

"What about him?"

I was on my guard.

"Well, if you had to depend on him, would you feel safe in his arms?"

I couldn't tell if she was making a joke or if it was a serious question which would require a serious answer.

"Do I need to be safe?" I asked.

She said no more. Neither did I. I hoped she hadn't noticed my shaking hands.

We arrived back to the lobby of the flat and Miss Balgrave's bag went upstairs with us. She put it on the sideboard by the entrance door, and went into her bedroom.

Without giving it another thought, I grabbed the bag with the wallet inside and reinserted all the cards and notes. A few minutes later, Yasser and Miss Balgrave came around the corner.

Had they been intimate?

No, not with her. She's old. Had they?

I knew it only took three minutes.

Miss Balgrave picked up her bag, and sat on the sofa. Yasser gave me a nonchalant look, the same look he had given me in the boat house after our liaison.

I knew they had. I felt nauseous.

It took me a minute to focus on the situation when there was a knock on the door. Eda and Mohatmed, the Blitz twins entered.

"Amira, get us some drinks," commanded Miss Balgrave.

My head was spinning and my hands were sweating so much that I nearly dropped the glasses as I was putting them on the kitchen tray.

I couldn't help glancing at Miss Balgrave as I re-entered the living room. Eda and Mohatmed had thrown themselves onto the couch in such a fashion that I thought they were taking a permanent nap.

"Amira knows a lot about history," Miss Balgrave scoffed.

"She can show you all the sites," Yasser teased as he looked at the brothers. His face was perfectly straight. "She's very efficient. It wouldn't take any time at all."

Yasser looked to Miss Balgrave for approval. It's amazing how pure sex can make an attachment seem real. Miss Balgrave smiled back at Yasser.

"I'd be happy to be a tour guide," I scowled.

F-in boat ride. F-in Miss Balgrave.

The two brothers looked at me like it was a big joke.

"Get your feet off the furniture," Miss Balgrave said impatiently to them. "This is my home. You're not in some army camp."

"It would be better if we were. Nothing is the way it should be here in the Middle East."

That was Eda. I wondered if he lived in a perpetual state of *Intifadeh*. I held out a glass of *Karkadé*.

"Would you like some?"

He took the glass of cold Hibiscus tea without looking at me or saying a word.

"Thank you, Amira," I chirped at him.

A lack of manners really gets to me. Besides, sometimes I like living dangerously. Lucky for me, he ignored my stupidity. He was a typical angry type, full of hate and blame, full of frustration that he chose to deal with by being violent.

"That's fine, Amira," said Miss Balgrave.

Her tone was deliberately low key, making sure she managed all her players so that nothing blew up in the living room. I didn't know if she was as terrified of the man as I was.

The other brother settled back in the sofa.

"You're looking well today," he spoke to Miss Balgrave the way a son would speak to a mother. "I see Yasser is well. How's Steinman?"

Well, maybe a really different kind of mother.

"He's fine. He's been busy checking out the boats."

"So, you think that might still be a possibility," Yasser said. "Have you planned anything definitely?"

She shook her head.

She flicked her eyes towards me and back at Yasser and said, "Perhaps doing a bit more sightseeing might be in order?"

I could tell she still wasn't sure about me. Although the group had grudgingly consented to my inclusion, I still didn't know what was going on. I was feeling annoyed. I felt my face growing red. A hangover was starting to form in my brain.

"I'll clean up in the kitchen," I announced.

It would give me something to do. If I had had my transmitter, I could have contacted Omar, but what would I tell him?

I didn't actually have any useful information, just a lot of speculation about where the political attack might take place and none about who the target might be. My choice to retreat to the kitchen probably wasn't incredibly effective since I couldn't hear or see a thing the gang was saying or doing.

The kitchen had an outside door that went out to a tiny dark landing and a filthy staircase that weaved back and forth all the way down to the ground. The garbage cans for the flat were on the landing.

When I opened the door, there was a huge ruckus. A black cat jumped out of the garbage, turning it over. I put my hand over my pounding heart. The door on the opposite side of the landing burst open. A woman stood there with a broom in her hand.

She hooted at the expression on my face and lowered her weapon.

"Good day. I'm Amira."

"Haima. You American?"

"No, Canadian. Big difference," I said.

"Yes. Friendly Canadian."

"That's us. Where did you learn English?"

"I work for many doctor American Hospital."

"Yes right. You told me that before."

Haima was a wonderful young woman with absolutely no prospect of any kind of success. She told me she cleaned and shopped for foreigners. Her English language skills had obviously kept on improving. However, the world she was being introduced to, the world of affluence as she saw it, was a two-edged sword for her.

She was determined to see that the life of her parents was not going to be repeated with her. She had already refused two offers of marriage which typically would have secured her financial future. She judged she could do better.

The foreigners she worked for treated her well and took her on trips she said. She had travelled all the way to Alexandria. They had stayed in a one-star hotel. She thought it was amazing. There were beds in the rooms. Towels in the bathroom.

I knew the hotel.

It was the most amazing dump.

Once I had had a room on the top of that hotel. The room could only be reached by a set of old rickety stairs on the outside of the building. Despite the stairs, the rooftop room and the huge veranda was wonderful, until I discovered that the veranda doors wouldn't close.

The Alexandria wind blew off the ocean into my room all night. All night, and it was freezing cold. The bed was a slab. In the morning, I was an ice cube. I went to take a hot shower to thaw only to discover the water was as cold as the night wind. I was very sick after that with a raging case of Bronchitis.

I smiled at Haima's story and said yes, Alexandria is a wonderful place.

"Where do you live in Cairo?" I asked.

Her face fell. Haima lived with her parents in dirt. Their place, you couldn't call it a flat, had been dug out under the foundation of a high rise. There were two areas only, not rooms but areas. The water ran down the walls and made rivulets on the ground. They defecated in the street.

"I can work for you Miss?" Haima was apparently always looking for another job.

"No, no. There is no work here," I said to her.

"Yes, yes. They very busy. I see."

"Oh? What do you see?"

"They give money."

I was surprised by this bit of information. "What do they give you money for Haima?"

"To buy. Buy wire."

"You mean like, like wire for electricity and stuff?"

She nodded. My expertise with light bulbs is turning them on and off, but I knew enough about detonators to know you needed wire, sometimes a lot of wire.

"Package. I pick up package."

"At the post office?"

She nodded. "They busy."

Indeed, they had been far busier than I knew.

"I think, spies."

"What? You think they are spies?"

She nodded energetically. When Sadat was moving Egypt away from relationships with the Soviets, spies were everywhere. The government expelled hundreds of foreigners. Cracked down on any dubious activity. The effect of his suspicions had obviously lingered among the population.

"I like America," she stated.

They always do, the ones with no future.

I smiled and tried not to let it show that her enthusiasm made me sad.

"Moment," she said.

Haima dove into her kitchen and came back with a plate of *Konafa*. The sweet dessert looked very appetizing.

I thanked her profusely. Egyptians are so generous.

I used the cake to explain my absence from the living room. I felt it prudent to dispel any possible thought Miss Balgrave might have had that I was going through her bedroom drawers, which I wasn't, but sure wanted to.

However, I got the impression there wasn't anyone in the living room who was all that curious about what I had been doing for the last hour.

"Here's a little something I just whipped up," I proclaimed as I placed the cake on the coffee table.

In my absence, Steinman and Nancy had arrived. He had brought a black case with him, the kind you put a musical instrument in or a machine gun. She had brought her bad attitude toward life.

"A cake," Nancy scoffed. "Just what a good servant would do. Bake cake."

She nodded to me to serve her.

"Help yourself," I teased.

I looked at her arm in the sling.

"Oh wait, let me do it for you Nancy, you being a cripple in body and soul."

Mohatmed's body started shaking so much from laughter that I thought he was going to have a fit and end up on the floor.

"You should leave now. Back to the kitchen," Nancy said through her teeth.

She had a habit of speaking like that I noticed.

"Amira," decreed Miss Balgrave. "Go to your room."

Wow! I hadn't heard that command for a long time, but with cloak and dagger sitting on the couch in the living room, I viewed it as a good suggestion.

I curtsied with all the dignity I could muster.

"Give them cake," I scoffed at Nancy.

I'm not sure the reference to Marie Antoinette was fitting since she had lost her head under the blade of the guillotine and I might lose mine.

Whatever. It was a dramatic exit.

The flat is actually quite large. The rooms are definitely separate, none of this open floor plan stuff. My room was at the far end of the hallway, of course, just before the kitchen. But, you guessed it, I had to pass Miss Balgrave's room on the way down the hall.

Yes, I did. I figured since they were all in the living room, here was my chance to search her room.

Her room was close enough to the living room to hear the murmur of their conversation, so if they stopped talking, I should be able to hear the silence. If someone walked in, I would simply say I got confused and thought it was my room or thought Miss Balgrave meant for me to go to her room etcetera.

I do fake confused really well.

You never know what you will find in people's bedroom drawers. She had an astonishingly large amount of jewellery which was odd because she never wore any of it. The quality looked quite good. I laughed to myself thinking of her hawking the stuff at a pawn shop to fund her nasty little plans.

There were some books on her nightstand beside the only telephone in the flat. The large book was the one I had picked up at the bookstore for her. It was part of an alphabetized series on sites in Cairo. It was far more detailed than your average tourist compendium. The volume was 'M'. The second book on the nightstand was a puzzle to me. I couldn't make out the language of the book, but it was definitely a Slavic tongue.

Interesting.

Where would she stick the blueprints?

That was why I was searching.

Ah, the wardrobe.

Sure enough there they were rolled up at the back of the closet. I paused to listen. Couldn't hear anything. I went back to the bedroom door, opened it a bit, and could hear murmurs coming from the living room.

Suddenly, I heard Eda shout out, "The Jewel of the Nile!"

I don't know about you, but I loved that movie. It was a huge hit in Cairo; everyone went to see it. The plot line is that writer Joan Wilder is off on an adventure at the behest of a charming Arab ruler who wants her to write his biography.

At one point, her boyfriend, Jack, had a boat which explodes from a bomb placed by the ruler's henchmen. The dots were starting to connect on this one. I could also hear the group moving around.

I quickly left Miss Balgrave's room and hurried down to mine. I had to get in contact with Omar to let him know they were planning to place explosives in a boat, ferry it down the Nile to a specified location, and BAM!

The volume in Miss Balgrave's book was 'M'. That letter was for the Marriott, maybe even Mena House. I was proud of this deduction. Omar would be pleased and I would be free of the police. My services would no longer be required. Most importantly, I would be free of Miss Balgrave when the SSIS nabbed her.

I couldn't have been more wrong.

I took my simple deductions to bed with me. The alcohol was wearing off and I felt extremely tired. I woke up at four o'clock in the morning. It was now or never. After I was out of the apartment and had closed the doors, I slipped on my shoes and ran down the stairs.

I had to find a telephone.

CHAPTER TEN

I had a hangover from my Mena House excursion. It was the kind of pounding in my head I used to get on a school night after I had consumed alcohol at an alarmingly fast rate because I had a curfew and had to get back to the dormitory.

In my haste to find a telephone, I hadn't really considered that it was an obscenely early hour. Nothing was probably open.

True.

Not even the telephone exchange was open.

What was today going to look like? Whatever was going to happen was probably going to occur very shortly.

I looked around for the SSIS. After all, Omar had indicated Miss Balgrave's gang was being watched.

Nothing. There wasn't a soul in sight.

My only hope was that they had seen me out searching for a telephone while they were surveilling Miss Balgrave and would think my behaviour out of the ordinary. Perhaps then the SSIS would contact me, instead of me trying to do it the other way around.

There was no hope of getting back into Miss Balgrave's flat undetected. I didn't have a key.

Was it luck or misfortune that Eda was coming into the apartment building the same time as me?

"Hey Eda," I flipped my salutation toward him. "It's too early to be up."

He just gawked at me.

"Too early. Take my advice, I'm not using it."

I headed up the stairs. He was taking the elevator. That would be a long wait. The elevator was ancient. There was no way I was getting in that elevator box with him. I sprinted up the stairs and arrived at the door of the flat before him.

I could hear the elevator clanking and pulling. It made a real racket. I was wondering how on earth I was going to get into the flat when I noticed the door had been left ajar, probably to let Eda in.

"Alhamdulillah."

I slipped into the flat. I could smell coffee brewing. There was no one in sight. I hesitated for a moment, but just a moment, and firmly shut the door behind me. I sat down on the couch and picked up a magazine.

There was a knock on the door. After a few seconds, there was another, a little more insistent this time. I didn't budge. After the third set of pounding knocks, Yasser came from down the hall.

"Why didn't you get the door?"

I shrugged. "I didn't hear it."

Yasser opened the door for Eda saying, "I left it ajar, that's weird."

Eda brushed past Yasser, clearly annoyed.

"How did you get in here?" he demanded glaring at me.

I think that's the first time he has ever spoken to me.

"She lives here."

I love it when people come to my defense. Dear Yasser.

I smiled again and shrugged. "Coffee smells good," I said.

As I was no longer cooking, Miss Balgrave had arranged for the meals to be brought in, and since I didn't want to be punched in the face by Eda, I stayed clear of the food until I was sure he was done and then grabbed some breakfast for myself.

After breakfast, Miss Balgrave had arranged for the chauffeur to come at eight o'clock sharp. Miss Balgrave hadn't requested my driving expertise since the last Sheraton visit. A personal skill that was put in the same category as my cooking, I suppose.

I went down the elevator with Miss Balgrave, Mohatmed, and Eda. My shaky legs felt weak. My palms were sweaty. I concentrated on not thinking about being trapped in that small backseat with three people, all three of them being my absolute favourite people.

Our destination was the Sheraton, again. The brothers were moving locations. Miss Balgrave decided it was best to divert attention by having a third person carry some of their luggage. The term luggage was used for the benefit of the chauffeur.

"Why can't Yasser do this," I whispered to Miss Balgrave as we crossed the lobby of the Sheraton.

"Yasser has things to do."

"What things?"

Miss Balgrave glared at me. I felt like an errant child on a vacation I didn't want to be on. All I wanted to do was to go sit by the pool.

"Room 420."

I stared at her.

"Go to room 420. Help with the bags, Amira. Do I have to spell everything out for you?"

She did not.

I was just thinking that's all. I gave her my best smile. It took me a while to get there though before I figured out she hadn't said 1420 but 420.

I was on the fourteenth floor heading for room number 1420 when I came across a young couple. They were obviously from Saudi Arabia. He was the picture of a prince in a brilliant white *Galabeyah* and white headscarf. The *Keffiyeh* was a black and white chain-linked pattern, held in place with a black *Agal,* complete with tassels. He was a tall, slim, good-looking dude with a cropped beard and clear smooth skin.

She was dressed in white too, very pretty, feminine. Slim. Young, with doe eyes gazing up at his face.

His eyes were jet black. It was clear he was angry. I mean the type of controlled boiling that happens inside a pressure cooker.

I didn't hear any words as I passed them by, but it was apparent they were communicating. Her voice tone was pleading *don't do this*. His was *I decree, you obey*.

I heard the door click. She had gone back into the hotel room. He was striding down the hall with his *Galabeyah* and headdress blowing in the wind of his sovereignty. It made my blood boil to see the outcome. I imagined she was weeping. Confined to her room as per command. Her room was 1422.

As I knocked on the door of room 1420, it slipped open. These heavy doors need an extra push to make them shut properly. The brothers were getting careless.

I strode in without a word and just caught a glimpse of a white naked butt and backside turning to adjust the bedside lamp.

It definitely wasn't Eda, nor was it Mohatmed.

Oops! Wrong room.

About face, and out of the room before the man could see it was me. That's the moment I figured out it was room 420 not room 1420.

When I finally reached the room, there was a *Do Not Disturb* sign on the door, but Mohatmed was waiting for me in the hallway. The room was a mess. Eda didn't acknowledge my existence.

I leaned against the wall and pretended I was a painting.

Whatever they were planning, the date must be getting close I figured. Eda was as jittery as a cat jumping out of a garbage can in a back alley.

"You go," Eda said to Mohatmed. "I will do a final look."

Mohatmed handed me a smaller black bag, instructed me to keep walking through the lobby to the side exit and then to the parking lot. A taxi would be waiting for me to travel alone back to the flat on El-Sobki.

Clandestine.

We went to the elevator lobby together. I felt like a real spy. I was enjoying myself so much that I didn't pay attention to Mohatmed who got into the elevator without me. A couple of tourists swooped in front of him with a trolley full of bags.

Hey, I'm not a Velcro person. He was at the back of the elevator and couldn't get out. I couldn't get in.

As the doors slowly closed, I caught his eye.

I shrugged and said, *"Mahlish,* I'll take the next one."

The elevator doors had shut like a curtain closing on an act. I had a brilliant idea when I spied a telephone on the hall table.

Of course there was a phone; it was the Sheraton with access and convenience for all. The line made a connection to the switchboard and then out to the real world.

I was panting so hard I had to repeat the number twice for the operator.

Omar's phone rang.

Pick up. Pick up.

The phone rang.

Someone picked up Omar's phone.

Eda walked into the hall.

"What are you doing?"

I hung up casually.

"The elevator," I said motioning to the closed doors. "It's not coming. I was phoning the concierge."

"So why are you not talking to the concierge?"

"I did. He said the elevator will be right up."

Lo and behold, right at that moment the elevator doors opened. I walked into the elevator box with Eda.

I felt like I was going to hell in a kitchen dolly.

"You will take this bag as Mohatmed instructed," he commanded sternly.

I was so rattled. I didn't even remember Mohatmed's instructions about where to exit, yada yada.

In addition, Miss Balgrave had told me to wait somewhere where she could find me. I guess the tennis courts were it.

That was a nice central location, right?

When the elevator landed on the lobby level, I pretended I didn't know Eda. I can tell you that wasn't hard to do.

I settled into a chair at the tennis courts. Hoping to take my mind off my anxiety, I lapsed into a trance of watching the tennis ball go back and forth.

The *British School of Alexandria* had a rigorous tennis program. One time, I was paired with my instructor to play doubles. We played a match against two professors from the university. The courts were red clay, managed by Mahmoud who wore rags and different shoes on each of his feet. He maintained the courts for ten piastres a day. It wouldn't do to pay him more; he might get ideas I was told.

I'm a good player, if I may say so. We regularly beat the doubles teams of two men at the club. Since I wasn't truly Egyptian, being half Canadian, they turned a blind eye to the infraction.

Of course, the men would never tell their wives they had been beaten by a woman, even if it was mixed doubles. The wives might get ideas and want to play tennis too.

Anyway, back to the two professors. We were shellacking them pretty well, when I hit the coup d'état of tennis shots for suppressed women tennis players the world over.

It was a zinger of an overhead smash landing a foot to the right of the midline, a deep shot with a fast pace.

It bounced in front of the professor. Straight up into his crotch. But that wasn't the funny part.

Oh no. The fuzzy lime green tennis ball got stuck up there.

To release the ball, the professor did a perfect plié. The ball dropped straight down, two little bounces and rolled away.

To hide the fact that my eyes were popping out of my head with unrestrained astonishment, I whirled around and stared at the tennis court wall.

I was gulping frantically in my attempt to stop the laughter.

It was hilarious.

I couldn't risk laughing at a professor, a male professor. They'd never let me play tennis again if I did. Everyone carried on playing as if nothing had happened. It was never referred to, ever.

As I was sitting at the Sheraton tennis courts thinking about the ridiculous, my ridiculous current situation was no less laughable.

Whatever was in the black bag at my feet probably wasn't legal. Should I be caught with it, then I'd be in big trouble. My anxiety drove to the memory of a story about a wife and husband. Big trouble.

I first heard the account when I was sitting in the dentist's waiting room in Cairo.

An Egyptian born dentist, from Canada no less! He had lived in my birth country for decades. Knew more about the prairies than I did.

Anyway, my friend was with me because I hate dentists. Justified in my terror after many dentists, who should never have electric drills in their hands, had gone after me.

In the waiting room with me was my friend and two middle-aged Egyptian women. I had been conversing in English with my friend. I guess the two women figured we were foreigners who didn't understand Arabic. They were discussing the recent story in the newspaper of a woman who had been divorced by her husband. He had said *I divorce you* three times and that was it.

The only thing left for the now ex-wife was prostitution. However, being quite ingenious, she decided to kill him first before degrading herself.

The discussion continued between the two women until my teenage friend who could contain herself no longer, jumped in with her verdict. She thought the husband had gotten what he deserved.

The two women in the waiting room were shocked. I'm not sure if they were shocked at my friend's opinion or the fact that she spoke Arabic. They were maybe partial to the divorced woman's plight because they felt it was unfortunate that she had gotten caught.

How it was that the police had nabbed her?

Dogs.

If dogs have a full belly, they lay down and don't move.

There were so many stray dogs in the street outside the woman's apartment window that the police became curious and investigated. They found the remaining bits of the ex-husband's body that the woman just couldn't get those pooches to eat.

Like I said, big trouble.

I could feel my apprehension galloping toward catastrophe.

In addition, I hadn't seen hide nor hair of the Bombardier twins or Miss Balgrave. My dread rose in leaps and bounds.

Since the three B's weren't showing up, I went to the parking lot and got into a taxi. I understood my instructions to the taxi driver regarding the El-Sobki apartment destination to be pretty clear, but apparently not.

"What are you doing? You're going the wrong way!" I screamed.

"Sheraton here. There airport, airport," the taxi driver replied. He had insisted on conversing in English. To practice.

"I'm not going to the airport!"

"Mahlish, hadar. Okay, okay. I turn around."

I didn't want to linger. Getting rid of the bag was the first thing on my mind. Getting to El-Sobki was my second.

"Yes. Yes Miss. El-Sobki."

Unfortunately, it was not quite so simple. The road gives no opportunity to simply turn around. The driver would have to go through the airport, go past the terminal, and come back out. That's where the problem occurred.

The drive up to the airport makes a curve around the airport entrance drop off zone. I don't know why, but the Egyptian police had set up tall red pylons to block the lane of traffic immediately by the curb. A little further down there was another tall red pylon in the passing lane. The taxi driver could see that the uniformed police were stopping vehicles to conduct what amounted to a fairly thorough search of persons and contents.

Under normal, what's normal I ask you, under normal circumstances this would be terrifying on its own. The look of immediate alarm on the face of the taxi driver did confirm this opinion.

This was not good.

It occurred to me to drop my black bag outside the taxi window.

In my panic, that is just what I did.

The taxi driver saw me do it.

Could he be more alarmed?

He gave me a horrified look, jumped out of his taxi, and kicked the tall red pylon out of the way. His hysteria was unnerving. I was absolutely mute in the back seat. He slammed the vehicle into drive and floored the little beast. The Fiat leapt into the bypass lane, weaved past the pylons, and sped away.

He didn't even look in the rear-view mirror. I certainly hadn't moved.

I was listening for the sound of sirens.

Nothing. I waited.

Nothing.

I don't know how we survived because neither of us was breathing. I'm sure about that.

After about ten minutes, all I uttered was, "El-Sobki."

Why did I go back to the flat? Why didn't I just run?

To tell the truth I don't have a good answer. Maybe because I didn't have anywhere to run to?

Omar Mohammed was waiting with a prison key. I was a beaten dog that still runs home.

It was a long slow walk up the stairs to the flat. I concocted my story, my plan, in that stairwell. I knocked on the door. Yasser opened it.

"She's here."

They were all there, in the living room.

"About time," someone said.

"Where's the bag?" Miss Balgrave immediately queried.

The edge in her voice was unmistakable.

Confusion. That was my plan.

"What bag?"

Eda stood up and glared at me.

"The bag Mohatmed gave you in the hotel room."

I looked confused and mumbled, "Oh, the one I carried down in the elevator."

He was ready to explode, you guessed it, like a bomb.

I put on my curious confused look and queried, "Ah, I guess it's in the elevator?"

He was stupefied I suppose because he didn't say anything, but Miss Balgrave did.

"You mean you left it in the elevator?"

"Well, I didn't take it." The emphasis on the pronoun was just enough to indicate that I thought the act of carrying the bag would be immoral.

"Eda told me to wait at the tennis court. That's what I did. I just do as I am told."

I put on an indignant look to indicate anything less than total compliance on my part was totally unacceptable.

"He didn't say take the bag."

Well, that was it.

To put the blame on Eda was a very risky move, but the story just seemed to go that way.

"You left it in the elevator." I guess Nancy assumed it was time to chip in with a statement.

I held my breath.

Silence.

Eda broke into a torrent of swear words. I thought Miss Balgrave was going to tell me to go to my room again.

"You failed."

Well, that comment was quite narrow-minded.

My grandmother had said that to me once, just like that.

Oh yes.

It was regarding computer coding class or something like that, all those ones and zeros. I never did get it. It had been a grave disappointment to my grandmother, but it wasn't my fault.

The teacher in the class had been an abusive sort. He regularly devised an excuse to make sure I was the last pupil to leave the class. After a few weeks of groping, well, you know, I started failing the class.

I told the headmistress I couldn't do computers. She transferred me out naturally, just to keep up the perception of success in her school; it wouldn't do to have failures in the classroom.

I let Miss Beatrissa think I was an idiot, and my grandmother too. The truth, the alternative, was worse, just like now.

"I went to the tennis courts," I declared in my defense.

"I told you to go to the parking lot," scorned Mohatmed.

I don't think he was my friend any more with that tone of voice. I had understood he was the nice one.

"I went there too," I was perky.

I gave them all my best smile.

"Can it be replaced?" Miss Balgrave turned to the twins.

Mohatmed nodded thoughtfully and replied, "Yes. I believe it can. We still have time."

The brothers stood up to leave to rectify the situation immediately. Apparently, they believed all that early bird catching worms and no grass growing underfoot stuff.

I wished they had left without another word, but my biggest fan, Eda, spoke, "She can't do it."

Miss Balgrave made a calming motion with her hands.

"She'll do it."

She turned to look at me. I felt chills going down my spine.

"Like she said, she does as she is told."

Not to be outdone, Nancy jumped in with, "You're an accident waiting to happen, Amira."

Seriously?

You can only come up with cliches?

I didn't say anything to the woman who had her arm in a sling because you can't speak logically to an idiot, that would just be idiotic.

I let out a long slow sigh because I thought I was in the clear.

CHAPTER ELEVEN

I started to point out that the situation wasn't my fault, but no one was listening. Miss Balgrave disappeared into her bedroom. Yasser and Nancy glowered at the wall.

The boss came out five minutes later.

"Right," she said. "We're going sightseeing and shopping."

That was unexpected.

"All of us," Miss Balgrave proclaimed.

"With her?" Nancy was incredulous. "You want her to come with us, with me?"

I could tell Miss Balgrave was reconsidering. She was like a parent who realizes they made the mistake of having another kid.

"Well, we can't leave her behind."

A dog yes, a child no.

Still not to be trusted. Whatever. I was getting a little tired of it and said so.

"You are being paid to fetch and carry. Remember? You do as you're told," snapped Miss Balgrave, "or is four thousand pounds not enough incentive for you? Besides I believe I have you on record?"

There was that word *incentive* again, and reference to my taped confession. I couldn't return to Jerusalem until she returned the tape recording.

Yasser drove. I sat in the front with him.

The other two got in the back.

No one said one word all the way to Khan el Khalili. The bazaar is a shopping expedition and tourist ambush all in one, the beating heart of Cairo. The world of the bazaar is like going on a stage in the theatre. Everyone plays their part, the clever, the poor, the solemn, and those who mock. The bazaar probably hasn't changed much since Sultan Ashraf el Khalil had it built in the thirteenth century.

It was fairly clear that in my little shopping group there was plenty of resentment going around, and not only directed at me. Yasser was out of sorts for having to drive. Nancy was annoyed as usual. Miss Balgrave was just Miss Balgrave, in a foul mood.

Yasser dropped us off with instructions from Miss Balgrave to drive the route and make sure there were no glitches. I eavesdropped with a nonchalance that I assumed was convincing, but when Miss Balgrave was finished speaking with Yasser, she turned to me and said, "You have quite a rubberneck, Amira. I would like to twist it."

I was a little embarrassed actually.

Here I thought my stealth and detective skills were on the up and up. Apparently not.

The day was turning out to be quite a doozer. I could only hope Omar Mohammed had enough people on the job to handle the activity with Yasser driving the route, the twins galivanting to replace their bombing mechanisms, and Steinman probably beating up someone in a back alley.

The SSIS was no longer shadowing me specifically, but I found it hard to believe that they wouldn't be keeping tabs on this motley crew. I still couldn't identify an agent from Omar's department no matter how much I scanned the crowds. They were either very good or just plain absent.

I needed to speak with Omar about the situation.

Miss Balgrave and Nancy strolled into the bazaar, but their shopping technique was full of strange stops to look at merchandise I could tell they were not interested in at all. The Khan el Khlalili bazaar is a den of tourist traps, merchandise, illicit this and that, and some especially fun shopping.

Two of Miss Balgrave's prolonged stops were the leather goods shop and the lapidary shop.

A lapidary is an artist who creates with stones, minerals or gemstones. They are sometimes collectors or dealers in gems as well. The tiny lapidary shop we visited was only wide enough for one person enter.

Imagine two rows. One row contains the counter which runs the length of the shop wall. The other row is for the customer.

146

The three of us entered single file. There were mounds of gemstones under the glass countertop, semi-precious nuggets, polished and unpolished. I laughed at the big scoop shoved into the ruby pile indicating you could buy your jewels by weight.

Miss Balgrave asked some specific questions about sending gifts abroad. Was this a cover for the drugs?

Were they going to ship the narcotics out of the country along with jewellery?

Did it work that way?

"Get out!" Nancy hissed at me.

"What?"

"Move you idiot."

How was I supposed to know it was time to go?

I backed up and stepped out into the street. Miss Balgrave and Nancy glared at me like I was infested. We wandered out of the Khan el Khalili bazaar and sauntered down a side street. The next stop was the leather shop.

The building containing the store was a classic leftover from the colonial days. The curved staircase wound up three flights. The entrance doors of the leather store gracefully swung open to reveal a magnificent room with lofty ceilings and soaring windows.

Like I said, shopping is fun and a good leather place is a delight for the eyes and the nostrils. I love the warm smell of leather. The entire experience is just smooth.

Miss Balgrave was being her usual annoying self. Do you have this? Do you have that? What colour? No, not quite right. Can it be cut to fit?

The proprietor had his hands full trying to please her. He couldn't seem to give her a straight answer. Not an uncommon occurrence in the shops I grant you, but still.

Finally, he admitted the tailor wasn't on the premises. The jacket Miss Balgrave was inquiring about wasn't actually in the store, but the tailor might have it at home. He could check.

Was he the middleman for the drugs?

Did he arrange the shipment or was that the lapidary guy?

The conversation was going on so long that I began to wonder if it wasn't all in code or something.

And there it was.

My line of sight was dead-on. If I hadn't been looking in that direction, I would have missed it. I had spied a black telephone in the back recesses of the shop behind a tall rack of leather jackets.

I needed to speak with Omar. I was a bee heading for the hive. I picked up the phone, called the number.

The phone rang twice.

"Omar!" I whispered.

It wasn't Omar.

"Just one minute."

It felt like an eternity. I didn't have one minute. I leaned back and glanced anxiously through the racks of leather jackets separating the back of the shop from the front. Miss Balgrave was at the front of the shop, but not Nancy.

"Hello."

What a relief to hear his voice. I nearly dropped the telephone.

"Where have you been?"

"Never mind that Amira. What do you have?"

Omar scoffed at my idea of drug trafficking.

"Amira, you watch too much television."

"I do not. I don't watch any television. I read."

I was piqued, as if watching television was a crime and I had to defend myself. He was being quite judgmental. I love television by the way, but he didn't need to know that.

"Have you seen the blueprints Amira?"

I hung up the phone as Nancy's hand, her good hand, pushed a leather jacket on the rack to one side. I had no idea where she had come from.

She smiled wickedly, turned on her heel, and headed for the store exit. Miss Balgrave had already left the shop and descended to the street level.

I fled after Nancy and burst out onto the street just behind her. Nancy headed straight for Miss Balgrave who was window shopping a few stores ahead of us.

Now I know you might think that I pushed her, but I didn't.

It wasn't my fault.

The sidewalk pavement, what there was of it, was a jumble of uneven bits of concrete. Nancy went flying. She fell on her bad shoulder, no doubt cracked that collarbone again, and smacked her forehead on the cement with a resounding thwack.

People stopped to stare.

It was that spectacular.

Of course, I ran immediately to help the poor woman.

Just joking.

I did my best to not let Miss Balgrave see that I was laughing with delight. It had been that good.

Nancy had really smacked herself. Wow.

She was groggy and didn't know what had hit her.

Needless to say, Miss Balgrave was her usual empathetic self and insisted Nancy pull herself together immediately.

Khan el Khalili is a maze of walkways. We had to get back to where Yasser was picking us up. So, off we went.

Egyptians are very helpful. Miss Balgrave immediately issued directives for assisting Nancy through the streets. Two locals jumped at the chance for which Miss Balgrave paid them a hefty *Baksheesh*.

Once Yasser sighted us, he jumped out of the car to help. Nancy had basically been dragged through the bazaar to the car. I had followed discreetly behind. I hadn't enjoyed a shopping spree like this for, well, I can't recall when I had had a better time at the bazaar.

Back in the flat, Miss Balgrave was all business. I guess prep time for whatever they were planning was over. Steinman walked in and sat down. Nancy had been deposited on the couch. She looked positively green. That she hadn't passed out again astounded me.

"She's making phone calls. I don't trust her," said Nancy as she pointed an accusing finger at me.

I let out my breath slowly. She had seen me on the phone, but I hadn't been overheard. She certainly would have repeated what she had heard. Maybe it had been knocked out of her in that fall.

"Of course, I was talking on the phone." I was careful not to say I had made the call. "You had inquired about the tailor. The guy in the back happened to say the tailor was on the phone. I took the opportunity to speak with him about possibly fulfilling your order for a jacket."

Smile. My best I-was-doing-it-for-you smile.

"I was going to tell you, but with Nancy's acrobatics, it slipped my mind," I finished off casually.

To Nancy I mocked, "You should really be in the Cirque du Soleil. It's an acrobatic troupe we have in Canada. I can write to see if you can audition."

Nancy flinched as she stood up. She was shaking and wincing at the same time. I was certainly starting to enjoy myself, so I turned it up a notch.

"Actually Miss Balgrave, Nancy approached me about a bigger cut in this job."

It was lie of course. I didn't even know what the job was.

"I never did," Nancy's voice was becoming shrill.

"I've nearly had it with you. You always say too much," Miss Balgrave directed the comment to Nancy.

That was a close call, for a moment I thought she was talking to me.

"Yasser, take her to the American Hospital. Get her checked out."

What a relief, get that cracked nut out of here. But, Miss Balgrave wasn't done with me.

"You're a stupid low life, aren't you?"

What was I supposed to do, agree with her?

Steinman was looking eagerly at me.

It was on my tongue to mock her with a 'yes ma'am' but I thought better of it.

"Yes, Miss Balgrave" was all I said like I was back in school.

I almost messed that up too. I nearly said, "Yes Miss Beatrissa."

Crisis averted or so I thought.

I caught the quick nod Miss Balgrave gave Steinman, but I wasn't fast enough. His open-handed slap caught me square across the face and sent me flying.

"Steinman, not the face. Remember, it's," she paused, "so unsightly."

She was a true aesthetic, I could tell.

Steinman got a sour look on his face and sat back down in his chair. Miss Balgrave turned her full attention to the man.

"You took your time getting here today."

Steinman nodded and said, "It's wise to make sure."

"Did you have your tea?" Miss Balgrave was asking Steinman.

She certainly didn't care if I had had tea or not.

"I've had my tea."

"Enough tea?"

I picked myself off the floor.

My, my. Weren't we being motherly?

"Yes. Thank you. Two cups in fact."

Miss Balgrave smiled with satisfaction. Despite the burning on my cheek, I had the distinct feeling that this phony tête-à-tête was happening purely for my benefit. Not that I could have paid much attention to it with sun bursts happening in my eyes.

Suddenly, Miss Balgrave stood up. The abrupt movement caught me by surprise. I instinctively jerked back. In addition to my face which was now absolutely blazing from the smack, the day was turning out to be exceptionally hot.

"Relax."

She gazed at me with amusement.

"Perhaps you would like to watch a movie, Amira? Something like *Death on the Nile*?"

The sweat trickled down my spine. I watched Miss Balgrave head for her bedroom and wondered idly if she were referring to my death specifically. Steinman was chuckling at her jab.

Were we back to explosions, boats, and murder on the Nile?

Was she going to take a nap?

Was she a light sleeper or a heavy sleeper or did she just need some alone time?

What I needed was to see those blueprints. With Steinman on duty in the living room, there was no opportunity to leave the flat or search for anything. Steinman didn't utter a word. He didn't look like the napping sort. I was stuck with the two of them in the flat.

Worse than that, I was stuck with Omar and a looming prison sentence if I didn't produce. Miss Balgrave I might be able to hide from, but the SSIS, never.

I went to my own room. I cursed the theft of the transmitter. I cursed not mentioning the theft of it to Omar. I cursed about everything.

I felt like I needed a good glass of Scotch. I can hold my liquor fairly well. I know you're thinking no I can't; however, in my defense, I had had a lot to drink at Mena House and had a hangover, but those were the flouncy drinks they ply you with at the poolside.

Now Scotch I can drink. My exquisite good taste started with my Canadian grandfather and his little still in the shed. Manitoba can get quite cold in the winter. Besides, he was keeping up tradition. His family had run booze across the border to the United States during the prohibition years. I can turn on a dime, drink or not drink, ever since I was three years old which was when I started having afternoon tea with Grampa.

Now, some wouldn't be able to say they can turn their drinking on and off like that. My grandmother had a friend in Cairo who let their three-year-old take little sips from the beer bottle when company was visiting. Company visited a lot in Egypt. Pretty soon the little guy was actively petitioning for beer.

At first everyone laughed, thought it was cute, this little tyke begging for his bottle. Soon, he had a huge problem and they stopped giving him alcohol. Well, that kid had a fit. It was really awful. He went through episodes of screaming, pleading, and then he got the shakes. The withdrawal was enough to break your heart.

Once I got over feeling sorry for myself, it occurred to me that I didn't need to be cursing to myself in my room. I could just leave. Would Steinman let me?

Would he follow?

I marched down the hall, into the living room, and out the front door of the flat. Unfortunately, the elevator wasn't right there. Before I could make it to the stairs, Steinman was beside me.

"Where do you think you are going?"

He grabbed my arm pulling me back. I wanted to slap his face, but held back. One day.

"I have to get some tampons," I said jutting my face into his ugly mug. "I can bleed out in front of you if you like?"

I shook myself free and spun on my heel.

Steinman didn't know what to say. I didn't give him time to think. I was down the stairs, through the lobby, and out onto the streets with him grumbling behind me. I hoofed it down to the druggist who stocks such things.

The shop I had chosen was below street level. Once down the stairs and in the store, I could see Steinman's feet pacing back and forth on the sidewalk. Tampons were contaminated items, I guess, because Steinman stayed on the street. He wouldn't be caught dead near a hygiene product.

I had all the time in the world.

"May I use your phone?"

The druggist looked skeptical.

Come on you frickin' asshole.

I put on my best smile and tilted my head for effect.

"For a fee, of course."

I placed my hand over my heart.

He pointed to the back of the shop. I quickly stuck my head out the front door and called to Steinman.

"Want anything?"

I was so glad I wasn't close. I swear he would have hit me.

"No? Okay. Just a sec. I have to get the correct size. You know how it is."

Smile. Smile, on my part, not his.

Omar Mohammed was still in. This time he answered the phone. I told him all about the visit to the bazaar, the lapidary, and the leather shop. I left out the details about Nancy, those were for me to savor. I mentioned the reference to the two movies, explosions, and death.

He agreed it was strangely suggestive.

Omar, of course, was especially interested in the Sheraton, the airport escapade, and the visit to Mena House. I forgot about some minor points like my drinking, the visit to the book shop, the fact that I was no longer cooking, and sex with Yasser.

All in all though, I was pleased with the amount of information I could give him.

I could hear Steinman yelling from the street at the druggist to hurry up. What did he think the guy was doing in the shop anyway? Trying out a custom fit?

I apologized to the man, made some excuse about why I had to use the phone, pointed to Steinman and shrugged my shoulders. I gave the druggist a hefty sum of coins since I didn't need him coming out into the street explaining to Steinman that the length of time I had been in his shop was due to the telephone call.

Steinman was not in a jovial mood. I couldn't tell if it was totally due to my tampon emergency or if he was just a born prick.

On the way back, I stopped at a street vendor to order a *Shawarma*. The smell of the seasoned marinated camel stacked on a rotating skewer wafted into the air. The vendor shaved the meat off as the spit slowly turned. I had him stuff it into the bread with plenty of tahina. The sandwich was savory, a real delight.

I mumbled to Steinman about food for the soul and headed back to the flat. I elected to walk up the stairs. Steinman followed. I could hear the slap of his feet on the stone steps. In the corridor, he selected the chair outside the flat door to sit down on. Looked like he was going to stay put.

Nothing like a tampon emergency to make a man keep his distance.

The flat was fairly quiet when I returned until I heard the sound of the shower coming on. Like a dog that spies a squirrel, I was instantly alert.

I turned the knob on Miss Balgrave's bedroom door. The door swung inward silently. I shut it behind me. I waited for my eyes to adjust to the dim light. The curtains were still drawn. The bed was rumpled from her nap. Yasser wasn't there. It would have been an awkward moment if I had bumped into him in Miss Balgrave's bedroom. I hadn't considered that.

I hadn't thought of anything except taking this opportunity to search Miss Balgrave's room. I could hear the shower running. The blueprints had been in the wardrobe. I edged toward it and pulled the latch. Stuck. I jerked it again. I couldn't make too much noise wrestling with it.

Then I realized it was locked.

Of all the F-in luck. Didn't that woman trust anyone?

She would lock it, just when I was going to take a look.

I backed away from the wardrobe to scan the room. My eye landed on the table by the window. There they were, the blueprints, on the table, unrolled, underneath her tourist compendium volume of 'M'. The book was so large that I had nearly missed seeing the blueprint. I'd have to be careful about moving the volume out of the way. It would need to be replaced in the exact same spot. Any shift, Miss Balgrave would notice.

The shower shut off.

Being a little jumpy, I recoiled into a pedestal table behind me. The alabaster carving of Nefertiti's head crashed to the floor. I quickly righted the table and replaced the replica.

"You're a poor specimen," I whispered to the carving. "Very poorly done if I may say, serves you right."

Luckily, the thing weighed a ton and hadn't broken, but it had made a noticeable smash mark on the floor. Miss Balgrave wasn't one for walking around with downcast eyes, so I'd have to hope she wouldn't notice.

When Miss Balgrave walked into the living room with a towel wrapped around her head, I was slouching on the couch making pretend knitting motions with my hands.

"What on earth are you doing?" she snapped.

"Knitting. Can't you tell?"

I was so rattled by my sleuthing escapade it was all I could think of doing. You might say I had wool in my head.

"Surprisingly, you can get fantastic wool in Egypt from Europe and Greece," I told her. "Lovely quality, colours, a great selection. My grandmother taught me to knit, astonishing as well, I know. I have made a scarf, and a sweater. The scarf was a success, but the sweater, yes, well. I'd knit the cuffs a bit tight. It's difficult to wear a sweater if you can't get your hands into or out of the sleeves. I can make you a sweater Miss Balgrave."

I'd love to see her with her hands stuck in the sweater of my youth.

She ignored my generous offer with a sneer.

"Where's Steinman?"

"Seriously, I can knit. I'm not trying to pull the wool over your eyes."

I pointed my imaginary knitting needles to the door.

"He's been a bad boy, so I sent him into the hall."

She yanked open the door and told him she required his presence. Without another look at me, they went to her room but left the door ajar. I could hear them conversing.

I had only seen a corner of the blueprints because the huge volume of the tourist compendium lay across most of it, but I had gleaned some vital information from it. The drawing on the blueprint was the corner of a two-story neo-classical building. Printed on the blueprint were two large capital letters.

The first was the letter 'M'. The second letter underneath it was the letter 'G'. I knew it! The Marriott hotel or as it was once known as, the Gezira Palace. That was the location.

It all made sense. It wasn't drugs; it was a political attack, bombs and all.

Nothing particular seemed to be happening in Miss Balgrave's bedroom. There was a steady flow of conversation. There was nothing urgent or emphatic about their speech. I peeked into the bedroom. They seemed settled and had a self-satisfied air about them. They might have been discussing plans for dinner. I thought it prudent to keep going down the hallway and headed to my bedroom just as they came out of Miss Balgrave's room and headed back toward the living room.

"... if I go in?" I heard Steinman's growl behind me as he walked down the hall in the opposite direction.

"It's my idea," she answered. "Let Yasser handle her. After it's over, it doesn't matter anyhow, even if she does the job well."

Steinman scoffed. "That mule? With her looks you don't even need explosives, anything she looks at shatters. She'd be effective just sending her in alone, she has a stench about her."

Miss Balgrave snickered.

Steinman asked, "When do Eda and Mohatmed return?"

"Tonight. Yasser knows ..." she whispered surreptitiously.

They began speaking in lower tones and disappeared around the corner. I couldn't make out the words. I went into my bedroom and lay down on the bed. I had to consider what I had learned.

The only thing that kept coming to mind was that I was ugly and I stank. Why did I care what that big ape thought?

It reminded me of my classmate at school in Alexandria. She had found out that my mother's family name was an Egyptian name. She taunted me with it. One day, I was walking in the city and came upon her with a group of what I had assumed were my friends. They didn't know I was behind them. She was, of course, going on about lowly Egyptians and how they reeked.

"Do you mean Amira?" one of my supposed friends inquired.

"Well, I don't like to say."

The group had giggled.

"You don't have to *say.*"

They had all burst out laughing.

"All you have to do is smell."

In unison, the group inhaled deeply and fell into a hilarious uproar.

I had slunk away. They never knew I had heard it all, but I remembered each one of them in the group. It carried a pain that only true betrayal can give. They had made me feel dirty and ugly. It made me want to take a shower and scrub the skin off my body, just like now.

Expect nothing. That way, you will never be disappointed.

My grandmother's words had never rung truer.

Never try to pretend to be someone you are not.

I look out for number one, me.

I heard someone coming down the hall. I rolled over on my bed, my back to the door. I heard the door open, but whoever it was didn't say a word. I nearly turned over to tell the world to go to hell, but if it was Steinman, I didn't want to get beaten up just then.

Besides, I was already black and blue inside.

CHAPTER TWELVE

I spent the rest of the afternoon on the couch watching television, thinking of Omar, and my situation. I was convinced Miss Balgrave's group would be moving against the Egyptian government or some notable dignitary connected with the turmoil in the Middle East.

Eda and Mohatmed stormed into the room and threw their jackets over me as if I wasn't even there.

"People are a little jumpy since the assassination of Anwar Sadat," argued Eda. "He was pivotal in the removal of King Farouk in the 1952 Revolution. Sadat had been a close advisor and Vice President to President Gamal Abdel Nasser whom he succeeded as President in 1970."

"That's not my point," retaliated Mohatmed. "I know my history."

"Obviously you don't," spat Eda. "Anwar Sadat served Egypt for eleven years before his assassination. He led Egypt in the Yom Kippur War of 1973. Took possession of the Sinai Peninsula. A hero in the eyes of many."

Mohatmed put his hands on his hips.

A sure sign he wasn't going to back down.

"Not all Arab nations agree. He had his own ideas for Egypt's future and departed from many policies of Nasser."

I had always thought that Sadat was an active campaigner for peace in the Middle East. However, the Takfir Wal Hijra faction approved of sacred terror and felt Anwar Sadat was leading Egypt astray.

Eda pointed his finger at Mohatmed's face in a fierce motion and shouted, "No consultation with other Arab states! He refused to reconcile with them over the Palestinian dilemma. Sadat just went and made peace with Israel."

Was I going to pipe up to point out that every action has a reaction?

I don't think so.

I knew that in reaction, the PLO started terrorist acts against Egypt and seventeen Arab countries imposed economic sanctions against Egypt. These were tough years for Sadat.

I shrank further into the couch.

"There was a fateful day," warned Eda. "And there will be another fateful day."

Oh ho. I'm not sure which fateful day he was referring to, but on the fateful day of October 6, Sadat, dressed in his new field marshal uniform with a green sash, went to the parade.

My grandmother had talked about that day often. It had been one of those life-changing events. It had stayed with her, a type of wake-up call you could say.

A member of the Takfir Wal Hijra had substituted one of the trucks in the parade. They were against peace initiatives with Israel and wanted a new Islamic era. When the truck drew near Sadat, an extremist jumped out, and threw a grenade in the stands. The others opened fire. Sadat was fatally shot.

"Don't!" Ed yelled at Mohatmed. "If you recite those words one more time I'll…"

"You'll what?" taunted Mohatmed. "Sadat's own words live on and I quote: *For the sake of our people and for the sake of civilization we have to defend man everywhere against rule by the force of arms so that we may endow the rule of humanity with the values and principles that further the sublime position of mankind.*"

"Grrr," exploded Eda as he covered his ears.

"Arguing," said Mohatmed. "You're always arguing. The League of Arab States argues, Saddam Hussein argues. Egypt is out. Egypt is in. The PLO is in. Yasser Arafat is accepted at the Cairo summit."

"It's a unique political history," retorted Eda.

"The current situation is no less intense, brother," said Mohatmed. "Recently, Hamas, an extremist group, has emerged. More violent conflict in Palestine will happen since one of its mandates is the total eradication of the Israeli state."

They make Arafat look reasonable, I thought to myself.

It made me sad to think that at this point, Egypt was still excluded, shunned if you will. I felt it personally, having experienced being shunned myself.

My grandfather believed that extremists derailed peace, but it doesn't mean that people should give up trying to bring justice.

"If you want peace, work for justice," I mumbled to myself, not sure what these two crazy brothers wanted.

I moved the cushions on the couch closer like I was trying to build a fort. This argument couldn't go on forever.

"President Mubarak treads a shaky path between political parties who hate each other with passion," said Mohatmed. "That will not be us."

My ears perked up.

Wouldn't be them? Really? How so?

Eda had calmed down enough to nod. "Mubarak even encouraged the Muslim Brotherhood to run for office in the Parliament, only to discover some plot to overthrow the government."

"No one can be trusted," said Mohatmed.

"We will set it right," agreed Eda. "Come, we must meet with Yasser. Grab the bag. We should go."

As the door slammed shut, I suspected their anti-government scheme to set things right was no different from schemes of the past.

How wrong I was.

By the time evening rolled around, I was decidedly ticked off.

Steinman had avoided me as much as he could, but he commandeered the one bathroom with a shower. It was a good-sized room; I will say that much for it. There was plenty of space between the sink, toilet, and where the shower head came out of the wall. The force of the shower water sprayed the entire cement room and made it effectively the shower stall. There was no divider, no shower curtain.

I finally got into the bathroom after two hours. It was a steaming mess.

He had left his litter everywhere. I mean everywhere. To top it off, his cologne was accentuated on every bead of mist. I could hardly breathe. To avoid the flooding on the floor, I hung my clothes and towel on the back of the door.

Under the showerhead, I welcomed the drenching stream of hot water. The tiny drain in the middle of the room couldn't handle it. The excess had made its way to every corner of the room. It drained down the inside of the wall to the apartment below.

The owner on the floor below was home because he started banging frantically on the exposed water pipes in a type of Morse code. I suspected the flooding in the apartment below was a regular occurrence.

After I had finished my toilette and as I was walking down the hall, I could smell that dinner had been brought in. This time, it was from *Le Chantilly*. The food made the gathering bearable.

I didn't know how much more waiting around I could take.

When the three men, Eda, Mohatmed, and Yasser, walked in, Miss Balgrave brightened at their arrival. I guess dining with Steinman and myself was not to her liking for she hadn't said one word to either of us the entire time.

Although Eda and Mohatmed had a violent history, as far as I knew, Miss Balgrave, Nancy, and Yasser were relatively clean. It put them well off the radar. No doubt it made them valuable operatives if one wanted to convey a political statement.

However, it occurred to me they might also be planning another assassination.

What information did I have to support my theory?

Political dissatisfaction obviously, a blueprint for a Neo-classical building, explosives, and a boat on the Nile. Those translated into motive, opportunity, delivery, and escape.

I could check them all off.

Mission accomplished.

They seemed very sure of themselves, yet they were the moodiest bunch of people I had ever met. One minute they were glowering and snapping at each other, the next rubbing their hands together and winking at each other.

When the time came to execute their plan, be it a political coup or a drug trafficking ring, I wondered which version of the gang would show up.

I was musing at a level of disquiet that was beginning to make me fidget, when Nancy piped up and broke into my contemplations.

"Dinner is finished. It's time you went to your room."

Now see here.

They all looked at me.

Their looks said, "Now is a good time."

Well, I had had enough of them too. I retained my dignity and left the room.

To keep control of my own destiny and show them a thing or two, I impulsively slipped into Miss Balgrave's room to have a closer look at the blueprints.

The document was on the table.

I heard the doorknob turning behind me. The only thing I could do was jump into the wardrobe and pull its door shut behind me.

Miss Balgrave came into her room. She sighed and kicked off her shoes. One of the shoes must have hit the wardrobe. I sucked in my breath. My gasp stuck in my throat.

I shut my eyes and was back at school in Alexandria.

Just get through it.

I said the phrase over and over in my head.

My eyes shot open as soon as I heard his voice.

"Humar. They're a pack of donkeys I tell you," sneered Yasser in his silky voice.

He must have come in at the same time as Miss Balgrave.

"I don't want to hear about them," said Miss Balgrave.

At least I think it was her. It sure didn't sound like her.

"Come here."

"Ouch. Easy."

"Oh, I'm easy all right," replied Miss Balgrave.

Yasser laughed, a low sound. It was a sound I had heard before, down in the shed by the Nile River. The bastard. They weren't?

Yes, they were.

Then the rhythm began. The bed creaked with the weight of the two of them. I tried not to giggle. It reminded me of those silly schoolgirl jokes about authors and book titles. You know the ones, like I. P. Knightly who wrote the book Rusty Bedsprings.

It wasn't the three-minute special. Their breathing became louder. He grunted. She squealed. Maybe it was the other way around. She was a bit of an A-type personality.

The whole time, I had to stand in the closet and remind myself to not bang my head against the wardrobe door in frustration. It was getting hot in the closet. I could feel the sweat starting to run down the curves of my body. I had a vision of me fainting and tumbling out of the closet, prostrate right at the foot of the bed at the moment of their climax.

The denouement arrived. I matched the drawing in of a deep breath of air with it. I was suffocating in that wardrobe. I was sure I was going to pass out, and desperately pressed my nose on a crack in the side of the wardrobe to try to get some fresher air into my nostrils.

"Was everything completed today?"

Yasser replied, "Everyone knows what to do. Steinman has served the tea."

"How well does he know the guard?"

"Well enough. The guard will be very sick and will definitely be off duty tomorrow."

Yasser spoke with conviction, "I want that baboon to know that when I tell him to do something, he needs to do it."

Miss Balgrave soothed her lover.

"I'll have a word with Steinman. Don't worry. I'll deal with that situation."

Yasser mumbled something I didn't hear.

"Perfect. We have work to do," said Miss Balgrave. "I want to go over the entrance again."

"I like that idea."

"Hey," she giggled.

"What were you saying about entering again?" asked Yasser playfully.

The groaning started again. It was definitely her. I had managed to suck in some fresh air, but my neck was in such an odd position. I imagined that instead of passing out, I would explode out of the wardrobe like a rupture with a multitude of spasms racking my body.

"Where are my pants?"

"I get the shower," she said back in command again.

There were some more muffled sounds. Then silence. One more minute. I couldn't have lasted any longer. I was impressed with my self-control as I inched open the wardrobe door and spied the room was clear. It was ten feet to the door. Miss Balgrave was in the shower and the clanging of the pipes echoed from the apartment down below.

Like the hunchback of Notre Dame, I managed to scurry to my room without anyone seeing me. I felt sick from being cramped in the wardrobe. For the next twenty minutes, I tried to regulate my breathing and clear my head. I changed my clothes and combed my hair.

When I thought I wouldn't keel over, I did some calisthenics exercises. As soon as I felt better, I sat down on the edge of my bed to review what I now knew.

After my escape from the wardrobe, I should have taken a look at the blueprints. I had had the time.

If I had thought to view the blueprints instead of hearing the orgy fest, things would have turned out differently for Miss Balgrave and Yasser, for all of them in fact, and especially me.

But I hadn't.

I certainly wasn't going back.

Instead, with a glass of water from the kitchen, I sauntered down the hall to the living room.

Nancy glared at me.

I had the most incredible urge to walk up to her and accidentally bump the arm in the sling.

Just because.

I didn't have a chance to fulfill my dream of hurting Nancy because I felt someone brush up beside me. Eda. The sight of him made me shiver.

In the corner of the room, Steinman was having an earnest conversation with Mohatmed. I could tell something was going to happen soon.

As I understood it, some guard wasn't going to be there tomorrow. So tomorrow it was.

I suddenly felt incredibly flustered and walked back down the hall to my room. It was obvious that my days in Cairo were coming to an end.

Yasser had been organizing a boat either for approaching the Marriott or leaving the scene or both. In addition, I remembered Miss Balgrave had had a particular interest in charters when in Ashkelon.

Were they planning an ultimate escape via seaworthy vessels?

This wasn't a piece of information I had shared with Omar.

I had just thought of it now.

It probably wasn't significant or was it?

Then there were the explosives, taken care of by Eda and Mohatmed. The target, the actual person I still didn't know, but the location and the means I did.

If the brothers were linked to one of the many extremist groups, that was big trouble. Those two follow the *Jihad*. Yasser seemed almost like a pretty boy in it for the ride.

Steinman was surprisingly even tempered. He seemed to be astonishingly practical. He only acted out of necessity. Any mistake he would make would have to be a big one. I also realized Steinman was more than just a bag-snatcher with a sadistic fist. He had a role dealing with the guards or at least a guard. Getting someone out of the way was just up his alley, that was for sure.

As for Nancy, whatever her role might have been, let's just say she kept tripping up. She was on the fringe, if not out of the picture. Nancy I could see as being a bit bent, and for myself?

Was I her replacement or did they have a new job for me?

Obviously, they were keeping me around for something or was I too inconvenient to let go?

I knew a lot, but actually no details.

Miss Balgrave?

I couldn't quite figure her out, but I was sure there was a malicious streak in her I would have to watch out for.

Was tomorrow the day for death on the Nile? My death?

It was obvious, in retrospect, that I should have searched Yasser and Steinman's rooms as well.

Why were they out on constant errands?

What was in the bags in their rooms?

But all of this only occurred to me later, when it was too late.

The fact that Steinman could actually be in charge of anything never occurred to me. I had always assumed he was the stooge, not the general.

It wasn't my fault that I hadn't considered it. Omar hadn't thought of it either, not once. Not in any conversation had he indicated that he believed the person in charge was none other than Miss Balgrave.

Well, maybe, but … Steinman must be an underling, was he?

This situation was all Omar Mohammed's fault.

Why hadn't he seen this coming?

I had no means of communication with him. He wasn't sure of my location.

But if he had Miss Balgrave and her crew under surveillance then he would know I was with them.

The problem was I had never seen anyone trailing us or watching the flat.

Was Omar letting me go it alone?

CHAPTER THIRTEEN

The Heliopolis flat on El-Sobki was fundamentally a rectangle with a long hallway dividing it in half. The living room, the dining room, and the veranda were on one side. The bedrooms, bathrooms and kitchen were on the other side of the divide.

My room was basically my own personal closet. It was located right beside the kitchen. The kitchen was the last room in a row of rooms along the long hallway in the flat. Therefore, I was well positioned to hear the commotion in the kitchen next to my room and went to have a look.

"Haima?"

She was bouncing around in the small kitchen space. The kitchen door was open to the tiny dark landing between this flat and hers. The garbage cans were overturned on the landing.

"Haima! What on earth are you doing?"

"I come in," she shouted at me.

"Yes, you certainly did. What's wrong? Are you ill?"

"You American?"

"No, Canadian. Remember? Big difference," I said.

"Yes. Friendly Canadian."

"Right. Are you unwell?" I asked again.

I didn't try to stop her. She was flinging the cutlery out of the drawers and was now going after the pots on the shelves.

"I work," she stammered, "but not now. No more."

"You don't work here, but over there, Haima."

I pointed to the flat across the back landing.

"Why are you here?"

"I shop. I clean. I work. I get the post," she sobbed. "I work."

Okay, this was getting a little hysterical, but I didn't know what to do with her. Steinman appeared in the hallway behind me. I knew this because he started to yell at Haima in Arabic. He wanted to know what she was doing. To which she replied she was working.

I was shocked at the transformation in her. Where had that kind wonderful woman with no future gone to?

My guess was something significant had happened.

On a hunch I asked, "Haima, have you been travelling?"

I made a motion with my fingers to indicate walking.

"Travel," she yelled at me. "I go to Cairo."

Now Cairo isn't very far from Heliopolis, but for her that was probably a big trip. She was after all determined to better her life. When the opportunity presented itself to move beyond her circle, she certainly would take it.

Steinman, who was still in the hallway, was his compassionate self, as usual. He indicated she should leave this flat. She nodded her head in submission. He then turned on his heel and left. Obviously he thought this was no place for a man, because he hadn't even crossed the threshold from the hallway to the kitchen.

I remembered Haima had been to Alexandria.

"You went to Alexandria?"

She stared at me.

"I mean before Cairo, you went to Alexandria, yes?"

She began to cry. I mean really wail.

"Shh, shh, Haima. What is wrong with you?"

I had been speaking to her in English, not letting on that I understood Arabic. I don't know if that made her feel safe and that was why she started to speak to me in Arabic. She was probably thinking she was just talking to herself but it all came pouring out, and I understood.

She had been to Alexandria but not with the doctors in the flat across the landing but with a man. He had taken liberties.

Although, those weren't the words she used.

She became distraught. She lived in dirt. Now she was dirt she said. The doctors in the flat had found out about the trip and kicked her out. No job. No money.

"I can work for you Miss? He give money."

"Who gave you money? What did he give you money for Haima?" I asked.

She began to wail again.

"Haima, stop it!"

"He bad."

"What?"

Surely, she didn't mean the man was someone from Miss Balgrave's flat?

I mean they weren't good men, certainly not, but were they what she referred to as bad?

On second thought, I don't know what I was so surprised about, of course they were.

She nodded energetically.

"I like America," she said.

America is the answer for everything that is wrong for the downtrodden, apparently.

I smiled to cover the fact that I found her desperation alarming. It didn't work. She descended into an abusive stream of Arabic that would have made a prison guard blush.

"I kill him."

Her statement was uttered with such simplicity that it shocked me. I believed her.

"Now, Haima. Is he worth killing? I mean just move on."

That's what I do, did in fact, many times. So far, I haven't killed anyone.

Her face contorted. She was having quite a struggle with my suggestion.

"Tell you what, I'll have a chat with the doctors or even find you a new job. Why don't you go home now?"

Nothing doing. That seemed to ignite the injustice of her situation quite significantly.

"No home. Here. I stay."

She pushed by me and started running down the hall. She opened every door along the way. Finding no one, she continued to the living room.

I wasn't going to stop her.

To heck with that.

She was carrying a large kitchen knife.

There was plenty of shouting happening by the time I made it to the living room. Everyone was on their feet. Haima was pointing the knife at Yasser and screaming obscenities at him.

Eda and Mohatmed had the disadvantage of being on the other side of the sofa. Nancy was sitting in her chair with a gaping mouth.

Suddenly there was a crashing sound. Haima fell to the ground, but not before she gave a good swipe at Yasser.

Miss Balgrave had saved the day.

I laughed to myself.

She had been standing unnoticed, slightly behind Haima, and had hit her with a heavy ceramic vase. Thwack.

What a farce.

I stood back to survey the scene.

The twins leaped over the sofa and grabbed Haima. Nancy looked like she had fainted. Steinman, I noticed, had been on the veranda for the whole thing. Yasser had blood on the front of his shirt. Miss Balgrave looked like a cat just released from a cage.

I restrained the impulse to clap at the performance.

"Why didn't you warn us?" Miss Balgrave snapped at me.

I shrugged and said, "I forgot."

She turned her attention to Yasser. I restrained the impulse to laugh again. It was only a flesh wound. Besides, he had taken poor Haima to Alexandria and screwed her. He deserved what he had got.

Haima was being held in a vice grip by the two brothers.

Miss Balgrave turned and smacked her across the face. Now see here, the girl was only doing what anyone would have done. There was no call for that.

Miss Balgrave shot me a look that said, "I dare you to speak."

I'm not much of one for dares, so I kept silent.

Yasser was bleeding fairly steadily, but he wasn't going to die. Although, he was beginning to have a bit of a fixed staring look as the shock settled in.

"I'll get the car." Steinman finally spoke. "Mohatmed bring Yasser down to the street."

Yasser was still sitting on the floor. Miss Balgrave was trying to wrap his arm and torso in a sofa blanket. Pretty ineffective, just like Nancy who still hadn't moved.

Mohatmed left Haima in Eda's custody and got Yasser to stand up.

"Yasser knows where the nearest hospital is. He's taken Nancy there many times," I couldn't resist a jab at her.

It seemed to snap Nancy out of her daze.

"Not the hospital," she said. "I know a doctor."

"Take him there Mohatmed. Nancy go with them. Steinman go as well," Miss Balgrave barked her orders.

I volunteered for emergency duty thinking it would provide a good opportunity to contact Omar with this tidbit of drama, but nothing doing.

"The rest of us will stay here." Miss Balgrave was emphatic and gave me a good long look.

Jeesh. You'd think I had been the one wielding a knife.

Yasser was away just over two hours. When he returned, he looked extremely pale and wobbly. Pain killers no doubt. I didn't look at anyone directly because I was feeling extremely satisfied about events and didn't want to encourage another stabbing with me as the target.

Yasser displayed his war wounds to Miss Balgrave. He had a neatly taped wide bandage across his chest and left bicep. Fifteen stitches. That was all it took.

I was disappointed; there had been so much blood.

"Where's Haima?" Steinman asked.

"She's gone," Miss Balgrave stated. "She won't be coming around here anymore."

No doubt the threat of the police was enough to keep her in her parents' hovel for the rest of her life. Steinman nodded. Yasser was too far gone on pain killers at this point to care.

"Amira, get Yasser into bed."

"Yes ma'am."

I said it crisply with innuendo. I heard Miss Balgrave suck in her breath sharply.

I tucked Yasser into his bed and whispered in his ear, "Serves you right asshole."

I don't know if he heard me, but it sure made me feel good to say it.

I had been stuck in the living room and was glad to get away from the scene of the crime. I headed for the kitchen where I put the bloodied sofa blanket into the refuse bin on the landing. The cats and the rats were going to have a heyday with that garbage.

No one had thought about the kitchen door, so I made sure it was locked, just in case Haima had a real moment of insanity and felt compelled to finish the job on Yasser. I left the cutlery and the pots and pans on the floor where Haima had flung them.

It wasn't my kitchen.

It was getting on to midnight. I had absolutely no feeling for any of them. I wasn't one bit sorry.

Well, I was sorry for Haima.

The incident highlighted just how tired I was of all the black looks and comments directed toward my supposed defective personality. Those comments from Miss Balgrave's gang, in fact a lot of people throughout my life, had left me with nothing.

I had always thought the criticism had just rolled over and off me. I had noticed the jabs and the criticisms to be sure, but I had received so many jabs during my life that they no longer emotionally wounded me. There was nothing, no searing impact, a void.

So I had thought, but the void was reacting.

I used to believe I was truly defective, that I would never get the social emotional game right.

The aftershock of the evening was that I was reminded it wasn't necessarily me.

Although granted, I did have moments of being unkind, but that wasn't it. I realized there were just a sizeable number of rotten people in the world with really big issues.

It was these people who kept popping into my life, influencing events, and pointing their finger at me. Maybe. Maybe it is that way for everyone. After all, even in fairytale land, you just can't sail through without meeting an ogre or two.

Maybe. It was too much to think about.

I slid into bed for the night.

In the morning, there was a knock on my door. What a polite gesture! Usually, they just open the door and give commands. I had slept like a brown bear hibernating in a Canadian winter.

I was ready to meet a new day.

Immediately alert at this new exhibition of manners, I was very suspicious. I was called to breakfast with Steinman and Miss Balgrave on the veranda. The brothers were off doing what terrorists do during the day. Nancy was mooning over Yasser in the corner.

What a pair, the two of them.

Before I could stop myself, I quipped, "Are you two getting married? You seem suited to each other."

"Have a seat, Amira," invited Miss Balgrave.

She was being incredibly civil.

Now I was really getting worried.

I decided to return the courtesy and said politely, "How is everyone today?"

The wedding couple ignored me, but I caught a quick glance between Miss Balgrave and Steinman.

I braced myself.

Miss Balgrave served tea and offered me a pastry from a white china plate. She took her time, as if she needed to collect herself for the big moment.

"Amira," said Miss Balgrave.

That's my name, don't wear it out. Come on. The suspense was killing me.

"Amira, Steinman and I were having a friendly chat. We thought we would confer with you about who's right."

Confer? Really?

"Sure," I said.

My voice was about as non-committal as I could get. The soft morning sun flowed over the veranda. I thought Steinman had fallen asleep in his chair.

He hadn't. His eyes were slits.

He was peering at me.

Watching.

"The light on the wall," said Miss Balgrave as she pointed to a sconce high on the wall, "needs replacing. Do you think you could change the bulb?"

"Seriously?" I chattered.

This was a new one.

"You want me to get a ladder and change a light bulb?"

"No. We want you to do it without a ladder." Steinman's voice came out low, just above a growl.

It sounded like it was a test for a new job. I was at the point where the job interviewer breaks off the verbal discussion and suddenly asks you to draw a picture of a bicycle going backwards, just to test if you are flexible and compliant.

Okay. Being an easy-going person, I played along.

"Well, the chairs and table are too low. Stacking them is just plain unsafe."

Steinman made a grunting noise, which really irked me. I was solving a grand problem here. I didn't appreciate animal noises from the peanut gallery.

I goaded him by saying, "Maybe I can use Steinman's broad manly shoulders to stand on?"

I looked with satisfaction at Miss Balgrave.

She laughed and spoke to Steinman, "See I told you she could do it."

"She hasn't done it yet," said Steinman as he rose to his feet and motioned to me to get on his shoulders.

"You don't actually want me to climb on top of you?"

I was incredulous.

"Nancy can do it," said Miss Balgrave.

"Nancy is practically in a body cast," I shot back.

Nancy gave me that you-can't-do-it look. As I already pointed out I am not much of one for dares, but this was from Nancy.

"Fine. I'll do it," I tossed a wicked look in her direction.

Steinman was already crouching. I put my foot on Steinman's thigh, my knee on his left shoulder and grabbed his right hand. I made sure to dig my knee into his trapezius muscle extra hard, but the man didn't even flinch.

I grabbed his left hand as he stood up and placed my foot to the right side of his head. I was a little wobbly getting up onto my left foot but with the wall to place my hands on, I managed the rest of the motion with a fluidity that made me proud. I was still short of the sconce, however.

"We need one more person," I said as I waved one hand with achievement.

You'd think I had scaled Mount Everest or something.

Steinman moved away from the wall which he thought was a fine joke as I nearly fell off his shoulders backwards. I have good balance though and have always leaned to the athletic side, so I recovered.

Whereas some people find sport ridiculous and a waste of time, I have always found any type of athletic competition enticing. I win fair and square. You can always tell everything about a person by how they compete in sports. You can tell the whiners, the cheaters, the fake injury types.

Miss Balgrave raised her eyebrows as she was looking at Steinman.

"What do you think Yasser?"

Yasser? What did he have to do with any of this?

"Yes. I will be okay. Indeed, it's not until tomorrow. It gives me time. It will be fine."

It sounded like Yasser was trying to convince himself.

I didn't like it.

"What will be fine?" I was curious.

"How would you like to earn some more money, Amira?" Miss Balgrave asked.

"It depends what it's for?" I said immediately. "A trip to Alexandria?"

They ignored my reference to the Haima escapade.

"Sit down," commanded Miss Balgrave.

So, this wasn't a job interview after all, but more of a we-have-one-more-thing for you to do directive.

"We will double what we have already paid you."

Paid me?

I hadn't seen a piastre of the money. That was a lark.

"When?" I said and stuck my chin out.

Miss Balgrave took a deep breath like she was getting ready for a deep-sea diving plunge.

"Tomorrow," she stated. "The instant the job is finished. You will get the money tomorrow."

I looked skeptical, I'm sure.

"With your tape recording from Ashkelon," she added. "Just a little incentive."

My father used to blackmail me with the same tone of voice that Miss Balgrave had just used. He used access to my half-sister as punishment.

If I didn't think the way he did, then he would get very personal. He could be quite nasty. What's a kid to do when a father doesn't do his parental job?

When I tried to use my voice to defend myself, it only got worse. Just use your words my mother would say. As if. What needed to be said were words I didn't even know existed.

My father would often be very upset about something and his voice would rise. I admit I was quite a cheeky five-year-old. I would try to nip it in the bud by pointing out he didn't need to get so angry. That went over like a lead balloon.

He'd retaliate with comments about how I was the nastiest and meanest person in the world. He got that line from my mother, I think. Oh, how they could really dig it in.

Emotional stuff like that sticks with you.

I was young but I remember it like it was yesterday.

After a deluge of criticism, my father usually chucked in comments about how overbearing and difficult I was. Needy was a word he often used. Go figure. He didn't like the way I talked to my mother either. Hostilities he called them. I told him they were discussions, even my mother thought so, but there was no convincing him. I was there. I heard it.

In response he would say, "You were at each other's throats".

His perceptions were ridiculous. He thought what he thought. There was no changing that. He'd finish off his diatribe with the sentiment of how much he loved me.

Whatever.

The kicker of course was that he was nasty, like I said. He wouldn't let me see my sister if he didn't like what I was doing or saying. That's what genuinely hurt me.

You don't keep a loved one away from someone because they don't agree with your point of view. That's not right, but he did it.

I loved my sister. We never fought. We were kind to each other and had a great time together. If my behaviour wasn't just right or what he considered was just right, I couldn't see her. I couldn't even talk to her on the telephone. And Canada was a country where you could just pick up the phone and dial the number!

He could poison her love for me too, which he did whenever he spoke with her, saying one well-placed negative comment here and there, over and over.

People with power over other people can affect your life in extremely negative ways. He could do that you see because she didn't live with us. My half-sister lived with her mother. I didn't have a chance.

I smiled sarcastically at Miss Balgrave. "Do I have a chance to change my destiny? Do I even have a choice?"

I focused on what I could do with that amount of money.

The problem was I knew I would never see it from Miss Balgrave. I'd be lucky to get away from her alive, with or without my tape recording. Even if I did keep my life, Omar would have me in prison on charges of terrorism.

"I'd love to help," I continued. "Whatever I can do. I'm all yours of course."

CHAPTER FOURTEEN

The four of them were watching me the way a leopard targets its prey. I leaned back in my chair and ate a piece of fruit.

"Tea please," I made the request to Miss Balgrave.

The tea pot was right next to her elbow so she could hardly refuse. The thought of telling me to do it myself flashed across her brow, but since she was going for the Miss Congeniality award, she poured me a cup.

When she handed me the cup, it was only half full.

I smiled sweetly, made a comment about it being just right, and filled it up to the brim with a good helping of milk.

"Aren't you even going to ask what we want you to do?"

Nancy's voice held a note of vexation.

I took a delicate sip of my tea and savoured it.

"I am going to do what you were going to do, sweet Nancy," I murmured. "Your job."

Miss Balgrave laughed and Steinman disclosed his philosophical opinion of me by commenting, "You're not as stupid as you look Amira, and you look pretty stupid."

I wasn't quite sure what to do with his comment. It felt like a backhanded slap.

"What job is that Amira?"

Now Nancy was just being churlish.

"Nothing profound, I'm sure," I replied.

Steinman interrupted, "You are going to be a woman. You are going to shut up now and do as you're told. You are going to keep your eyes down."

I looked at Miss Balgrave.

She nodded and said, "That's the first part."

Steinman continued, "Make sure she is ready. Get there in time."

He stood up to go and said, "Miss Balgrave, I will meet you later, as we have arranged."

After Steinman left, the other three sat in silence.

I was peeved and retorted, "That's it? I think I have the right to know a little bit more about what I am getting myself into."

Miss Balgrave looked questioningly at Yasser and Nancy.

Yasser, who had been basically mute, made some comment to Nancy which I didn't catch. It was Nancy who stepped up into the leadership role.

"You don't need to know anything right now. You will find out later, as necessary, not before. Everything is in order. Just shut up. Do as you are told."

That was a fine piece of advice. She certainly made me feel better. Not.

"You won't be coming back to this flat, so pack your things," Miss Balgrave added. "You can move into Steinman's room for the rest of the day. Nancy, you can take Amira's room."

Why? That was strange, but Nancy nodded. There was a little gleam in her eye.

Then it hit me. Miss Balgrave would be in the room on my left. Nancy would be on my right. To get to either exit door, I would have to try to get by them, and then there was Yasser who was at the end of the hall.

"Well, that's trust for you," I said.

Miss Balgrave had a pistol, a fact I had become acquainted with in Ashkelon. I didn't doubt Nancy had one too.

"We won't shoot you Amira," crooned Miss Balgrave.

"Not if you behave," Nancy mimicked her tone.

I wondered what Nancy's definition of behave was.

Before I could make a witty comeback, she added, "Maybe the Pofem brothers can blow you up too."

No one said a word. There was little else I could do but Nancy had given me plenty to consider. I didn't have too many things to pack to complete the move to Steinman's room. A room, by the way, which was only slightly larger than my previous bedroom.

Upon returning to them in the living room I proclaimed, "Peace. I just want us all to get along. After all, we are all in this together, just like family."

Miss Balgrave looked at me curiously.

I figured if they were going to throw a spanner into the entire Middle East negotiations, the least I could do was make one final attempt to stop them. I wasn't supposed to know anything about Eda and Mohatmed, so I also figured that being a bit alarmed about the explosive comment would be playing the part.

I launched into it. "Genuine peace is brought about by achieving justice for the oppressed. Couldn't we advocate for that instead of blowing something up?"

No one said a word.

"Terrorists and countries who use similar tactics love to create chaos."

I was convinced I needed to speak out. Accepting everything they had told me without a reaction would not have been convincing. Besides, they were a suspicious bunch, best to keep them guessing.

"Have you ever considered going on a speaking tour, Miss Balgrave? You seem to be quite astute."

"What would I be lecturing on, Amira?"

"Well, things that bring about peace, especially here, in the Middle East. You know, things that build, recreate and create,"

I waved my hand in the air like a magic wand.

"You could talk about hope," I suggested.

"The only thing I'm hoping for," interrupted Nancy, "is that you will shut up."

I ignored her. She was an ignoramus.

"You could be for positive change in the status quo. Then peace would be real, full."

I made a shape with my hands like I was holding a loaf of newly baked bread.

"What's brought all this on?" queried Miss Balgrave as she shot a nasty look at Nancy. "Why don't you go out onto the veranda, Amira?"

Miss Balgrave had a little smile on her lips. Her suggestion was, of course, a command, not a request.

I had tried. My political acumen is rather vague. My statements sounded ridiculous. To believe that Miss Balgrave would think about peace or reconciliation or anything other than herself was equally ridiculous.

Does peace ever truly last, especially when it's forced?

Did I really think my little plea would change anything?

Yasser sat at the table, but I hesitated going out onto the veranda. What a pickle to be in.

I couldn't talk to these guys. I couldn't communicate with Omar. Hey, don't get me wrong, I wasn't trying to be a heroine or anything.

I was trying to figure out a way out of my predicament.

I had to contact Omar, but short of throwing a message over the balcony railing it didn't appear that there was any way to accomplish that. I had a distinct longing for my handy dandy walkie-talkie. It was for emergencies, which this certainly had the makings of becoming; a transmitter would have come in handy, no pun intended.

"Amira, come here."

It was Yasser's voice. He was beckoning me to sit down at the table. There was a white plastic bag in front of him.

"*J'arrive*," I announced my submission with a flair.

"Open the bag. Take it out."

I could tell he was still in a fair amount of pain. The movement would have been difficult for him. I involuntarily raised my eyebrows.

"It's not a bag of spiders, Amira. Just take the stuff out."

"All right, all right," I grumbled. "Don't get so testy."

It was a white rope ladder.

"Are you trying to help me escape?" I whispered to him in mock secrecy.

"Not from here," he replied. "From somewhere else."

"Where are the wooden rungs? This thing is going to be tricky to climb without wooden rungs."

I viewed it with scepticism.

"There are no wooden rungs," explained Yasser. "You step here and here."

He showed me the woven rungs.

"Besides," he continued, "when rolling the ladder up, wooden rungs make it a fairly large bundle, too large in fact. This one has been made so that it is portable. It is all from one piece of rope, following a traditional pattern."

"What is this made of?"

"It is white nylon. Simple. Strong."

I examined the rope ladder. "The ends are unfinished."

"That's because the ladder will be attached to hooks and fastened to the ..."

Yasser stopped himself.

"To what?"

"You'll see."

"Where are the hooks?"

"They're metal. They wouldn't make it through security screening. Don't worry. The hooks are already on site."

I wasn't worried, just damn curious.

"How many ladders are you using?" I asked Yasser.

"Two."

"We need two ladders to get down?"

"You'll see, Amira," said Miss Balgrave. "It's not really that complicated. Just do as you're told."

She had come out onto the veranda with Nancy to inspect the two white nylon rope ladders.

"Are they long enough?"

Yasser replied, "I am just measuring them."

Yasser took out a tape measure.

"You're leaving it rather late, aren't you?" I quipped.

They ignored my question.

"The hooks?" Miss Balgrave posed the next question.

"Steinman has taken care of that."

"Good," Miss Balgrave said.

For a long time, she watched me tapping the table.

"You're getting agitated, Amira."

"Well yeah," I yelled. "You would be too if you had absolutely no idea what was going on. For all I know that rope is for me to hang myself."

"Okay. All right. Calm down," soothed Miss Balgrave.

Oh, that was really helpful, especially since it came from her. "She needs to relax," concluded Yasser.

I think he was afraid I might pass out from a panic attack. I was afraid, but I needed to know what the plan was in case I had the opportunity to relay the information to Omar. I increased my breathing and moaned. My hand came to my forehead. I collapsed onto the chair.

I thought I might be overdoing it but apparently not.

"Tell her," snapped Miss Balgrave. "Just about the exit."

"Amira, look at me," said Yasser.

I wiped the tears from my eyes. I felt like a five-year-old child who has just tumbled off of a swing.

"The top of the ladder is going to be woven into two hooks, one on each side. See."

Yasser held up the ends of the rope.

I nodded.

"The ladder will be placed, hooked, onto the metal bar that runs along the bottom of the window ledge. That's it," finished Yasser with a curt nod.

"I don't get it. What do you need a ladder for if you are hooking it onto the bottom of the window?"

It didn't make sense to me at all.

"The window is twenty feet off of the floor."

I retorted, "Well, you would need a ladder to get to it, wouldn't you?"

"Exactly. We are making a human ladder. You will be close enough to hook the rope ladder to the window."

"Who is comprising this human ladder may I ask?"

I wasn't going to like the answer.

"Well, you," Yasser said, "me, and Steinman."

"You have got to be joking!"

"It's no joke, Amira," Miss Balgrave declared.

I was trying to picture it. I had stood on Steinman's shoulders which were fairly broad. He was strong, but Yasser? I looked Yasser up and down, bandages and all.

"You are going to stand on Steinman, and I am supposed to stand on your shoulders, Yasser? Is that what you nuts are thinking?" I asked, totally flabbergasted.

"Nancy can do it. No problem." Miss Balgrave flipped the comment at me.

I clamped my mouth shut. I was snarling inside.

Nancy was sniggering in the corner.

"Look," implored Yasser. "You climb up on my shoulders to the window. Between the three of us, you will get close enough to the window ledge. The grappling hooks, which will be fastened to the end of the ladder will be placed on the rod which runs along the base of the window."

"If they have hooks, why not just throw them up there?" I made a point.

I shook my head at them like they were daft bats.

"And break the window?" Nancy sneered. "Brilliant idea."

Obviously, that was a possibility.

Yasser ignored our spat and continued, "Once the ladder is secured, we can climb up to the window. Another ladder will also be fastened on the hooks for the exterior wall. We climb down and we're done."

"Exterior wall? So, this stunt is to get out, not in?" I exclaimed.

"Correct."

"Why don't we just walk out the door like normal people?" I asked vying for more information.

I must admit by this time there probably was quite a bit of condescension in my voice.

"The doors are alarmed. We can't use them," said Miss Balgrave getting exasperated.

"And the windows aren't?" I asked in disbelief.

"The windows are alarmed," clarified Yasser, "but only the lower windows. The transoms that run along the top are not."

"How do you know they aren't alarmed? How do you know they even open? They could be painted shut. It's not like they ever get opened, I imagine."

This plan sounded like a disaster waiting to happen.

"The transoms are not alarmed. They do open. In fact, they are large enough to get you, Yasser, and Steinman through," added Miss Balgrave.

Nancy made a snorting sound.

"You figured this out?" I responded making a face. "You guys can't even walk down a street without getting hurt."

I shot an angry look at Nancy.

"You can stop being childish right now," commanded Miss Balgrave. "You are having a temper tantrum."

I was too.

I excused myself to go to the loo. Once I was in there, I splashed water on my flushed face and told myself to pull it together. I was trapped in the flat. Soon I'd be climbing a rope ladder on my way to paradise. Then they'd shoot me.

I had to leave, recording or no recording. Omar would understand. He wouldn't just throw me in prison. What would he gain by that?

Perhaps I could make it to Alexandria and from there slip on a boat. This was not worth it. I'd be strung up on some rope ladder trying to escape after the gang had finished their dirty work. I was out. My decision to resign from the SSIS was final.

Yet, it was all I could do to open the bathroom door to make my escape. I immediately turned to the right as I came out of the bathroom.

Nancy was at the end of the hall guarding the kitchen door. I kept walking toward her and turned into my bedroom.

Okay, that exit wouldn't work; I'd have to use the front door and run for the stairs.

If I slipped out quietly, I would have a head start. I quit my bedroom and turned left down the hall. I could see the door in front of me.

Miss Balgrave came from around the corner and stepped in front of me.

"Ahh, Amira," she sweet-talked since she was all polite again. "We were wondering what happened to you. Feel all right? Come join us on the veranda."

She placed one hand on my shoulder and waved the other in the direction of the balcony. I clearly was going nowhere, except where she wanted.

I joined Yasser and Nancy once again on the veranda. Miss Balgrave pulled a black garment out of a carry-on bag and laid it across the back of the chair.

I smiled my one-for-all-and-all-for-one smile.

Miss Balgrave sneered back. It was reassuring to see she was back to her usual self.

Maybe I could pull this off after all.

"Okay, so how do we get in?" I asked.

"We walk in," Yasser said simply.

"Well, that's a relief," I said.

"Lunch will be in thirty minutes," announced Miss Balgrave.

I didn't know if I would be able to eat. My stomach was tied in knots. I said as much.

It was already one o'clock in the afternoon.

The lunch delivery arrived from *Sahans*; the restaurant Miss Balgrave had taken me to when I first met her in Cairo. I thought of Wanda in her fish tank and her treasure chest with the hidden metal key.

"You had better eat up, you won't be eating for a while," Yasser coaxed.

"Time's ticking," pressed Miss Balgrave. "We need to get you dressed. Hurry up Amira."

I was dawdling, but not on purpose. I was feeling quite out of my depth with recent events. I watched Miss Balgrave hold up the black garment she had laid across the back of the chair. It was an *abaya* complete with a *niqab*.

"Are you thinking that I am wearing an abaya?" I inquired distrustfully. "What for?"

"How else are you going to get the rope ladders inside?"

"I'm carrying the ladders?"

Nancy couldn't resist and jabbed, "Wow, Amira. You are a swift one."

"Maybe I should go slower so you can catch up to me," I shot back at Nancy.

To Miss Balgrave I emphatically said, "I'll wear a hijab over my body, but not a niqab. I'm not covering my face. Besides, this whole thing is an insult to Islam."

"You're not even religious. What do you care what you wear?" scorned Nancy.

"I have principles."

"Those I haven't seen," smirked Miss Balgrave, "I wouldn't know about your principles."

She was actually upsetting me.

I blurted out, "Well, I don't know much about anything, do I? Here I was told you need me for a job. I don't even know what it is. You have me standing on shoulders. Wrapping rope around my body. What are we doing? Raiding a circus?"

I was emotionally escalating, again. Just getting started.

"I was told you would tell me what is going on. You haven't. Maybe I will stay here in the flat and let you hang me with that length of rope."

I went into the living room and threw myself on to the couch.

"All I have is hysteria and heartburn, my two good friends ever since I have met you three. Whether I eat enough or wear that get-up or twiddle my thumbs is no matter to me because I don't care."

I had had an episode like this with my grandmother once, only once. I don't even remember what it was about, but the same sentiment was there. I do remember that my meltdown was right before she decided she had had enough of me living with her in Cairo.

The next day she shipped me off to the British boarding school in Alexandria. I had felt a dreadful pang of guilt for having spoken to my grandmother like that. It was a feeling that resurfaced with regularity.

Guilt seems to be a staple in my personal relationships.

Safa, one of my best friends at boarding school, was often the unlucky recipient of some of my guilty deeds. She frequently let me use her schoolwork as my own, but one time, she was accused of just the opposite.

I didn't defend her so she was punished and had to do an extra school assignment over the weekend. It was exactly the weekend her family had me as a guest at their villa on the Mediterranean in El-Arish. While I was frolicking on the beach in the waves and the sand, Safa was hard at her schoolwork. A huge pang of guilt hit me when I complained that Safa wasn't joining me. I was rebuffed by her mother with very curt language. My guilt didn't last, of course, but it was there.

I have always managed to wangle out of tricky situations.

That I am a lucky person, despite some of the truly unlucky things that have happened to me, has struck me more than once.

As I mentioned before, Safa's father, Tarek, carefully watched whenever I was swimming in the strong current of the Mediterranean Sea. One warm evening, after Safa had completed her daily lot of schoolwork, we were having a late dinner on the cozy veranda in the garden which was separated from the street by a low wall. The crescent moon was already high in the sky. The minarets were encircled by stars.

A mother was calling for her son. I can still hear her plaintive wail as she cried his name. The moment she saw us, the mother inquired if we had seen her little boy. Alas, no.

Tarek's wife shook her head with grief. It was a common question apparently. Tarek expressed his regret to the departing mother but then wagged a finger at his wife.

"That's because the parents don't look after their children."

This was, sorry to say, something I was well aware of, but in a different context.

His wife had waggled her head.

"Unluckily, it happens. They think the child is with this person or that person on the beach. Everyone is having fun. They don't keep an eye on the child."

"The child goes into the water, and is swept away," said Tarek as he wagged his finger at me. "No one even notices!"

Safa's father was very much about making life the best for people around him. Group success in Egyptian society is very important. If one person succeeds, everyone succeeds. If one person fails, everyone feels the shame. That concept was never more prevalent than at school.

Luck, some people have it, some people don't.

Some say you make your own luck.

I don't know about that; I guess if you are lucky you can.

I pushed my luck to the outer limit.

I continued wailing, "The hall mistress, Miss Kervan, had a daughter in the British school who was just a bit smarter than a bag of nails. Naturally, to pass the final exam, she needed a lot of help!"

"What?" exclaimed Nancy totally perplexed. "What has that to do with this?"

I wailed even louder, "That's what her classmates were for, but unfortunately, there was a new teacher from England who was supervising the examination. She held the opinion that giving Miss Kervan's daughter thoughtful suggestions for the correct answer was cheating."

"The British…" mumbled Yasser.

"I know! I know. We all felt that the British perception was an outrage and kept the new teacher quite occupied with questions. Those sitting closest to Miss Kervan's daughter gave the correct answers to the girl. She passed with fifty percent, much to the relief of her mother."

Miss Balgrave made a move toward me.

I stepped back, just in case.

I always felt a pang of guilt about the whole thing. Although I was glad no one from my class had failed their examinations, I hadn't really been a team player. When I had the chance to give the daughter some answers, I said I wasn't sure if they were the correct answers and didn't.

It wasn't my fault though, Miss Beatrissa had me on tenterhooks. If I made one more slip up she intimated, she would expel me for good. No cash donation from my grandmother would set it right.

I had the feeling Miss Balgrave, Yasser, and Nancy weren't playing fair.

How could I be a team player if they wouldn't tell me what was going on?

In some strange twisted fashion, my inability to contribute to their lawbreaking made me feel tremendously guilty.

My outburst astonished them, that was for sure.

There was an awkward silence.

"Fine," enunciated Miss Balgrave as she left the room.

I thought she might be going to get her pistol to shoot me dead and put me out of my misery, but instead she returned with a set of the blueprints. She rolled them out on the coffee table.

At first, I believed I was looking upside down at the plans of the Marriott Hotel in Zamalek.

It wasn't the Marriott.

I thought there must be some mistake and nearly blurted out, "Where's the Marriott Hotel? This map is wrong."

This was a disaster for me. What would Omar think of this?

Various locations on the blueprints had been circled to emphasize key sites. The locations were two smaller rooms, one on the first floor, another on the second, and a fairly large area at the back of the building on the second floor.

The newest question was how would I get this information to Omar? The answer was I couldn't.

"First, Amira, we are going to wrap the rope ladder around your body and then cover you with a thin layer of padding. That's in case anyone accidentally bumps you. They will just think you are plump."

"Better to be fat than caught with rope wrapped around your body," I chirped.

Miss Balgrave stopped talking and glared at me. She was probably thinking of how many ways she could kill me.

Yasser jumped in. "Then we will place you in this lovely black robe. You will be transformed into a plump well-endowed wife. You will also wear a scarf around your head and neck to complete the illusion."

Miss Balgrave found her voice. "You will be accompanying your husband, Yasser. You will defer to him in all matters as a dutiful wife should."

It was my turn to stare and be speechless.

"Once inside the building, you will make a direct line for the public washrooms on the second floor. You will find the last stall not only has a toilet but also a broom closet. The lock has been changed. This is the new key for that closet."

Miss Balgrave held up a key.

I was all ears.

"You will leave the abaya and the rope ladders in that broom closet. Lock it. Keep the key. Leave the washroom. You will not rejoin Yasser at this point, but mill about with the crowd inside the museum."

"What are we doing there?"

It still didn't make sense to me.

"I'm getting to that, just listen. Ten minutes before the museum closing time you will go to the utility room on the second floor. It is located here."

Miss Balgrave pointed to a location on the blueprint.

"Do you understand, Amira?"

It took me a minute to orientate myself to the building plan.

"Why don't I just go straight to the utility room? Why all the rigmarole about the abaya and the rope ladders in the closet?

My voice held a note of you-guys-are-all-idiots to it.

It wasn't surprising that Miss Balgrave's reply came back with the same tone.

"You are somewhat noticeable in an abaya among all the pant-loving tourists. You will be a minority in the museum. Just disappearing into the utility room might be noticed."

Miss Balgrave tapped the blueprint.

I dutifully looked and chatted, "Yes, I see the location of the loo and the broom closet. We're going to rob the place of its brooms?"

"She's as dense as they come," interjected Nancy.

"Isn't it obvious what we are doing, Amira," said Yasser.

"It's the coins, isn't it?" I deduced.

I had observed that Miss Balgrave had spent plenty of time staring at the coins in the Egyptian Museum of Antiquities.

"Tut, tut," Miss Balgrave made the strange sounds. "Not the coins."

"The coins are on the first floor," remarked Yasser.

"We are aiming at the second floor," hinted Nancy.

"There are only mummies on that floor, and ..."

I gaped at them.

"That's right," grinned Miss Balgrave.

"You don't mean, King Tut?" I yelped.

My astonishment seemed to delight them.

"Yes, the Tut Ankh Amun exhibit."

I guess they thought they were really clever.

"The stuff weighs a ton!" I exclaimed.

"Not the stuff we're nicking."

CHAPTER FIFTEEN

The objects were priceless. Miss Balgrave had her sights set on the successful theft of selected pieces from the Tut Ankh Amun collection.

"You never wear any jewellery." I gawked at her.

"You don't need to wear it," Miss Balgrave proclaimed, "just possess it."

"Besides, we have eccentric buyers with millions of dollars," Nancy quipped. "They put in their orders."

Miss Balgrave shot her a malicious look. Nancy always did give away too much information.

King Tut Ankh Amun has sparked international fascination since discovery in 1922. Pectorals or chest ornaments, amulets, headdresses. The most famous in the world. The jewellery in the collection is composed of bracelets, earrings and necklaces.

Miss Balgrave was back watching me with her usual hawk-like stare.

"You followed me to the King Tut exhibit, Amira. You have known all along what the target was, haven't you?"

I must be getting better at hiding my emotions because I was totally blown away by their entire scheme. It was a compliment that she thought I had figured out what they were planning.

I hadn't had a clue they were going to rob the King Tut Ankh Amun exhibit in the Egyptian Museum of Antiquities.

"Of course, I did," I asserted. "Right from the start."

I gave her my best your-secret-is-safe-with-me smile.

"So, your emotional outbursts about not knowing what's going on are just an act," Miss Balgrave said.

It was a conclusion, not a question.

She had me there, but I'm quick when it comes to deceit.

Without a blink, I shammed, "Knowing versus being included with knowledge of the details are two different things. I'm still upset, but feeling better about the whole thing."

I wasn't feeling better.

"It's a great choice. Jewellery was worn to increase fertility or prosperity. The colour, material, and shape of the jewellery endowed it with specific magical properties."

I stared straight at Miss Balgrave. Wink. Wink.

She wasn't buying it.

"Jewellery was also a show of wealth and status," I continued, "Like today. You guys can all pretend it's a reward given to you from the Pharaoh. Heck, honorary gold collars and bracelets."

"Even the gods were adorned with jewellery," Nancy chimed in.

Miss Balgrave gave her an irritated look.

What a moron, Nancy.

I continued, "I can tell you know what you are doing since you are all professionals."

They didn't. They were all idiots.

I understood it to be a dreadful plan destined for failure.

I clapped my hands together and inquired, "So, what does the utility room have to do with a jewellery heist?"

Miss Balgrave didn't pursue her argument.

Yasser spoke up, "I have the second key. It is for the utility room. It's a glorified closet, but it will serve its purpose which is to conceal us as the museum shuts down for the night."

"No one is going to check that room? It seems a little lax, if you ask me."

I wasn't impressed.

Miss Balgrave took offense and spoke defensively, "The guard for that section has already been taken into account."

Yasser continued, "The guard has called in sick for today. Painful stomach cramps, apparently."

Nancy chortled, "Steinman's special tea."

They all laughed.

"Once a guard is absent, they don't replace him. Being short staffed already, they just do without. The security is a mix of hired guards and civilian watchmen."

"Surely, there are other guards on that floor? What if one of them decides to be efficient?" I argued.

"That's been taken care of as well. First, the lock to the utility room was changed yesterday. I have the new key. No one else," instructed Yasser. "Second, the guards on that floor are civilian watchmen actually, not hired guards. The civilians have all been offered tickets by Nancy."

"Which they gladly accepted," said Nancy, quite pleased with herself.

"Tickets to what?"

Nancy looked like a student in class who has pinched another student and then points to the girl beside her as the teacher looks to see what's going on. She thought she was being super tricky and was reveling in self-glory.

"It's a special club near the museum. Very exclusive. The strip show has been arranged to start fifteen minutes after the closing of the museum. No latecomers," chortled Nancy.

"Those civilian watchmen won't be doing anything efficiently," laughed Yasser.

"Well, nothing to do with work anyhow," sniggered Nancy. "They will be rushing to get out of the museum."

"What if some of them are not interested?"

I love to play devil's advocate.

"Peer pressure. Even if they don't go, they will be out of the museum. No one is going to check the utility room."

"It's important that you enter the utility room at ten minutes to closing time. The guard watching the internal security monitor will be distracted by Nancy at that time. Tap on the door like this," explained Yasser as he showed me the special knock.

"Seriously? We're doing a special knocking code? Isn't that a little juvenile?" I questioned the tactic.

Yasser shrugged, "Hey, it works."

I figured it could work, but with any heist, especially this one, we would need a fair bit of luck. Miss Balgrave made me repeat the procedure.

"Carry rope ladders into the museum under my flowing black robe. Next, deposit the entire shebang in the bathroom closet on the first floor."

She raised her eyebrows.

I assured her I wouldn't forget to lock the broom closet nor lose the key.

"I pretend to be a tourist until I slip into the utility closet on the second floor."

I gave a smirk.

"I use the coded knock. Yasser is waiting for me."

It occurred to me that having Yasser in an enclosed space all to myself might lead to some extra-curricular activities. I caught his eye, but then I remembered his recent war wounds courtesy of Haima, and figured probably not.

"Make no sound, don't talk, just wait," said Yasser.

I raised both my hands in the air. "Right. The museum closes. We jump out of the closet, grab the loot. Victory!"

I did a little victory dance.

There was unanimous deep breathing from the three of them. When the pause was over, Miss Balgrave spoke.

"You will enter the utility closet. Remain there until four o'clock."

"Four in the morning!" I shouted.

"Stop yelling," insisted Yasser. "Once the guards finish their sweep, the internal visual monitors are switched."

"Super," I said enthusiastically.

"Amira, shut up," snapped Miss Balgrave.

Yasser took a deep breath through his nose. "During the day, the monitors are set for the corridors and the key points in the museum. For the night, the monitors only survey the entrance and emergency exit doors."

"Who is watching the monitors?" I asked.

Yasser laughed. "That's the beauty of it. No one. The monitors just run all night. The tapes are reviewed in the morning."

"The museum's entire security is based on taped recordings from the monitors?"

If I had gone to school in this building instead of the British school in Alexandria, I would have been in a lot less trouble.

"No, the entire system is not based on recordings."

I could tell Miss Balgrave was being very patient with me, but was almost at her limit of tolerance.

"Once the guards leave the first and second floors of the museum and the internal monitors are switched over to exit doors only, the lasers come on. There are sensors every foot horizontally and every two feet vertically."

I interrupted, "So, all the corridors are a grid of laser beams once the museum locks down and the guards have left."

"The alarm sensors are only activated at night," revealed Yasser. "Once the sensors come on, they cannot be shut off without an eleven-digit code which is only known by the director of the museum. Movement will trigger the alarm."

"Accessing the code has proved impossible." That was glum Nancy's contribution from her corner of the living room.

Every time I look at her, especially when she is shrivelled in the corner, her head covered with bandages, and her arm in a sling, I get an irresistible urge to chuckle with satisfaction.

"Oh, don't tell me," I put up my palm to tell them to stop with the explanation. "Yasser and I will exit the utility room and waltz our way to the jewels. Our dance will be carefully choreographed to avoid the lasers, right?"

I was close to hysterics. They all ogled me.

"It's on an automated system for the night?" I asked stifling a bubbling giggle.

I still didn't see how we were going to get out of the closet.

"It is automated," explained Miss Balgrave, "but it shuts off at four in the morning for the cleaning crew."

"That's when we will go to work," declared Yasser.

"What about the cleaning crew?" I asked.

Before they could answer, I continued, "Sure. I know. They would be willing to help us."

I flipped my comment out to the group.

"They won't be in the building," said Miss Balgrave through her teeth.

"Why not? What's to stop them from coming into the museum?"

Miss Balgrave didn't answer my question.

"Enough talk! It's time to get you dressed."

She picked up the black abaya and motioned to me to stand to attention.

The abaya is more than just a preferred choice of clothing. It is a cultural and religious symbol which fits the criteria for the Islamic dress code to cover the entire female body. Traditionally abayas are made from one piece, both for head and the body, going all the way to the floor.

"The body of this garment is separate from the head covering," said Miss Balgrave.

I stood mute.

Abayas can be covered in ornamentation, elaborate, stylish. In turn this style sparks the modesty versus fashion debate. Nowhere is that debate more prevalent than in Europe where freedom of expression is a right. The abaya is a religious and cultural statement, and also a political one.

I found my voice and said, "I recall sitting at a café on a street corner in Europe when two women walked by in the very traditional one-piece abaya. The black garment covered their heads and torso, and then the abaya basically stopped."

I gave a mischievous wink to Yasser.

"It ended just underneath their tush. They had beautiful long slender bare legs finished off with stiletto black patent shoes. It was stunning."

The rebel in me laughed with delight. I wished I had had a camera.

"Shut up Amira," snapped Miss Balgrave.

What was she going to do? Kick me off the team?

I kept talking.

"When I was a child I saw my first sea blue abaya at the main Cairo train station. The woman floated past me with a confidence that I found astounding. She was elegant and stylish. The fabric flowed around her body, her curves. It was also stunning. The traditional black abaya is like a stiff tent, hiding everything. Not that one. Wow."

Miss Balgrave gave a vicious tug on the ropes as she picked them up to twine them around my body.

"The abaya has obviously changed," said Nancy as if I was the dumbest person in the world.

Yasser, Mister Expert in women's dress argued, "Although in Saudi Arabia, all women must wear the abaya in public as a matter of law."

"Reminds me of the book *The Handmaid's Tale* by that Canadian author," I said glad to educate them. "It just came out three years ago. Knocked my socks off as I read it, it did."

Miss Balgrave held up the black abaya she wanted me to wear. Right now.

"Not a fashion statement then," laughed Yasser. "It's definitely a tent."

Nancy moved off her web and scurried over to pick up the rest of the rope ladder. She had a gleam in her eye that bothered me. She moved toward me.

"No way," I hollered.

She stopped.

"Not you," I was emphatic. "You're not touching me. Don't even try."

Yasser interceded. "Give it to me, Nancy."

Her face held the expression of a child denied a special treat. She dropped the rope ladder on the ground and darted back to her chair.

"It's fine Amira," he was doing his best to console me. "You understand what needs to be done. Let's just get on with this."

He picked up the rope ladder.

"I can tell you are truly professionals," I remarked.

Miss Balgrave looked at me with amusement. Why, I do not know. I wished I had a snappy comeback for her too, but I didn't. I was all tongue-tied.

"I'm going to finish wrapping the rope ladder around your body," Yasser replied. "Not too tight. Not too loose."

"Shouldn't I be sitting down?" I questioned his approach.

"How am I going to walk around draped in rope?"

"We're not going to wrap you up like a mummy, Amira."

"Wait," I said.

"What for?" she asked.

"I have to make a trip to the loo."

The moment I returned Miss Balgrave took charge. I was still not convinced about the plan and started to question it.

"You ask too many questions," snapped Miss Balgrave. "Just make it work."

"Hold up your arms," directed Yasser.

He wrapped the rope around my torso, and made one figure eight around my shoulders. Most of the ladder was around my girth.

The second ladder he draped off of the first so that it hung like a long skirt. Then there was a vest of soft padding so if anyone bumped into me, they would just think I was an obese and cuddly wife. It had enlarged my bulk, but the shape was not unbelievable.

Yasser stepped back to survey his work.

"Now for the abaya."

It fit the girth but the length was too long. Nancy, who was supposed to have been wearing it, was quite a bit taller than me.

"I feel like a sumo wrestler," I complained.

"The rope does not show," concluded Miss Balgrave. "No one is going to pat her down."

"What if I'm stopped?"

"I will speak for you," declared Yasser, "as your husband."

"Keep your eyes lowered, Amira," instructed Miss Balgrave.

"What if they pull me aside for a search?"

I wasn't convinced the plan would work.

"I will deal with any situation," asserted Yasser. "As your husband, what I say goes. Follow my lead."

"Yes, follow Yasser's lead by keeping your mouth shut," menaced Miss Balgrave.

She grabbed me by both shoulders and looked me in the eye.

"Do you get it?"

I nodded.

She pulled out the niqab.

"You want me to become Darth Vader?" I sneered.

"Stop being so insolent," Miss Balgrave sneered back at me.

I made a stop sign with my hand. "I'm not covering my face. I'll get claustrophobia or something."

"Fine," she said through clenched teeth. "We'll go with the Hijab."

I was fitted with the Hijab over my head and around my neck. I looked in the mirror.

All black.

It didn't even look like me. Underneath the abaya were the two rope ladders, the padded vest, and me. I had absolutely no confidence that this would work. They must have suspected my inner feelings for Miss Balgrave gave an unexpected pep talk.

"This will work. We know what we are doing, Amira."

I honestly didn't think they did.

Miss Balgrave mistook my silence as a lack of confidence on my part.

"You can do it Amira, don't worry," she reassured.

Her effort at sympathetic consolation was freaking me out. She was like the guidance counsellor at the British school in Alexandria. I couldn't stand the counsellor but had to spend an hour per week with her because Miss Beatrissa deemed it would be good for me. Needless to say, the counselling sessions were a disaster. Stuff like that doesn't work if one party doesn't want to be there.

"What if I freak out? What if I have a panic attack?" It was a real possibility.

There was a long pause.

"Well Amira," warned Miss Balgrave in a tone that told me the next part of the sentence I was not going to like, "if you don't manage to do your part, we will have to make sure you don't play any part. Ever."

"Are you afraid of going to Hell?" sneered Nancy from her cave in the corner.

"It will be fine, Amira," said Yasser trying to counteract the death threats. "Just think of the money you're making."

I doubted I would see any of the money. I didn't want money at this point; I wanted help.

It occurred to me that if I left a note for Omar in the apartment, surely his men would search the flat after we had left with our bags. I couldn't believe the SSIS didn't have at least one of this group under surveillance. The only question was where to stash the note. I smiled at my clever brainwave.

"Why are you smiling?" Nancy asked suspiciously.

"I'm thinking of my next vacation," I retorted. "I'm going to Hell, remember. My grandfather always said if you're going through Hell then you should just keep going."

Miss Balgrave was watching me again with her unwavering stare. I was glad she had stopped the pep talk and was back to normal, but still, I couldn't help wondering what she would do to me if she knew I was working for the State Security Investigations Service.

"It's time to leave," announced Miss Balgrave. "Get your bags. Remember, we won't be coming back."

Yasser was in charge of wiping the place down. A procedure I thought was rather silly. Nancy was in charge of the final check.

I went to my bedroom to get my small bag. I didn't have anything of value; I could have left the bag behind. I only had time to scribble two words on a blank sheet of notepaper, museum and antiquities. I crumpled the paper up tightly into the palm of my hand and walked back to the front door where they were waiting for me.

"I have to go to the loo," I announced.

"Again?" inquired Nancy.

I turned without a word and went into the main bathroom.

Where to put the message?

There was a knock on the bathroom door.

"Give me a minute!" I yelled. "This is tricky with all these ropes around me."

"If you crap on those ropes, I'll kill you," growled Yasser.

"Shut up!" I screamed.

Where could I put the message so it could be found?

Someone was trying the doorknob.

I pulled the chain to flush the toilet.

"Honestly," I said pulling the door open. "It takes time you know."

They were all standing there looking at me.

"Nancy, check the bathroom."

I broke into a sweat. If they were to discover I had left a message for someone, I was dead meat. Nancy looked in all the usual places, the toilet water tank and behind the vanity. She looked at Miss Balgrave and shook her head.

"Have you taken all the garbage from the kitchen?" Miss Balgrave questioned Nancy.

I knew the answer to that one. A resounding NO. Miss Balgrave said it just the way Miss Beatrissa always asked a question when she already knew the answer.

I snickered just loud enough for Nancy to hear, "The maid hasn't done her job."

"Take all the refuse Nancy, even the paper baskets, all the rooms." Miss Balgrave snapped.

Miss Balgrave gave me the same look of disapproval as she pushed me toward the front door.

"We are on a timetable!" Miss Balgrave was getting brusque.

"Got it all," said Nancy as she came to the front door with the garbage bag in her hand.

"All of it?"

"Yes. All the refuse. I emptied every paper trash basket in the flat. There wasn't much."

Through the clear plastic, I saw the crumpled note I had left in plain view in the bathroom paper trash basket.

Now in Nancy's garbage bag.

My heart sank.

CHAPTER SIXTEEN

Eda and Mohatmed were waiting for us at the curb as we emerged from the lobby of the El-Sobki flat. There were no words exchanged but Mohatmed and Eda gave Miss Balgrave curt nods and loaded their two black bags in the boot of the taxi.

We had left our luggage in the lobby for the porter to take to a location unknown to me.

Nancy and Miss Balgrave got in one taxi. Yasser, the boys and I got in the other. Mohatmed was sitting on one side of me, Yasser on the other. They were taking no chances that I might leap out of a moving taxi.

As if.

It gave me quite a feeling of pride though to think they even considered I would be capable of such a masterful feat of prowess.

Eda turned slightly to address Yasser in the back seat, "Keep your wife in line."

I thought he was making a joke, but no one laughed, not even a smile.

I knew we would be driving to Tahrir Square, *Midan el Tahrir,* which by the way is the Arabic word for Liberation Square. Freedom.

Quite ironic for me currently trapped in the back seat of a Cairo taxicab.

I launched into a history lesson to quell my escalating anxiety, like I always do.

"Did you all know that Tahrir Square has quite a history to it. Before the 1952 revolt, a statue of Khedive Ismail, King Farouk's grandfather, had been ordered. In a twist of irony, it arrived shortly after the overthrow of the monarchy. Of course, it never made it to the empty pedestal in the middle of Tahrir Square."

"Nasser left that empty perch untouched for years as a reminder to the populace. It finally came down when the metro station was constructed," Eda finished my spiel with a good solid glare at me.

I guess the reception to my little history lesson about Tahrir Square was mixed.

"You know your history, Amira. Just don't get so wrapped up in it," snarled Eda.

"I thought you might be curious, sir."

"Don't call me sir."

I'll call you anything I like, you old Humar.

"Hey, did you hear the joke about the *Fellaheen* and the donkey that went to get a train ticket?" I twittered nervously.

They all looked at me in amazement, but I kept on going anyway. The knots in the rope dug into my backside. I couldn't sit properly. It was starting to hurt.

"The Fellaheen went to the ticket window to ask how much a ticket cost. The attendant said five piastres for you and twenty piastres for the donkey. When the Fellaheen asked why so much for the donkey, the attendant said that's because the donkey is allowed in first class."

The taxi driver thought it a good joke, laughed heartily, and encouraged me to tell another.

Before anyone could stop me, I continued, "There was a *Fellaheen* who was waiting for a train. Another man came up to him and asked him what was in the sack he was carrying. The *Fellaheen* replied there were geese in the sack and added he would give both of them to the man if he could guess how many were in the sack. The man replied three."

The taxi driver hit the steering wheel with his hands. He was truly enjoying himself now.

"Enough!" Eda barked.

We nearly swerved off the road.

"You idiot, *Fellaheen, Ya Humar!*" Eda was bellowing at the taxi driver who was going the wrong way.

The driver had taken an off ramp. Once you are on one of those, it takes you forever to circle back and get on your route again.

And we were on a timetable.

The driver slammed on the brakes, right in the middle of the off ramp. He started backing up. I could see his crazed eyes in the rearview mirror as he floored the gas pedal.

Eda, Mohatmed, and Yasser started screaming, but it was too late. In panic they waved their arms out the side windows for the cars behind us to get out of the way.

The taxi driver swerved and curved his way back up to the main road. It must have been a good hundred metres.

What a feat!

Not a car had been hit.

Back on the main strip, the taxi driver slammed it into drive and sped down the road.

Everyone in the taxi was speechless.

The driver dropped Yasser and me off at the main Cairo train station by the colossus of Ramses the Great. I wondered if Eda was going to tip the driver.

Maybe not.

I looked to the Ramses statue to give me comfort, as I was a little rattled. A tourist bus blocked the departing taxi long enough for me to hear Eda tell the driver to go to the Nile Ritz Carlton hotel. Hmm, not the Egyptian Museum of Antiquities, but the hotel kitty-corner to it?

What was up with that?

Yasser took my hand and pulled me toward the train station.

"Stop, stop," I hissed at him loudly.

"What's the matter?"

He was swearing under his breath.

"I'm fat remember! I can't walk that fast!"

Indeed, I couldn't. With the rope and the vest around my torso I was having a hard time breathing. The rest of the rope skirt kept slipping between my legs underneath the abaya.

Besides I wasn't sure I wanted to do this.

"It's sacrilege," I grumbled. "It's just wrong to use this dress as a disguise. It's meant to be honoured Yasser. I'm not…"

Yasser ducked down in the crowd, pulled his jacket off and placed a cap on his head. As he stood up again, he grabbed my arm and steered me back to the taxi stand.

We got another taxi and made our way to the Egyptian museum.

"What was all that change of attire for?" I puffed. "You really think you look that different?"

"Just making sure, that's all," he exhaled noisily. "You do your part Amira. You don't have much of a choice."

If Omar Mohammed's crew had been tailing us, they certainly weren't any more. That stunt with the taxi driver on the off ramp had certainly shaken off any surveillance.

I was definitely on my own.

Yasser was getting nervous I could tell. The last thing I wanted was to have him screw up, Miss Balgrave blame me and put a bullet in my head. I patted his hand and smiled with my eyes. I didn't let the taxi driver see though; it would have been unseemly.

The time schedule had been to leave the Heliopolis flat by three o'clock to make our way down to the museum. Entrance into the Egyptian Antiquities Museum always generates a fervour before its scheduled closing time at six o'clock. As the hour approaches, there are a fair number of people desperate to get in before it shuts.

Today was no exception. Tahrir Square was packed. The roads leading into it were backed up to and past the Egyptian Museum of Antiquities.

Yasser made sure the taxi dropped us off at the museum as close as possible considering how difficult it was for me to walk in this get-up. We had to have bought our tickets and be inside the museum before the last call, which was at a quarter to five.

We had left the flat late. The time was now close to half past four. Yasser couldn't stay with me. I was moving too slow.

"I'm going to go ahead and get into the ticket line," he decided abruptly.

"Good idea," I replied.

He leaned over and whispered into the area where my ear was on the other side of the black Hijab, "Wouldn't it be funny to see Eda and Mohatmed here?"

I gave him a sick smile.

Well played you bastard.

He knew the possibility of meeting the terror twins would keep me moving toward the museum entrance, just in case I had any further thoughts of ducking out.

I played the part of a submissive wife to perfection. Yasser obtained two tickets, one minute before the last entry time, and guided his dear wife into the grand hall.

I thought I was going to collapse either from anxiety or from the immense relief of finally being inside the museum The closet in the public toilet was on the first floor. I made a beeline for it, a big fat bumble beeline.

I was expecting to go directly into the public restroom and go straight to the toilet stall with the closet in it. My expectation of an easy access to the public restroom was thwarted at every turn. First, I kept tripping over the abaya and had to remember to hike it up as I walked.

Second, when I finally got to the restroom, I discovered there had been a problem. The janitor had been called to mop up. The closed sign hanging on the door made my heart stop. As I stood there waiting, numerous museum guides kept coming up to me to suggest using the public restroom on the second floor.

All the while I was wondering if I should save myself?

What would the guards think if I told them my story?

I ran the scenario in my head. There was a good chance they wouldn't believe me. After all, I was wrapped up in rope ladders and a vest. They wouldn't see a victim. They would see a woman wrapped in contraband and call it intent.

Would they even contact Omar Mohammed or just throw me straight into prison?

I had an overwhelming feeling of being ensnared. I just wanted to be left alone and stood silent with my eyes staring at the floor.

At long last, the janitor sign was removed. Everyone who was waiting could go in. There were only five toilet stalls in the restroom. I was in a very long lineup. This posed numerous problems, the most obvious being that I had to gauge when my stall would be vacant so that I would be next in line for it.

It wasn't as easy as you might think. I kept letting women go ahead of me. Then I missed my chance when a woman cut into the line, so I had to let a bunch of women go ahead of me again. By the time I actually managed to enter the correct stall with the broom closet, I had caught the attention of the restroom attendant which was the last thing I wanted.

My hands were slippery with sweat. I could barely close the latch on the stall door. I took a minute to calm myself. The first thing I did was pull off my Hijab. The air in the bathroom was stifling hot.

But even that was a relief compared to having my head and neck wrapped in black cloth. My hair was plastered down on my skull. The perspiration ran into my eyes. Next, I yanked up the abaya to pull it over my head. I had the bottom part over my head and my arms halfway out of the sleeves when I got stuck.

"Breathe Amira, just breathe," I whispered to myself.

I tried to pull my arms further out of the sleeves but they wouldn't budge; my sweat was making them stick to the fabric. And with the sleeves turned inside out I had trouble figuring out where the sleeve opening was.

After a long battle, I got one hand back out through the sleeve and reached around the back to try to feel what the abaya was stuck on. I was doing all this in the dark too, because half of the abaya was over my head.

Don't cry Amira, don't cry.

I was close to tears. I'm sure I was making small moaning noises as I tried to extricate myself from the garment.

I rubbed my back against the wall in the hope of moving the fabric over the padded vest and the rope knots.

Eventually it worked but not without making significant grunting noises.

I lifted the abaya over my head.

I was spent.

My back and neck hurt from the contortions; my shoulders were raw. The attendant had come to the stall door and asked if I was all right.

Mahlish, Mahlish.

"No problems," I said.

Compared to getting the abaya off, the removal of the ropes was not difficult, only time consuming. Yasser and Miss Balgrave had wrapped the ladders around my body and where more support was needed, to keep the rope from slipping down, had tied them together with extra twine but now there was just me to undo it all.

They had made sure any extra twine used to keep the ropes in place was always on my front side. I managed, but it took time like I said.

A lot of time.

I was still untying the ropes when I heard the chimes for the closing of the museum. The first warning comes twenty minutes to six o'clock.

I had ten minutes to get to the utility room on the second floor which seemed like it was a mile away.

"Concentrate, Amira. It's okay." I whispered to myself.

Where was the key to the broom closet in my toilet stall?

I will confess that for a brief moment I just couldn't remember what I had done with it. It wasn't in my pants pockets, nor on a chain around my neck. Then I remembered I had stuck it down my sock.

I heard the second warning which comes at fifteen minutes to six o'clock.

Five minutes to my rendezvous time.

A momentary distraction occurred due to an argument in the restroom. I peered through a slit in the stall wall and saw the attendant quarreling with a tourist. Apparently, it was about *Baksheesh.* The attendant was complaining about the amount. The tourist was obviously not interested in parting with more money.

During the clash between the attendant and the tourist, I flushed the toilet numerous times to conceal the noise of putting the abaya and the rope ladders in the closet.

Lock the closet.

Miss Balgrave's voice rang in my ears. I did.

Then I realized I had another problem. I could see via the slit in the stall divider that the attendant was the same attendant who had been in the restroom when I had entered. I had been in the stall forever. She would certainly notice that a woman in traditional garb had gone into the stall and that a woman in Western wear was coming out.

There was no longer anyone in the public restroom except the two of us.

I waited.

She waited.

I could see she was getting impatient. She looked at her watch. She looked at the exit door.

The third warning chime sounded. It was now ten minutes to six.

This is it. It's over.

This is how I go down, in the loo.

It was now or never. I moved my hand to undo the latch of the stall door just as another female attendant pushed open the outer restroom door and yelled to her friend to come on!

My attendant gestured toward my stall to which her friend basically told her who cares, let's get going, the workday is over. It wasn't actually over until the end of their shift at six o'clock but I prayed for youthful indiscretion to kick in.

It did, helped by the coins of *Baksheesh* I tossed her way from under the stall door. No sooner was she out of the restroom than I was out of the stall. I pulled open the door to the hall and glanced back at my toilet stall.

The black hijab on the floor. Damn!

I had forgotten to shove it into the closet with the rope.

I looked at the hall.

Back at the hijab.

No time. Out into the hall I went.

I couldn't run, too obvious, but I could speed walk, only slightly less obvious. I rushed to the grand staircase, praying again that my memory of the blueprint served me right.

The utility room should be on the right, about halfway down the hall once I reached the second floor.

A guard stopped me.

He gestured at his watch. There were only five minutes left before closing. I burst forth with an explanation that I had left my bag at an exhibit and would only be two minutes.

I was so agitated that he let me pass.

No doubt he had Nancy's strip club pass in his pocket and didn't want to deal with me.

If I had had to repeat the secret knock twice, I would have screamed and given the whole thing away, but I didn't

Yasser opened the utility room door on my last tap.

"Where the hell?" he hissed at me.

I fell into the utility room. He shut the door quietly behind me. There was a transom window in the room, way up high. Through its dirty dusty glass it let in a vague filtered light.

"What the hell?" I exclaimed.

"Quiet," Yasser shushed and slapped me across my shoulder.

I'd been staring at the third person in the utility room. I turned back to Yasser. My eyes were popping out of my head.

I hissed like an Egyptian snake, "Steinman? Steinman's in here too?"

"You knew Steinman was going to be here, Amira," Yasser was totally exasperated.

"What?" I cursed, took a step backwards. "Ah!"

I had completely forgotten that fact. It was a dreadful shock to be reminded.

Steinman loomed before me and put a finger to his lips.

"Shh."

Then the panic of being in an enclosed space with the bad-tempered beast hit me.

"What! Not on your life."

I made a mad dash to get out of the utility closet.

Yasser grabbed me by the arm and yanked me back.

"It's too late Amira."

Steinman's bulk loomed in front of me. The look on his face said shut up or I will knock you senseless.

I threw myself down on a sack of dirty linen sheets. Dust and dirt flew up from the brown sack. You would have thought the bag had come straight from the Sahara. I could hardly see and started to wheeze and gasp as the dust settled into my throat.

Steinman shoved a bottle of water into my hand. I guzzled the entire bottle. After the air had cleared, I peered at Yasser who was standing behind Steinman. Yasser just shrugged his shoulders and sat down on the floor.

Steinman was obviously listening to the happenings outside the room. No doubt he was trying to gauge if my spectacular entrance had been noticed.

Nancy was also in the museum building, and had called in a few favours to get into the security room. Her responsibility was to keep the guard from observing the internal monitor located outside the utility room. Let's just say that she must have had to do quite a bit of talking to keep that guard's eyeballs off the screen since I had arrived at least ten minutes late.

Yasser whispered to Steinman, "Nancy knows her job. The guards would have come by now if they had seen us enter the utility room. They don't know we are here."

It was well past six o'clock now, so those monitors should have switched to the exit and entrance door circuits.

Steinman nodded and motioned to Yasser to stop talking.

I had left the hijab on the floor of the loo. It was all I could think about. Although we had made it into the utility room undetected, I couldn't help noticing that so many things had already gone wrong. The timing seemed to be totally off. They had totally miscalculated the difficulty I had with getting the rope ladders off my body and into the restroom closet.

Where was the key for the closet?

In a startled action I looked in my sock.

Nope.

I jumped up. My pant pockets.

Nope.

Where was it? My shirt pocket?

Yes. The sigh I let out could have sailed a Felucca across the Nile River at breakneck speed.

Steinman loomed up before me.

He didn't say a word. He didn't have to speak.

I silently sat down, slowly.

My eyes wandered around the utility room. In the dim light, I could see there were lots of places where Steinman could stuff my dead body after he had done the deed.

It was getting quite dark in the utility room which only made that line of murderous thinking worse.

The evening darkness came quickly and was a fact of science that confused me when I first came to Egypt as a child. I was under the impression that Egypt was closer to the equator, the fatter part of the earth, the bulge, and therefore would be closer to the sun. To me, closer to the sun meant more sunlight, more daytime sunlight.

In Canada, we had lovely long summer evenings. The further north you travel, the longer the summer days. It's wonderful to have daylight until nine or even ten o'clock at night. I was expecting that in Egypt.

I thought Canadian hot summer days and long nights would be paralleled in Egypt which was even hotter and therefore would have even longer summer days.

How wrong I was.

It was such a disappointment to find out that the light and dark were basically fifty fifty. Around six in the morning the sun rose. Around six in the evening it was setting. There was a definite day and night with only a slight difference in sunrise and sunset during the summer months.

We sat quietly in the utility room for about an hour. Obviously, we couldn't turn on the electric light, but the city outside the transom window sent a yellow beam through the high window. I couldn't believe I was actually in the museum's utility room with two men waiting for four o'clock in the morning to arrive.

Every thirty minutes, I made a point of standing up, moving around, and stretching. We had been in the closet for three hours. There hadn't been a peep from the other side of the door.

"So far, all of this is about me carrying rope into the Egyptian Museum of Antiquities and locking myself into a closet with you two?"

The sketchy plan dubbed a jewellery heist was incredulous.

I know jewellery is no less important today than it was two thousand years ago, but honestly. I wished I had a piece of jewellery around my neck to protect me from what I felt was imminent disaster.

My grandmother had an astonishing collection of jewellery, but she only ever wore one piece a day. Any more than that she said would be ostentatious. It would deprive yourself of the chance to be the star, the personality that people should really see.

My grandmother had a funny mixture of wise encouraging advice for me — matched by an unfiltered regular, and at times, harsh criticism. I hoped she loved me as much as I loved her.

"Who came up with this plan?" I demanded to know.

Steinman looked at me like he would like to hang me.

At the time, it didn't occur to me to ask about the twins and their explosives. I was so stressed. I could only focus on one thing, which was that I was in the utility room closet with Yasser and Steinman.

When one of the teachers at the British School in Alexandria threw my notebooks out the window, it was all I could think about for days after; in four seconds, I had watched an entire year's work go out the window.

I had been particularly truculent towards the teacher the day of the launching of my schoolwork. I guess he was fed up with me too. My classmates all gasped at the teacher's actions and watched as my notebooks wafted through the air, out the window. They floated down, down, down into the dirt below the classroom window.

In defiance, I threw my pencils out the window too. The point about this tale is that stress makes you do the oddest things.

I must have dozed off in the utility room for a bit, because I woke with a start at the sound of a collision on the road immediately outside the utility room window. Yasser came over to reassure me like I was his best friend. If I messed up,

Steinman would leave me dead on the floor at the feet of my favourite pharaoh, Akhenaton.

I asked Yasser what time it was. He replied it was nearly eleven o'clock. What was Omar Mohammed doing now?

Why had I assumed so definitely that the blueprint was the Marriott in Gezira, the two-story neo-classical building?

I now understood my mistakes. The 'M' on the blueprints had stood for museum, not Marriott. The 'G' had probably been the name of the Italian construction company, Garozzo Zaffarani.

The words neo-classical, which is the term for the Marriott architectural style, had in fact been Beaux Arts neo-classical and referred to the Museum of Antiquities. I had only seen the last part, neo-classical.

I had made totally wrong conclusions from the partial information. I was convinced the plan was a political attack and had seen all my discoveries in that light.

Ahh! What was potentially worse, was I was sure that I had convinced Omar of it too.

Being in the closet with Steinman was like the time I went swimming in the Suez Canal.

A mistake.

I had made a trip to see friends who lived in a town on the canal. We all thought it would be rather cool to swim in the Suez. It wasn't far to go and there was no one else there.

While I was in the water, I noticed I had black spots on my newly purchased swimsuit. Raw petroleum. It's the same kind of ruinous spot on my life that had been left on me since I first met Steinman.

The bathing suit was ruined; those stains would never come out of the fabric. As I stood there in the canal commiserating over the death of my swimsuit, an oil tanker slipped by.

I'm not sure how such a massive tanker could have snuck up on me, but it was at such close range as to be unexpectedly overwhelming.

The ugly thing loomed over me as I stood in the water.

It was an ominous hideous thing.

Steinman's presence was just like that tanker.

After my friends and I left the Suez Canal, we drove through the town where the bullet holes from the war with Israel were still visible on the walls of the buildings.

The trauma of the war loomed, in the same way Steinman's presence did; there was evidence of damage already inflicted.

Moreover, just being in a locked utility room for hours would have been bad enough, never mind being in there with an attack dog like Steinman. I looked at the exit door with trepidation. My thinking was snowballing, but honestly, I couldn't stop it.

What was on the other side of the door?

I had had this same intense feeling at a friend's place in Mansoura. My friend had travelled from Canada to work with the city's agricultural sector as a development project supervisor. The Canadian company sold agricultural water towers and pumps. Specifically, his job was to supervise the installation.

Unfortunately for one development site near Mansoura, the Egyptians had attempted to put the tower up without any consultation. They constructed a tower of sorts, but it was upside down.

No matter. My friend just had them take it down and build it again.

It had been lovely to be with a Canadian friend but what wasn't great about that stay with my friend was not the work he was doing but where he lived.

Ah, yes. The door...

The house was right beside a steel mill. I mean right beside. If you looked out the window you could see the pistons and arms of the machines moving literally inches from the window. If you were in the flat during the day, everything rattled.

And then there was the front door.

What was on the other side of the door you ask?

The only entry door to the house was covered with hundreds of flies. No matter what my friend did, he couldn't get rid of the flies. He would have to stomp on the landing, hit the door. Hard. Just to get them off for a second so we could scoot inside.

We had to do the same maneuvers to get out of the house. After a while it wasn't a question of what was on the other side, but how many.

The hundreds of flies on the door trapped us inside with no hope of ever opening the door. We would be consumed. The mill next door made the place feel like we were in total warfare.

The parameters of the visit were totally unexpected.

Once inside the house, I was in circumstances that were unavoidable.

That was what I felt like in the utility room.

Around midnight, I fell asleep from sheer exhaustion and had a dream about Omar and the SSIS. It was no wonder considering the situation I was in.

In my dream, I had a complete feeling of having done a good job. But then again, I am not the best with self-assessment even in a dream.

Nevertheless, Omar seemed pleased. I reminded him this wasn't my regular profession. I'm an artist at heart, even in my dreams. I spoke to him on the phone. He agreed it was time I went home, to where I truly belonged.

Dreams kinda jump around, so the next scene is an hour later. A car is waiting in the street. I have to go down the stairs to the street but I don't have any luggage. That's not a problem. It's strange how some dreams can be so vivid.

I climbed into the back seat and lay down on the soft black leather upholstery.

"That's gratitude for you," I said. "What a beautiful car."

I was asleep before the car hit the road heading out of Cairo. When the car slowed down, I woke up. It was about two hours later.

Next, I am watching myself in the dream, an out of body experience. I see myself sit up in the car, trying to focus, trying to come out of the hazy just got-up state.

I can see we are in the desert, not home. Definitely not home.

The driver speaks as he looks at me via the front mirror, "Welcome home to the place you belong, ma'am."

The car had stopped in front of Building Number Four.

CHAPTER SEVENTEEN

It was now approaching two o'clock in the morning. If you've ever thought about spending time in a utility closet with two men, don't do it.

If you want to have everything you think, every idea you have ever had, every behaviour you have ever engaged in challenged, and I mean scrutinized, then go live in Egypt. There, they do things differently.

For example, Egyptians may not follow procedure or do things the way they are done in England, Canada or Europe but for Egypt and Egyptians, it works.

This fact is not appreciated by everyone.

My grandmother had an estate in the delta. It was a large house with a vast expanse of lawn behind it. I say lawn but in truth, it was dirt which happened to sprout two-foot-high grass stalks after the gardener had decided to flood the area with water.

The momentous day to cut this lawn came. For that express purpose my grandmother decided to purchase a sit-down mower.

I was on the roof of my grandmother's house with two other girls, a visiting friend from England and my best friend, who was Egyptian, to watch the event.

It was immediately clear the gardener was having a marvelous time with the mower. He carefully started the machine and revved the motor. Then he drove it around the field but didn't mow anything down. It was like he was laying out his plan of attack. Abruptly he made a sharp turn and purred down the edge of the grass in a perfectly straight line. Making a wide turn in the dirt patch, he came back alongside his first strip of mowed lawn to make another perfectly straight line.

My British friend beside me nodded with approval.

Then an odd thing happened. Out of the blue, the gardener decided to veer off course and go across the field on a diagonal.

What the heck?

He gave up on straight lines altogether and started to drive through the tall grass in amazing circular motions. He spun, turned and curved his way all over that lawn.

I laughed with delight. What a free spirit!

My English friend was scandalized by the gardener's behaviour and remarked it was typically Egyptian.

Insult noted.

My Egyptian friend was scandalized by my English friend's comment, and stated the gardener had done a marvelous job. She immediately went home, declining to stay for tea with my visiting friend from England.

The reason for my dear Egyptian friend's departure was that she thought my visitor was typically British.

Insults exchanged.

Another time this basic life difference was made clear to me was on a trip to Greece when my grandmother and I met three brothers who had married two Greek sisters and one British lady. The sisters' names were Athena and Persephone. The British lady was called Trudy. I always thought that was the type of name you give to the neighbourhood wandering cat you don't particularly like.

My grandmother and I were at an afternoon hotel party in Corinth. She naturally began conversing about where we had lived and so on. We learned that the three men had worked in Tanta, Egypt, on the railway as engineers about twenty years ago.

Two of the brothers, the two who had married the Greek sisters, spoke about their experience with fond memories. The other British fellow, Trudy's husband, found the lack of following proper procedure not only a disgrace but an absolute immorality. The indiscriminate starting times in the morning for example, the Mediterranean influence was how he termed it, was equally debauched.

He was so agitated by his recollections of his previous way of life that he had to leave the party. His brothers just shrugged at his departure; his Greek sisters-in-law smiled knowing smiles, and his poor wife looked distressed.

You see, there are differences. People do things differently. Next you're going to expect me to say we are all the same at heart, just one big happy family.

Not in this utility closet we weren't.

I checked the time. It was twenty minutes after two o'clock. As the minutes in the utility room dragged on, I tried to concentrate on being more Mediterranean than British or Canadian for that matter. Canada is part of the British Commonwealth so there is a bit of association going on there. I needed to shrug things off.

"I'm getting claustrophobia," I announced.

Steinman made a noise. "No, you're not," he argued.

"I have an excessive fear emerging about this confined space. I can feel it!"

"I'll make you feel an even smaller space," he informed me. "Would a coffin do?"

I started dry heaving, and felt dizzy.

"Give her some water, Yasser. Get her up and moving around."

"Look out the window, Amira."

It was more like looking at a foggy escape hatch.

"When do we get out of here?" I whined.

"Five minutes after four. After it's done," said Yasser.

"After what's done?"

It was more of a demand on my part than a question.

"Why? What's going to happen? What else haven't you told me about this plan?"

There was an awkward pause, but it didn't take Yasser long to figure out that he had better tell me.

"The cleaning crew usually comes in at four o'clock. The surveillance system is automated. It shuts down for one hour from four to five o'clock."

"There is no electronic security for that hour?"

"Correct."

"Unbelievable. What is to stop the cleaners from lifting every priceless object?"

I was thinking of applying for the job.

"They all enter and exit through one door. Each person is thoroughly checked. They even have to change their garments. The clothes they wear to clean the museum stay in the building."

Yasser shrugged and continued, "It works. They are short-staffed. For this type of security, they only need a couple of guards at the doors."

Steinman was watching me thoughtfully.

"What else? There is something else," I probed. "The cleaners are not just going to stand by and let us steal Tut Ankh Amun's treasures."

"We have to stop the cleaning crew," Steinman said.

I was aghast and exclaimed, "You mean we are going to shoot them?"

Steinman was clearly irritated and snapped, "No, you didn't let me finish. We have to stop them from coming into the building."

"We are in the building or hadn't you noticed? How are we going to stop them from coming into the museum?"

Yasser let out a long slow breath.

"It's a job for Eda and Mohatmed."

"You mean, they are going to shoot them?"

"Nobody is shooting anybody, Amira," Steinman clipped out his retort.

I wasn't so sure about that. I would have bet Steinman would shoot me if he had a chance.

"The chocolates."

The light finally dawned on me about what Eda and Mohatmed were actually going to do.

"They're using the explosives, right?"

Yasser nodded and said, "It's just a diversion. No one is going to get hurt."

I had a hard time believing that.

"Where?"

"The Nile Ritz Carlton. There will be enough of a distraction to worry the officials. The explosion is timed just before the cleaning crew is set to arrive at the museum. Procedures indicate the area will be contained. The cleaners will not be allowed to pass because the blast is so close to the hotel. Their usual route into the museum is the walkway and the entry door facing the Nile Ritz Carlton hotel. That area will be cordoned off."

"A bombing is not a distraction. It is an act of terror," I disputed their logic.

Steinman shrugged and mumbled, "Perception."

I glared at him. I sincerely hated the man.

"Think of the chocolates," he sniggered. "It's like a cooking lesson. We will be making chocolate souffle."

I didn't think he was funny at all.

"The automated system will continue its routine. The museum will be ours for one hour."

"Are you sure?" I asked.

Yasser tilted his head and laughed, "Hey, everyone loves a good fire. They're Egyptians; they will run to help. They won't be thinking about the Museum. They have already done their checks."

Yasser was in charge of gathering the selected jewels. Once we had our plunder, we would do the acrobatic climbing ladder stunt out the transom windows by the Tut Ankh Amun exhibit.

"As soon as we have made our escape via the rope ladders, we will meet Eda and Mohatmed who will be waiting at the end of the alley in a white van."

"They are just going to be allowed to wait there? That seems a bit much," I guffawed.

"The second explosion will go off at 4:48. It will give us the cover we need to make it to the van and down the Nile corniche for one kilometre to the wharf where a boat will be waiting to take us all down the Nile."

Plenty of loopholes in the plan. It was ridiculous.

I tried to control my breathing and relax, all the while knowing it was impossible. I would need plenty of luck to get through this escapade.

By three o'clock in the morning, I was sure all my luck had fled. I was so uptight that my eyeballs felt like they were permanently cross-eyed. Seriously, I don't know how much longer I could have lasted in there.

I thought about Omar's threats and how I hadn't spoken with him recently. I thought about the SSIS which I hadn't seen hide nor hair of for days. It was so frustrating that I started to count down the seconds and minutes just to keep myself occupied. At this point, Yasser and Steinman were just trying to ignore me.

Finally, the time arrived.

The first explosion went off at 3:30. It was the first thing in this cockamamie plan that was on time. In the utility closet, there were audible sighs of relief from the three of us as we made eye contact.

The next thirty minutes were filled with a hub of activity outside the museum. The response teams were set in place. They secured a wide area around the Ritz Carlton hotel which included the surrounding buildings.

It did prevent the cleaners from coming any place close to the museum. No doubt the guards at the doors who usually let the cleaners in, were more interested in what was happening outside the museum than what was going to happen inside.

Outside was a measured response. Inside the museum routine continued.

I was on the verge of physical collapse from the anticipation when Yasser spoke to me. It was exactly four o'clock.

"Why would I want to catch a cat?" I replied.

What a stupid thing for Yasser to say.

"What?" Yasser was gaping at me.

"You said go and catch a cat."

Yasser looked at me with exasperation.

"Amira, I said pull the latch back. You know, the latch on the door of the utility room?"

I was a little embarrassed, but I had been in that damn room for ten hours.

We crept out of the utility room into the wide hallway. I was totally disoriented that I was in the huge lofty space of the museum once again.

I really must have thought I would never make it out of the utility room alive. I dropped to the floor to steady myself. I felt like I had just descended from an alien planet.

"What are you doing?" exclaimed Yasser.

"Just give me a minute!"

Stop pressuring me.

He sounded like my friend at school when we were breaking into Miss Beatrissa's flat while she was away in Cairo. I can only accomplish so much under pressure.

It was now the 13th day after picking up Miss Balgrave from the Tel Aviv airport. My lucky thirteenth day, the morning of the Tut Ankh Amun heist.

"Now where are you going?" hissed Yasser. "You're going the wrong way. The broom closet is in the bathroom on the first floor!"

"I have to go to this bathroom!" I hissed back. "I've been in a utility closet all night."

Indeed, I wasn't sure I would even make it to the second-floor bathroom.

"Don't flush, it will make too much noise," said Steinman.

I shot Steinman a withering look. Seriously? Now the man was going to be a comedian?

I quipped, "That's important because?"

Steinman disappeared into the recesses of the museum as I ran for the second-floor bathroom.

Every minute was important. Due to my bathroom detour, I was now behind time, again.

The wide stone staircase down to the first floor held a dream like quality to it, belonging to a life beyond. I ran down to the first floor, past all the marvels, sights, imprints, gestures and faces of masterpieces carved in stone.

I had been to the Egyptian Museum so many times that even in the eerie light of the occasional pot light the artifacts and statues were familiar to me. I was filled with a sense of no longer being modern or remote from my heritage but alive and no longer oppressed. The ancient Egyptians of the museum were beautiful in their stillness. It was a marvelous sensation.

I burst into the public restroom on the first floor and was dismayed. It was pitch black. I didn't have a flashlight. It hadn't occurred to me that those dim little security pot lights wouldn't be on in the restrooms. Obviously, it hadn't occurred to anyone else either. The cleaning crew must flip on the regular lights. It was a move I figured wouldn't be a wise one. I'd have to blindly find my way to the closet in the toilet stall.

My greatest fear is that I will one day go blind.

I have no basis for this fear. I just think it would be the worst thing that could happen to me.

My grandmother always liked to be prepared. It's a quality or a vice, I suppose it depends how you look at it, which she instilled in me. I would, therefore, pretend I was blind by closing my eyes and feeling my way around the flat or house or wherever we currently were residing. It was in preparation for my inevitable blindness and became a sort of game I regularly played.

Because I felt I was being proactive, it helped me calm my fears about the future.

I was perfectly at home navigating through the restroom in absolute darkness. The only problem was this would take a lot more time compared to just walking into a perfectly lit room. I could picture the layout of the room in my mind and located the closet. I even found the hijab I had left on the floor which was lucky because I could have slipped on it.

I fished out the key from my shirt pocket.

Don't drop it, Amira. Don't drop it.

That's not part of the plan.

I didn't, but it wouldn't fit. I tried again and again.

Why wouldn't it go in the lock?

It's upside down, you idiot!

The rope ladders tumbled out and I dragged them behind me like a dead carcass.

"Where have you been?" Yasser exclaimed. "I thought you had blacked out or something."

I didn't bother to explain.

The moonlight was wafting through the high windows.

I imagined my grandmother and grandfather, and how they belonged to a different age. Yet, they had instilled in me a pride of a glorious heritage. The ancient land of Egypt is a land and a time seeped in mystery and myth. It is a land bounded by a gold scarab at the threshold of the world, by a sphinx at the threshold of death.

It is land that has been navigated by human inhabitants and Gods of an ancient culture. The fertile serpent breathed life into the land.

I hesitated.

"What are you doing now?" asked Yasser hurriedly.

The sporadic pot lights of the museum created a twilight. I was transported back in time.

The creations in the museum spoke over the centuries without words through a piece of fabric, a comb, a spoon. The countless objects told the narrative of the daily routine of a people I seemed to be in the presence of their religion, their myths, their anguish and wisdom — the soul of the people.

"There's someone else here," I whispered.

I could feel them.

"There is no one here, but us. Move on!"

Yasser grabbed me by the arm to get me going.

We covered the rest of the distance in silence.

There it was, the Tut Ankh Amun exhibit and in front of me was the Jewel of the Nile. The gold diadem of Tut Ankh Amun is the only one of its kind, incomparable and irreplaceable, a multi-coloured masterpiece.

The gold crown encircled the sacred head of the golden boy giving him the protection he would need on his journey into the afterlife. On the crown rests the vulture and the cobra.

The vulture representing Nekhbet protected Upper Egypt. The cobra, the goddess Wadiet, ruled over Lower Egypt. The eyes of the vulture are obsidian, a volcanic glass, the rest is solid gold. The cobra's head and hood are inlaid with lapis lazuli, faience, glass and carnelian inlay. Its long serpentine tail is curved to fit over the head.

The papyrus flowers on either side are made of malachite and the knob at the back of the diadem is of chalcedony. Together the vulture and the cobra protected not only the entirety of Egypt, but the King himself.

They were the magical protectors and Tut Ankh Amun's royal symbols of absolute power and divine authority.

The piece is extraordinary, an exceptional priceless artifact.

We were going to steal it.

Standing in front of the Jewel of the Nile was like having a thousand invisible doors open all at the same time. The diadem whispered intimate secrets to me.

The soul can only be nurtured with pure art.

Yet, how many people had stood where I now stood and merely saw its monetary value?

The deception sears the soul.

"Where's Steinman?" I asked.

He had disappeared immediately after we had emerged from the utility closet.

"He's gone to get the packing case."

"The what?"

"We need to pack the items, Amira. We can't risk damaging them," Yasser's voice was escalating with frustration. "Stop talking. I have to concentrate."

Each display section in the museum had pot lights illuminating the area, but they were so far apart the shadows created difficulties. It was up to Yasser to get into the display cases to steal the particular items we were after. In addition, the individual exhibits were not wired for security. Each collection was surrounded by four glass panels and one glass panel on top for easy viewing.

"What are you going to break the glass with?" I asked.

I wanted to appear co-operative and all on board, even though I still felt sick with apprehension.

Steinman arrived on the scene.

"Use Amira's head to break the glass," Steinman's voice was low, but it had an edge to it.

Wow. He was getting really funny.

I moved toward the glass case and gave one of the panels a good sharp tap with my finger.

Nothing. I tried again, harder, but it held firm. Steinman muttered something about tools. Yasser slid a thin wedge from his pocket. Slowly, carefully, they eased the panel free.

The glass just fell back into the case and smashed into pieces.

Well, that was easy.

Yesterday morning, Mohatmed had delivered the case in a cardboard box labelled with the words 'Jewel of the Nile'. In the Museum basement where the deliveries arrive, they never get to things right away. It's a maze of incoming artifacts, current artifacts, and I suspect, junk. Boxes sit there for days before anyone even notices. Steinman had easily located Mohatmed's delivery, one of the more recent boxes.

I looked at the hard black case Steinman had placed on the floor. It was a carrying case for a musical instrument, like a saxophone for instance.

"When we stroll down the back lane of the Egyptian Museum with a saxophone case full of loot which tune are we whistling?"

Yasser ignored my jest.

"We're late. Get a move on it." Steinman's voice sizzled like a piece of meat being scorched on a hot barbeque. "Why aren't you done yet?"

Steinman took the grappling hooks out of the black case and began working on attaching them to the two rope ladders.

Yasser motioned with his head toward me.

"She won't shut up."

Steinman swore. It was a frightful sound.

I took a few steps back and pretended I was a tourist admiring Tut Ankh Amun's scarab bracelet, while Steinman and Yasser smashed all the glass in the other exhibit cases. To keep my mind from thinking about what they were doing, I focused on the scarab, the symbol of new life after death.

Scarabs were made of gold encrusted or inlaid with lapis lazuli from the ancient land of Ariana, turquoise, quartz, malachite, and carnelian. Tut Ankh Amun's bracelet was found with a pair of earrings by Howard Carter in a cartouche-shaped box.

I moved out of the way.

Yasser took the gold diadem carefully from the exhibit case along with Tut Ankh Amun's bracelets. Next, he went for the necklaces, the falcon pendant and the scarab necklace. These two items had been found beneath the layers of linen bandages of Tut Ankh Amun's mummy.

The falcon necklace had curved wings and a solar disc on its head with Uraeus, the sacred serpent. The other necklace was a winged scarab holding in its forelegs the lunar disc, and in its back legs the basin.

Solid gold with cloisonné work. Stunning.

Being stuck in the utility closet with Steinman and Yasser had bordered on torture, but seeing their grubby hands fumbling all over these treasures tore equally at my heart.

There was no lost love between the three of us that was for sure. The only satisfaction I would get was when I left them behind.

Hopefully, that would be soon.

Yasser placed the diadem, the necklaces, the scarabs, the bracelets in the hard black case. He made sure the case was stuffed with some minor beauties. There were pendants of gold, the falcon and the vulture, gods and goddesses, pectorals with the scarab beetle and a necklace with the sacred eye, the Wedjat, also called the Eye of Horus which is a powerful protection symbol.

My grandfather had told me the myth of the mother and father of Horus, Isis and Osiris, who were rulers of the world. Set, Osiris's brother, was jealous and hated them. At a feast, Set brought a magnificent chest into the room and tricked Osiris to get into it. Set threw the chest into the Nile River but it was eventually discovered in the marshlands. Set was so angry that he opened the chest and chopped up Osiris's body into fourteen pieces and hid the parts across the land of Egypt.

Isis found out about the dirty deed and searched for the parts of her husband, but only found thirteen of them. His penis was missing, having been eaten by a fish. Therefore, Osiris could no longer rule the world. Isis reassembled him with the body parts she had found and sent him on his journey to the Underworld but not before becoming impregnated with their child, Horus.

Quite a feat. Not sure how that worked, but that's how the story goes.

Set was now ruling the world. When Horus was ready, he took revenge upon his uncle. During the battle, Horus's eye was ripped out by Set and torn into six parts before being thrown away. Very precise.

When my grandfather told me this fantastic tale, I was impressed. Set was really into mathematical fractions in a violent way. Wow. The measurements of the sections of the Eye of Horus were used by doctors in ancient Egypt to prescribe precise amounts of medicine.

The goddess Hathor and the god Thoth restored Horus's eye. In gratitude, Horus gave the eye to his father, Osiris, and brought him back to life. Osiris became the ruler of the Underworld.

I could see the eye peeking at me as Yasser shut the case.

"The extra bits are just for insurance," Yasser declared. "In case something goes wrong."

CHAPTER EIGHTEEN

"You said we had one hour! We have plenty of time," I argued with Yasser.

"One hour from start to finish, Amira. Climb up! Stop talking. Start climbing."

We were definitely off schedule, seriously behind the ticking clock.

I climbed over Steinman who had his back against the wall and the black case with the loot in his hands like he was going to make a suicide jump. It was the first time I noticed that Steinman had a distinct odour of cigarettes, cheap hair oil, and garlic. I'd definitely have to have an extra-long bath after this was over.

I placed my hands on Yasser and pressed close to him, giving his ear a little lick on my way up. I groaned at his touch and told him he was doing just fine, the way I had whispered to him in the boat shed by the Nile River during our sexual tryst.

I made sure to brush him hard on the chest and squeeze the arm with the stitches. Sure enough, when I looked down, there was blood seeping through his shirt in both places.

I was teetering on top of Yasser's shoulders. His hands had gone over my thighs in my ascent and now were gripping the bottom of my calves. I made another sighing noise like I was getting laid. His balance shifted.

"Higher, higher. I can't reach the window," I implored. "Steinman, stand up! Stop slacking!"

I wanted to make it as difficult for the two of them as I could.

I climbed the distance with one rope ladder swung over each shoulder. It was slow going. I had to be careful not to get entangled.

The windows were not alarmed. The diameter of the draw bolts was much too small for the fastener and pulled open easily. I swung open the window.

I took the rope ladder off my right shoulder, positioned the hooks onto the metal rod attached to the sill of the window casing. The exterior ladder fell down perfectly along the outside of the museum building.

It didn't go that well with the interior ladder though.

I was using my left hand. After I let it go, the ladder fell down but it was doubled over due to getting caught in the grappling hooks at the top. The interior rope ladder only extended as far down as me.

It was a mess of tangles.

"Wait. It's caught," I chattered a string of nonsense.

Steinman was cursing profusely.

"Stop moving," I hissed at Yasser. "Remember the time we were in the boat shed by the Nile. This is so exciting, just like the time we were fooling around. Thrilling!"

"What?" I could tell Yasser was trying not to think about our sex-capade. "Stop talking!" he bellowed at me.

If I kept it up, he would really get wound up.

"Twice! You know, when we were by the Nile in the boat shed. I can feel it even now."

Underneath Yasser, Steinman was making exasperated noises and grunts.

As I grabbed a rung on the tangled ladder I peered down at Yasser. He was in pain. The blood spots on his chest and arm were larger. There were beads of perspiration on his forehead. He looked like he was going to pass out.

"Give me the case," I beckoned to him.

"What? What?" I could see the agitation in his eyes.

"I'll undo the tangle in the rope ladder, but I need to make sure the case will fit through the window."

I motioned for Yasser to hurry up.

"Give me the black case. Tell Steinman to hand it up."

I panted with urgency like I was having an orgasm.

Yasser looked confused. "What for?"

"I said I have to see if it will fit through the window. Tell Steinman to toss it up."

I moaned again and yelled, "Hurry up! Hurry up!"

I was hoping that Miss Balgrave had had words with Steinman about listening to Yasser. I was also hoping that Yasser's ego would jump to the fore, making him the idiot boss I knew he could be.

Sure enough, Yasser had some pretty concise words in Arabic directed at Steinman.

Up came the black case containing all of the jewels.

The weight of it made me wobble for a second. Then I heaved the case out the window. I quickly followed. I flipped myself through and stood on the first rung of the exterior rope ladder. In Tahrir Square, the sound of the second explosion blasted in the morning air. The clock had struck 4:48 a.m.

Liberation.

"It's all good!" I yelled down to Yasser and Steinman.

I moved the interior rope ladder and its grappling hook off the metal rod where it had been anchored. The interior ladder fell down in one lovely floating motion and landed at Steinman's feet as I escaped.

I left behind me centuries of history in the museum building and two very angry men.

Climbing down the exterior rope ladder was a cinch. I dropped lightly to the ground. The black hard case was there waiting for me on the ground like an obedient dog.

I could see the van at the end of the alley and the silhouettes of Eda and Mohatmed. The Bombardier twins were standing by the two open doors of the van. One brother on either side of the white van.

I gave a wave and headed the other way.

After I turned the corner, I hopped into the car.

Was I ever glad to see Ahmed.

"Drive!"

Not missing a beat, he sped down the side street.

"Everything okay?" Ahmed asked.

"Fine, just fine," I urged. "Just go!"

"This works every time," Ahmed said with satisfaction.

Yes, it did.

Ahmed and I had a standard practice of pick-up points. If the situation was getting difficult with a mark, he could always be counted on to be just around the corner, the opposite corner, with a vehicle. I had escaped many a dicey situation that way.

Behind us, the alarms went off in the Egyptian Museum of Antiquities. The place lit up like a prison reacting to a botched escape.

"Oops," I laughed as I looked at Ahmed.

Yasser and Steinman had triggered the five o'clock alarm.

With satisfaction, I imagined Yasser and Steinman chained together, wearing black and white horizontal striped jumpsuits as they shuffled across the prison yard.

"Any problems on your end?" I asked.

"Nope. The guard, I paid him off for his blind eyes. Enough time for you to get down the ladder."

"I thought I'd never make it," I said, still shaking. "He could've turned around at any second."

"He didn't," Ahmed said. "Orders were to monitor the exterior perimeter only. I timed it when I saw you chuck the ladder out."

I nodded and pulled in a gulp of air. "Yup. You can't see the ladder behind that column."

"Only if you know where to look," Ahmed chuckled as he sped along the road. "These streets outside the museum are cleared. The checkpoints focus on the main entrances. No one's looking down the side alleys."

"Especially if they're bribed," I added.

"Hey!" Ahmed exclaimed. "It's just incentive, that's all."

"The patrols?" I asked. "They won't stop us now that the museum alarms have gone off?"

"It takes them time to adjust to a new development. That teeny window gives us time."

Ahmed eased around a corner.

"Cairo protocol after an explosion and the activation of the museum alarm involves doubling the perimeter and blocking roads. But they concentrate on visible access points. Service lanes and these side streets are official vehicles only."

I was holding my breath.

Ahmed glanced in his rearview mirror.

"And this car?" I asked.

"Official vehicle," he said slapping the steering wheel. "National Response Team markings, lights off, engine quiet. Perfectly legal to be at the end of the lane waiting for you."

Ahmed gave a whoop.

"They assumed you were part of the perimeter operation," I said quietly. "I'm impressed."

"Nobody questioned it. I love your faith in my abilities."

I exhaled sharply, letting the motion of the car calm my nerves. "Are we clear?"

"Almost," he said.

I leaned back. "You're insane."

A grin tugged at his lips. "Just insanely prepared."

Ahmed pulled over sharply and grabbed the black case.

"Quick, Amira," he instructed.

I followed his instructions and hopped into the new car.

"Nice Egyptian taxi," I commented laughing as I slammed the door shut. "Do you miss your West Bank taxi?"

"A taxi is a taxi," said Ahmed simply. "This one belongs to my cousin."

"You know the brothers were at the other end of the alley?" I asked.

"Yes, of course, Amira. I'm not an amateur," he replied.

I smiled at him. "Good."

"I had a heck of a time keeping track of your movements over the last days though. I almost lost you a couple of times," Ahmed exhaled.

My arms flew around his neck and I gave him a hug.

"Look," I said eagerly as I pulled the black case onto my lap to show him the jewels.

Ahmed took a glance. The car swerved slightly.

"Watch the road, Ahmed."

"Then put those away!"

"I just wanted to give you a peek," I said meekly. "You know, in ancient Egypt, jewellery played a protective role. I sure needed that tonight."

Ahmed slid a sideways glance at me. "You okay? I know how you feel about Tut Ankh Amun and his queen, Ankhesenamun."

I pondered his comment for a moment.

"True. Nothing I could have done to stop them though. At least the jewellery and diadem are with me now. That's something."

"Remember in school how we learned that the beaded necklaces and bone jewellery were actually worn over vulnerable areas of the body?"

"Yeah, the neck, the wrists, and the ankles. Amulets or pendants protected the wearer against accidents, repelling evil and diseases. I remember," I said.

"You're not diseased, are you?" he teased.

I gave him a goofy look.

Ahmed raised his eyebrows and asked, "Hey! They simply gave the case to you?"

"Yeah, I know. People are so stupid."

Bezaabt. Exactly.

"How did you manage it?" asked Ahmed. "Come on, give me some details. I always want to know how you accomplish it and handle the situation."

"Get Yasser hot and bothered, not difficult I assure you, so he can't think straight. Add in some physical pain and stress. Specifically, that's Yasser's sex drive, his injuries thanks to Naima, and the inability to stay on time. The result? By crunch time, he was ripe for poor judgment," I snickered. "He didn't know what to think when I said gimme the case."

Ahmed guffawed.

I had a fit of the giggles. Nervous tension released.

"Actually, I believed for a moment he might even pass out."

"Anything go wrong?" Ahmed asked.

"Not for me," I boasted. "We even have some insurance."

I told him about all the extra pieces Yasser had greedily stuffed in the black case.

Like I said, every crime does indeed need a bit of luck. When the interior rope ladder got tangled up and only fell half-way down the wall, I knew that luck was on my side.

"Steinman," I said proudly. "He felt the pressure as well. Behind schedule. Pressed for time. Along with the rope ladder mess and Yasser badgering him to pass the case up, Steinman made a mistake."

A huge mistake.

The bag would have fit through the window. That much was obvious.

How was Steinman supposed to get out if not through the window?

Always ask a man for something in the heat of a moment.

Chances are good for the answer to be yes.

I've known that for a long time, like I said, my British school education had been extensive.

"Frankly, I thought they still might hit the Marriott Hotel and the political gathering," I said raising my eyebrows and nodding my head.

"That's what I assumed too," Ahmed whistled. "I had trouble tailing you. The SSIS dropped the surveillance days ago. I didn't even have them to shadow."

I was really ticked. If things had gone wrong, I really would have been on my own. It was a fact I was glad I hadn't been aware of at the time.

"Those F-in bastards."

"Yup, they are."

"You did a good job Ahmed. Where would I be without my get-away car?"

We both laughed.

"I really believed Miss Balgrave's group was going for the jewels of the Sheikh's wife at the Marriott," I said.

"Me too. The big wig from Kuwait."

I contemplated that for a bit.

"Maybe if I had picked up on the boat rental and worked the whole thing backwards, I would have figured out what they were up to earlier."

"No matter," concluded Ahmed.

"True. It worked out in the end. I am just great at improvisation," I hooted. "Hey, I'm an artist!"

I lifted my hands in the air and took a mock bow.
Ahmed clapped his hands on the steering wheel.

"Still, it was touch and go. I didn't know what was going to happen," Ahmed said seriously.

"Me neither," I agreed. "Up until yesterday I also considered there was a really good chance that I was going to be caught in some political insurrection. If it hadn't swung to profit and gain, I would have been out of there. Day thirteen is always the last day for me. By the time I found out it was a jewellery heist, I had no way to contact you though."

"Like I said, I had a heck of a time tailing you," Ahmed spoke earnestly.

"You're the best. Yes, absolutely." I patted Ahmed on the leg. "How's your wife?"

"Good. She's gone to her mother's place for a few weeks."

Ahmed put his hand high up on my leg.

"Keep your hands on the wheel and drive," I exclaimed.

"Besides, it's your wife's turn."

Ahmed let his hand stray a little before putting it back on the steering wheel.

"Later," he chuckled.

"How are your kids?" I asked.

"Yup, good also."

I saw the huge billboard, the Miranda sign advertising orange pop, and knew we were already on the outskirts of Cairo heading north on the road to Alexandria in a taxi that looked like a million other taxis. It was over two hundred kilometres to El-Agamy, our destination.

You never know exactly how things will play out.

The entire thing could have swung to the political angle. The crazy brothers could have decided to make an angry attack on the world in the guise of a political statement. But I was fairly confident they would do something for profit; well, the odds were fifty-fifty.

Although it hadn't registered at the time, Miss Balgrave's look at Mena House was the same look her daughter had given me before I had taped the girl's mouth shut and locked her in the broom closet.

Yes, that's right. I had been at the British school in Alexandria with Miss Balgrave's daughter. The bitch had humiliated me more than once. I always swore I would get even. I didn't care to be told I stank, and that my Egyptian family was low and dirty. It was ironic Steinman had basically said the same thing as Miss Balgrave's daughter.

When Miss Beatrissa had discovered the daughter, the girl's face was bleeding from where she had managed to rip the tape off her mouth and cheeks. The tape was really sticky stuff and had taken skin with it. Upon healing, it left a delightful scar.

Oh well.

Punishing her daughter had been enough to satisfy me, at the time, even considering the humiliation she had caused me and in fact some of my friends. At school, I had been called by my British name, Margaret Alexander, not Amira Iskandar which was what my grandmother called me.

Obviously, Miss Balgrave had never made the connection. Maybe she never even knew about me anyway. An Egyptian waif named Amira Iskandar wouldn't figure too high on her daughter's priority list nor would my name come up during those precious and tender mother-daughter conversations.

Miss Balgrave's daughter loved to bully. Once she had found out my mother's family name was Egyptian, she taunted me with Amira, instead of calling me Margaret Alexander which was my official British school name. It was a paradox because the daughter's last name wasn't Balgrave.

At the school, we often quoted the line from the *Book of the Dead* regarding names. We were very intent on discovering the passwords needed on the road to eternity.

"Tell me my name. Shadow is your name. Tell me my name. He who leads the Great Goddess, this is your name. Tell me my name. He who knows the desert, he who lives amid the flowers, he who lives in the olive trees, this is your name."

I can't remember what the daughter's last name was, but I do remember the other students teasing her about her mother's name, come to think of it.

Your name is special. Taunting about your name, now that is serious stuff.

The connection between mother and daughter had come to me right before I had left the El-Sobki flat the day of the heist. It blossomed into a full realization as I was going down in the elevator with Miss Balgrave.

I didn't tell Ahmed about the connection. I kept that to myself as a special secret.

Funny how memory works. Once my brain made the association, the resemblance to her daughter had been unmistakable. I had seen Miss Balgrave at the British School in Alexandria before seeing her in Jerusalem.

It was no wonder she attracted my attention at the market and later at the Tel Aviv airport. It was weird that I hadn't made the link before that moment in Cairo.

I had already been plotting my revenge on Miss Balgrave but the connection to her daughter made it even more personal. Miss Balgrave was a certain greedy self-absorbed type.

I hoped she would stay true to form and she did.

Events are unpredictable, people are not.

There were times I had had to stop myself from laughing, especially when Miss Balgrave had said I was so predictable.

"I was counting on Omar Mohammed to round them all up, and see to it that Miss Balgrave spent a long time in prison," I said to Ahmed.

"Yeah, no," responded Ahmed.

"With the knowledge the SSIS hadn't even had them under surveillance, my hopes are dwindling," I said with dejection. "Curse the man."

"Amira," ventured Ahmed. "I see just how angry you are with Omar…"

"…with my parents, with living here instead of Canada, with Arabs, with Jews, the conflict in the Middle East…"

"… with yourself," finished Ahmed. "I know you better than you know yourself Amira. Your anger has called all the shots for most of your life."

"I just want all that to be over. I want peace. Just for things to be still, to rest, to stop changing."

"You feel you have too many enemies, people who hurt you in the past. It's all that hate and anger," counselled Ahmed.

I stroked the jewel case on my lap. I felt my ancestors were close, hovering in my thoughts. I had the hazy thought that for peace to occur, particularly peace in my life, there would have to be forgiveness.

Ahmed echoed my thoughts and said, "All those people in your life would need to be forgiven. That act of forgiveness would need to be initiated by the injured party, by you."

My fatigue was really setting in. I could hardly concentrate. I'd have to think about where my life was going, but not now; I'd think about it tomorrow.

"Almost at El-Agamy. We've bypassed Alexandria totally," said Ahmed.

"The city slumbers like a weary aristocratic old lady," I murmured slouching down in the seat. "Where are we exactly?"

"We are on the road to a relatively newer suburb."

"My grandmother had a villa in the seaside town of El-Agamy. Lovely place with terraced gardens and a view of the ocean until the city allowed high rises to be built around it."

"Then the view is gone and the gardens became unmanageable," said Ahmed.

"People from the upper floors in the high rises just chucked the refuse out their window. They figured the garden, which was an open spot with no building, equaled a garbage dump."

Ahmed shook his head and asked, "Why would anyone want to sit in a private garden when you could stroll down the street to the beach and sit right beside a million other people enjoying the seaside? Of course they threw garbage in there. People are so stupid."

I dozed off a bit while Ahmed sped along the dark road. When I awoke, we were nearly there.

Ahmed confirmed the boat would be waiting for us on the beach at El-Agamy. The wind was stiff. I could hear the waves hitting the beach.

There wasn't a soul in sight.

We abandoned the taxi car on the road and walked onto the sandy beach.

"I don't see anything," I was pissed off. "What's going on? Arrangements are arrangements, Ahmed. Where is he?"

I am usually so calm.

But this time his absence really annoyed me.

"If he is frikin' around again, I'll …"

"There he is," said Ahmed with relief.

A man stumbled out of the shadows of the buildings pulling a dinghy behind him.

I made a growling noise and shouted, "Ahmed, your cousin drives me crazy."

"A family trait."

Ahmed slapped his cousin on the shoulder and took hold of the rope attached to the dinghy. Together they dragged the craft over the sand and into the water. After a brief salute with his hand in my direction, Ahmed's cousin disappeared back into the shadows.

The electric motor on the dinghy took the small craft out to where a large yacht was anchored. *The Krysteeniha* bobbed in the waves. I could see a silhouette on deck. Waiting.

We quickly got out of the dinghy.

I wasn't glad to be on board the yacht but needs must.

The silhouette smirked at me and said, "No problems I see. It was good of Ahmed to finally let me know what was going on. Such loyalty. Otherwise, I would still be sitting in Cairo."

Only the three of us stood on deck.

I glanced at Ahmed who shrugged as if to say he had no choice and what could he do?

I understood Ahmed had had to tell him.

It still irked me.

"I have been waiting on the yacht for hours," the silhouette spoke the statement with a hint of superiority.

Whatever.

The sight of him reminded me that I hadn't left all the assholes behind me and that peace, my personal peace, was a long way off.

I scowled at him.

He hadn't been the one taking all the risks. My bruises were just starting to fade. His arrogant attitude was typical of people in his position.

"Where shall I tell the captain of my yacht to drop you off?"

The words slithered out of his mouth.

"Cyprus will do," I decided on the spur of the moment.

Out of the corner of my eye, I saw Ahmed clench his fists at the name of our destination.

Ahmed hates Cyprus.

"This is the last time I'm getting on your yacht or meeting you in secret locations or anything," I asserted. "This time I really mean it."

That would mean stop crossing paths with him, a problem unless one of us left the Middle East.

I lamented, "It was just my unlucky day to have bumped into you at the Gaza/Egyptian border crossing."

"Or your lucky day," he mocked and shrugged. "These last few days, I thought I had lost you in Cairo since you didn't call me to report."

"I got cloaked in secrecy," I sneered.

"I considered the notion you might be going it alone? How would I protect you then?" He was chiding me. "We had a deal. Remember?"

I rolled my eyes at his insincerity.

If Miss Balgrave's plan had been a political assassination attempt or terrorist attack, nothing would have saved me.

I really hate this guy.

"Did you know the SSIS wasn't even keeping me under surveillance? No support, at all," I complained.

He shrugged again. "You can handle anything, Amira. Besides, the SSIS would have just gotten in the way. It was a good thing to not have them watching you or any of Miss Balgrave's group for that matter."

"You weren't even sure it was a heist. All you knew was that they were thieves and terrorists. I was the one taking all the risks!" I snapped.

We glared at each other. Well, I was glaring. He seemed amused.

"Last time," I said with irritation. "This is the last time I am working with you."

He smiled at me. "With? I assumed you were working *for* me," he chuckled. "Tsk, Amira, such attitude. You're so angry."

I let the pause sharpen between us.

"I do what needs to be done to get the job done," he spoke concisely and held his hand out for the jewels which I dutifully handed over.

Well, most of them.

He was the scum of the earth.

He turned his back to me and started walking away, just the way he had in Building Number Four.

Over his shoulder Omar Mohammed threw a laugh and joked, "Cyprus is a good choice, Amira. Say hello for me. Your grandmother will be happy to see you."

THE END